# LOVE'S A CRIME

# LOVE'S A CRIME

*5/12/89*

*To Eileen,*
*I hope you can uncover the mystery!*
*Love*
*Joe*

## JOSEPH REDDEN

COPYRIGHT © 2009 BY JOSEPH REDDEN.

DUST JACKET PHOTO BY KRISTI EISENBERG

LIBRARY OF CONGRESS CONTROL NUMBER:  2008909128
ISBN:           HARDCOVER            978-1-4363-7687-7
                SOFTCOVER            978-1-4363-7686-0

All rights reserved. No part of this book may be reproduced or transmitted in any form or by any means, electronic or mechanical, including photocopying, recording, or by any information storage and retrieval system, without permission in writing from the copyright owner.

This is a work of fiction. Names, characters, places and incidents either are the product of the author's imagination or are used fictitiously, and any resemblance to any actual persons, living or dead, events, or locales is entirely coincidental.

This book was printed in the United States of America.

**To order additional copies of this book, contact:**
Xlibris Corporation
1-888-795-4274
www.Xlibris.com
Orders@Xlibris.com
40916

For Mom and Dad,

Thank you so much for your support on all my writing and photography projects. I would never have been able to do this without your help.

## Acknowledgments

I hope you enjoy the book. I just want to mention the people who helped me with *Love's a Crime* during the editing process.

Thank you Mom and Dad, for the many hours it took to proofread this book, and other projects I have worked on. Thank you for your help and suggestions. I also want to thank my friends and family for their constant support. Thank you Ray, Kay, Charles, and Steve for the suggestions on the parts I showed you.

I want to thank the members of the Rehoboth Beach Writer's Guild for their encouragement during our Free Write sessions.

I also want to thank Stephen Kushner, MD, for helping me with the correct medical terminology. Now you can read the rest of the book.

Thank you Lu Ann for helping me make sure the legal scenes were accurate. Now we don't have to discuss criminal punishments at church.

I especially want to thank the Xlibris staff for helping me get this book off the ground, and for locating mistakes I missed when I was proofreading.

# Chapter 1

"Come on, get the ball!"

"Over here!"

Spectators went wild three minutes to the end of the third quarter. Their shouts vibrated off the gymnasium walls. The players' shoes squeaked as they ran across the court. Broad Meadow Tigers star athlete Phillip Bishop leapt into the air and slammed the ball into the hoop. Fans screamed and whistled. The buzzer sounded, and the players went to the bench. Phillip looked at the bleachers and flashed a goofy grin at the pretty blonde girl, Susan Williams. She waved and smiled back at him.

She was not the only girl on campus who was infatuated with him. Maybe it was because he was tall and muscular. Maybe it was his bright blue eyes and short sandy hair. Maybe they admired him for his skill as a basketball player. He was truly a gifted athlete. His hard work not only paid off on the ball field, but he also scored academically. He was a leader. People respected his opinion.

Chad McAlpin's mind wasn't on the game. He secretly despised Phillip at the moment, and it had nothing to do with his athletic prowess. It had to do with the disgusting display of affection he just witnessed between Susan and Phillip. She was a source of extreme tension between them, and it would be hard to resolve their differences and remain friends. Last year, he had been the one flirting with Susan. He was tired of living in Phillip's shadow. He was tired of being the number two man on campus. He was tired of everybody knowing it. He was a damned good basketball player and wanted some recognition for a change.

Chad was blessed with good looks and had no trouble getting girls to go out with him. He could have been a movie star with his feathered blond hair and blue eyes, chiseled features and muscles. He wasn't as tall as Phillip, no one could be.

He slapped Phillip on the shoulder and said, "Good job!"

"Thanks, buddy," Phillip said.

Chad glared at him when he wasn't looking and took his seat.

Rudy Preston reached for his towel and wiped sweat off his face. He was gangly looking, with a nasal-sounding voice and a ruddy complexion. His hair was dark and curly. Though he wasn't as strong as Phillip, he made up for it in speed. He had an overabundance of energy and was a real asset to the team.

Andy Winchester had been Rudy's roommate since their freshman year. He was a lot shorter, with dark hair and a face peppered with acne. His body looked bigger than his head. A lot of strength came from his small package. He had powerful hands and legs that could propel him to great heights.

Rudy looked over at the exit door. Terry Dawson was talking to Headmaster MacPharlan. Terry's two-hundred-fifty-pound frame was all muscle. He looked like a giant, towering over the older man, just like he had intimidated opponents on the football field. But that was when he was a star. Now things had changed. MacPharlan backed away and shook his finger at him. They were arguing.

"I can't believe it," Rudy said.

"What?" Andy asked.

Rudy pointed at the exit door, and they all looked.

Phillip rolled his eyes and shook his head. "He's probably begging to come back."

"You'll probably make sure he doesn't," Andy said.

"And you would do anything to play well, wouldn't you, Andy?"

"Wouldn't you?"

Phillip was about to reply when Coach Reynolds called a huddle. He was a burly man, with a crew cut and dark, penetrating eyes. "Good job, you guys, but you've got to work on defense." He looked at Phillip and said, "Quit flirting with your girlfriend. Your mind should be on the game, not on her."

## LOVE'S A CRIME

He grinned sheepishly and said, "Sorry, Coach."

"It's not funny. We've got a lot riding on this game. Your shenanigans could cost us the state championships. Don't let it happen again."

Chad enjoyed watching the coach chew him out. At the sound of the whistle, they resumed their positions on the court. Fulton Rams players tossed the ball to one another like a hot potato. Rudy ended up with it and was surrounded by two opponents who were much bigger and stronger. He threw it to Phillip, who raced toward the hoop, Ramsman Bobby Baker blocking him the whole way. Phillip pushed him out of the way and threw the ball. It bounced off the baseboard and slipped through the hoop. Spectators screamed so loud, their enthusiasm created a high-pitched energy around the gymnasium. Cheerleaders were clapping and swinging their pom-poms. A newspaper photographer stood on the sidelines and snapped away.

Players darted around each other. Phillip ran next to his opponent and was unrelenting. They leapt off the floor, and the guy attempted to score. Phillip managed to hit the ball out of the way, and it missed the target. Ramsman Tony Morton caught it and threw it to Bobby Baker. Chad McAlpin pushed him out of the way and tore toward his side. He almost had it till Bobby Baker blocked his shot.

Spectators were at the edge of their seats. Another score for the Rams, then another. Andy Winchester scored for Broad Meadow. He controlled the ball until Ramsmen Greg Smith and Bill Ashcroft cornered him. He threw it to McAlpin, who darted across the court, and threw it hurtling toward the hoop. The ball ricocheted off the baseboard and slammed to the floor.

Tension mounted during the fourth quarter. Rudy threw the ball, but it missed the hoop. The Rams had the ball and scored. They were dead even. It was such a tight game at this point, anything could happen. Phillip forced the ball out of Bobby Baker's hands and practically flew into the air. With a thrust of his right hand, he slammed it into the hoop, nailing the winning score just as the buzzer sounded. Spectators stood and cheered. Friends and family members pushed their way down the bleachers and through the bustling crowd edging toward the door. Players got caught up in the crowd as they hugged and congratulated them. There was a lot of noise, and it was hard to hear.

Phillip wrapped a towel around his face and wiped sweat from his forehead. It was soaking wet now. Chad slapped him on the shoulder and said, "Way to go, Bishop!"

"What can I say but—?"

"Come on you guys!" Coach Reynolds bellowed.

The team filed into the locker room. After they showered and got dressed, the coach beamed with pride. "Good job, guys! But not good enough. You need to get coordinated. It was a close game. Too close. You can do better. Next time, I want you all to concentrate. You were too distracted tonight."

After the postgame talk, he dismissed the team with the exception of Phillip Bishop. At first, Phillip thought Coach Reynolds was going to congratulate him, but that was not how it turned out.

"What the hell did you think you were doing out there, Bishop?"

"What do you mean?"

"Your performance was half-assed!"

"I didn't think so."

"You were impressing your girlfriend and made a lot of careless errors!"

"What are you talking about?"

"Don't play innocent with me. I know what you were doing. Don't let it happen again."

"Coach, I think you're out of line. I played better than I have all season, and everybody knows it. At least, I know I did."

"You were slacking off—then started correcting your errors at the end of the game. Don't let it happen again. You've been warned."

The coach brushed past him and pushed through the double doors. Phillip sat on the bench with his face buried in his hands and heard Andy arguing with him in the gym. He had overheard their conversation and confronted him.

"Coach, you've got it all wrong."

"How so?"

"Phil played better than any of us tonight."

"Andy, don't butt in where you aren't wanted."

"You're being unreasonable."

"His careless mistakes won't get us into the state championships! This is between Phillip and me. Just mind your own business!" He stomped toward his office.

Phillip stuck his head out the door and saw the coach storm out. Andy went over to his friend and said, "You heard?"

He nodded and said, "Yes, can you believe him?"

"He gets like that sometimes, you know."

"I know. What's wrong with him anyway?"

"He was probably just blowing off steam. I'm sure in a few hours he'll be fine. You know how he is."

"I know."

They were on their way out when they saw Terry Dawson loitering in the lobby. He lunged at Phillip and said, "What do we have here, a little traitor?"

Phillip was about to punch him when Andy stood in between them and tried to push Terry out of the way. Dawson shoved him aside like an annoying little bug. Andy arched his back and almost fell but caught himself.

"Stop it," Andy said. "Get out of here, Terry!"

It took all the strength Andy had to hold Terry at bay. Terry loomed over him like a giant. Remaining basketball fans helped restrain him.

"I'll get you, Bishop!" Dawson shouted as they pulled him away.

He shook his fist at Phillip and pushed out the front door. When he had gone, Andy and Phillip went outside. They bundled up as a blast of cold air hit them like a ton of bricks.

"I never thought I'd see him around here again," Phillip said. His voice sounded shaky.

"Me neither."

They walked down the tree-lined entrance that led to the campus and waved at classmates who went up the steps leading to Hullien Hall. It was an impressive-looking stone building with a slanted roof and two large chimneys on opposite ends. In 1885, stones and rocks were transported to the campus from a quarry several miles away. It was constructed on what used to be ample farmland. Generations of young men lived in dorm rooms on the second and third floors and had wild stories to tell about their lives there. In the 1960s, first floor classrooms were converted into offices, and the basement was turned into a cafeteria.

The path meandered to the left, and Andy walked hurriedly to keep up with Phillip. A couple minutes later, they approached their dorm. Stewart

**JOSEPH REDDEN**

Hall was a two-story brick building built in the 1970s. It didn't have as much of the same character as other old buildings on campus but was like a home away from home for the young men who lived there. Students who stayed here had their own lively tales to tell about dorm life. Some of the stories were true. Over the years, most of them were probably juiced up to sound more exciting.

Phillip and Andy went to the lounge and played a video game for a few minutes then went to dinner. They sat with Rudy and talked to classmates about the game.

The next day, Andy and Rudy shuffled down the basement steps of Hullien Hall and got in the lunch line. The menu today was tacos and cling peaches. They went into the cafeteria and sat across from Phillip. They engaged in loud, raucous conversation. Mrs. Eudora Ashley adjusted her glasses and scowled at them from across the room. She had been there for a hundred years, at least that's probably what most of the kids thought. She was a stern disciplinarian and dressed the part. She always wore a collar that buttoned at the neck and outfits that looked like she was going to a funeral. She had heard kids joking about her over the years. She and her husband were the only ones who knew the truth. Yes, in fact, she did have a neck. And she did, in fact, once have long black hair that she occasionally let down to feel freely on her shoulders. She couldn't stand the current crop of educators on campus. The kids were unruly. There was no discipline.

She shook a long wrinkled finger at them to get their attention. "Be quiet!" she growled, finally having enough.

The boys cackled like a flock of birds. Rudy put his head on the table, unable to control himself.

Andy poured chili sauce on his taco and chewed carefully. He wiped sauce off his mouth and laid the taco on the plate, without spilling it on his white button-down shirt.

"You're the only person I've ever met who could wear white and not get his clothes all dirty," Rudy chided.

Andy grinned and said, "It's all in my upbringing, I guess. My mom always threatened to use my dad's huge fraternity paddle on me if I made a mess. It was huge! So I guess, you'd say, it kind of stuck."

Everyone except Phillip laughed. He saw Chad and Susan enter the room and glowered at him. Last year, Chad and Susan were Homecoming King and Queen and were voted the perfect couple. Who knew they would have parted in such a bitter way? Her warm, inviting smile melted the hearts of many young men on campus. She would probably be able to go anywhere and do anything she wanted.

Chad had gotten by on his looks up to this point, and probably would, years from now. His parents had enough money to send him to Broad Meadow. He had never had it really hard before. Things had always been given to him. It came as a major shock when Susan broke up with him. He had always gotten his way. People had never said no to him.

He had been Phillip's roommate for three years. During that time, they had shared many secrets. That all changed when Chad found out he was dating Susan a few months ago. They had to switch rooms. Chad felt like he couldn't win. Not only was Phillip a physical threat athletically, he took the one person who meant the world to him. Phillip outscored, outmaneuvered, and wound up with Susan.

Chad looked longingly into her eyes and reached for her hand, but she pulled it away.

"Damn him!" Phillip cried. "He's trying to worm his way back into her good graces."

"Come on, Phillip, it's not the end of the world," Rudy said.

"I know, but it just pisses me off."

"Come on, I know what will cheer you up," Andy said.

"What?"

"It's back at the dorm."

Phillip gulped down the rest of his meal and hoped he would not get sick on the cafeteria food if he ate so fast. He got up and glared at Chad on his way out.

Stewart Hall boys lived in cramped rooms with oppressive-looking cinder block walls. Some were starker than others, depending on the color. Andy and Rudy often joked that the mustard yellow paint in their room looked like puke. Supermodel posters covered most of the blocks, but there were a few patches that served as a constant reminder. They slept on bunk beds, so typical of a dorm. Desks were on opposite corners. Broad Meadow banners hung from shelves and on the door. Closet space was limited, so they had to pick sides to hang their clothes.

Andy picked up the latest copy of *Playboy* lying on his bed. With his back turned to Phillip, he carefully opened it and put a joint in his pocket.

"Be careful, Phillip might see it," Rudy whispered.

"What's wrong?" Phillip asked.

Andy tossed him the magazine and said, "Nothing."

They checked out the centerfold, then Andy went over to his laptop and opened the porn Web site on his favorite places list. He clicked View as a slide show. Phillip and Rudy gathered around, and they looked at more beautiful women. It wasn't long before they picked them apart and told dirty jokes.

"Think they're real?" Rudy asked.

"No woman looks that good," Andy said. "They have to be fake."

They broke out laughing when they saw the next scantily clad babe.

Andy cackled and said, "How does she walk without toppling over? Oh my god!"

"There's no possibility that they're real." He turned to look at Phillip. "What do you think, pal?"

He leaned back and laughed. "No comment."

Rudy pointed to the next woman and laughed at Andy. "Come on, Andy, she's dying to have you call her. Look, see, she's beckoning you. Go ahead."

"I think she's more your type, Rudy."

Phillip reached in his pant's pocket and whipped out his cell phone. "I don't want to miss anything," he said on his way out.

Rudy drew a deep breath and said, "That was close."

"Don't let Phillip see it."

"What if there's a surprise inspection?"

"We'll hide it." Andy reached in his pocket and stuffed the joint in a paperback book under his bed. When Phillip came back ten minutes later, they were talking about a model's head being pasted onto another one's body.

Phillip went over to the window and said, "Did you see him with her?"

"You'd think she would have sense enough to get away from him," Andy said.

He was about to respond when he saw them in the parking lot. "It looks like she's giving Chad the brush-off again. Maybe he'll finally get the message this time. Look at her. She looks really pissed."

They all stared down at the spat that was taking place. When it was over, she ran toward her dorm in tears. Chad looked up at them, shook his fists, and walked hurriedly into the building. Five minutes later, he appeared in the doorway and yelled, "What the hell right do you have spying on me, Bishop?"

"Susy made up her mind," Phillip said. "She obviously doesn't want to be with you. Accept it."

Rudy and Andy slipped into the hall to avoid the confrontation. Boys peered out their doors and looked intently at them. Chad slammed the door and they argued. They were about to tear into each other when the dorm supervisor forced his way in and separated them. He was a flustered-looking man with wafts of flaming red hair and a scraggily mustache and beard.

"What's wrong with you guys? Susan isn't anybody's property! Go back to your rooms and get a grip!"

Chad went out and glared at students who were still loitering in the hall.

He brushed past them and said, "Get a life!"

Frigid temperatures gave way to unseasonably warm weather the last week of January. Students who had been bundling up with thick sweaters and coats now wandered around campus with shorts and T-shirts and laid out in the sun.

On Friday night, students with cars could come and go as they pleased as long as they were not late for Sunday night's 9:00 p.m. curfew. Those who stayed went to a dance at the student center. It was a one-story brick building nestled beneath pine trees near the entrance road. It was reminiscent of a 1940s hangout, with pictures of kids from that era hung on the walls. Though the styles had changed, they basically had one thing in common. Teens were there to have a good time. Boys and girls sat at tables, playing games and eating junk food. Small jukeboxes hung on the walls in every booth. Some pictures showed classic cars parked outside the small brick building that was about a hundred years old. Athletes were wearing their school jackets that were crazy with metals on the sleeves. They were flirting with girls, who might have become their wives. They were probably grandparents now. Some of their grandchildren had long since passed through the school halls and had children of their own.

The music was drab, and the band was atrocious. Attendance was starting to wane. An odd assortment of couples took to the tiny section of dance floor. Rudy wrapped his arms around Wendy's pencil-thin waist. Her head came up to his chest. He awkwardly leaned down to rest his head against her mousy dirt-blonde hair, and they swayed to the music.

He stepped on her foot and said, "Sorry."

"That's okay."

Chad and Mary sat at a booth across the room, watching the happy couples.

She got to her feet and tapped his hand, "Come on, let's dance."

"Maybe later."

"Oh, come on. Don't be such a party pooper."

He was about to respond when Andy went up and pulled her onto the dance floor.

He spun her around, and they grinned dumbly at Chad.

He leaned in and whispered, "Wanna make him jealous?"

She smiled and said, "Sure, I'm game."

He glanced over at Chad, then slowly worked his hands down her back and pressed her body toward him. His head was in direct proportion to her breasts, and she had to get on tiptoes to stand taller.

"This music is terrible," she said.

"I know."

They bumped into Phillip and Susan, who were locked in a tight embrace. Chad gave him the evil eye from across the room. He didn't seem to care what Andy was doing with Mary. He was just going out with her to make Susan jealous anyway. But his plan backfired big time. She didn't seem to care that he was going out with Mary.

Phillip turned so his back was to him and concentrated his gaze on Susan. She felt a cool chill as she looked at her ex-boyfriend.

Phillip leaned in to kiss her. "Don't let him get to you, babe," he whispered.

"It's hard. I'm getting so tired of this."

When the band finally played rock and roll music again, students swung their arms and gyrated to the beat. Susan, Mary, and Wendy sat at a booth and giggled lightheartedly at guys who sat at the bar.

Michelle Martin slid next to Susan and joined in the latest gossip. She was a little bit taller, with high cheekbones and shoulder-length auburn hair. She was wearing a burgundy sweater that fit in all the right places. She pulled out her compact and dabbed red lipstick on, glancing over to see if the boys noticed.

They burst out laughing at something Mary said. The door swung open, and words failed them when John Fletcher entered the room. They always felt warm all over whenever he opened his mouth. It didn't matter what he said, it was the way he said it. That New England accent drove them crazy. Or maybe it was his long curly jet-black hair. Or that winning grin. He looked like a Greek god or something. Whenever he discussed poetry, their minds weren't on literature. They wondered if he ever suspected the real reason they spent so much time during his office hours going over important points with them.

He waltzed past them and said, "Good evening, ladies."

"Hi, Mr. Fletcher," they said in unison.

When he was out of earshot, they looked at each other and burst out laughing.

Chad was still not laughing. He hung his head at them. He didn't know what the big deal was about that guy anyway. Mr. Fletcher was twenty-three and not at all athletic. What did they see in him anyway?

John went over to his colleagues, the appointed chaperones and chatted amiably with them. Out of the corner of his eye, he glanced at the girls looking at him. He smiled at them as he talked to his co-workers.

Coach Reynolds went behind the bar and poured soda into a plastic cup. He watched the interaction between the star-crossed lovers with keen interest. It wasn't the first time he had been involved with the catfights of bickering adolescents. Every year, boys and girls with more hormones than brains thought they were in love, got into a spat, broke up, patched things up, and once again became the campus sweethearts. Love triangles were common. Best friends often clashed over the heart of a woman and vice versa. These growing pangs were just something that had to be lived through but worse than labor pains. Unfortunately, everyone on campus had to be a part of it.

It was a small campus, and boarding students were there all week. They lived, ate, and bumped into each other on a daily basis. Anger tended to reach a boiling point, and there was no outlet to release it. Everyone had to be on their good behavior. It was only a matter of time before . . .

Phillip went over to Chad and said, "Susy says we need to call a truce so we won't ruin the party."

Chad gritted his teeth and said, "You'll do anything she says, won't you?"

"Come on you guys," Andy said. "She's right. It's a party. Lighten up."

"Yeah, right," Rudy chimed in.

Chad glanced at the clock over the front door and groaned. It was about eight o'clock, and the music didn't show any signs of improving. He gathered his buddies together, and they paraded out the foyer door with their dates. At Susan's insistence, Phillip went with them as long as he didn't have to ride with Chad. They drove two cars down the road that led to a stream that wound around the hills surrounding the school. It was narrow in some areas, and a motorist had to drive slowly around sharp curves to avoid hitting an oncoming car or sliding off the shoulder and into the water. They pulled into a clearing and checked to make sure they had their cell phones. Chad and Michelle grabbed flashlights out of their cars. They went into the woods in couples.

Mary squeezed Chad's hand, and they walked in silence. He was unusually quiet.

"What's wrong with you?" she asked.

"That party was boring."

"Don't think about it." She darted ahead of him. He aimed the flashlight beam on her face. "It's so nice out tonight, isn't it?"

"It's great."

"Can you believe it's January and we're walking around like it's summer?"

# LOVE'S A CRIME

"I love it. I hope it stays this way for a while longer."

They sat on rocks near a tree that slanted toward the water. They held hands and sat in silence. She reached for his hand and kissed him. He wrapped his arms around her and returned the kiss. Then he got to his feet and walked over to the shore.

He looked back at her and said, "Can you believe that guy?"

"You're killing the mood. Just don't think about them."

"Come on, let's take a walk in the woods."

She took his hand, and they climbed the hill.

Andy rolled on top of Michelle like a rabid animal and pressed his lips to hers. His breath was hot and heavy. She wound up on top and scrambled to her feet. He sat there and looked up at her, puzzled.

"What's wrong?"

"I'm . . . I'm sorry. I can't do this right now."

He got up to go after her. He reached for her arm and pulled her toward him.

"Come on, I thought you wanted to be with me," he said. "It's okay if you don't want—"

"Not tonight . . . not like this."

He released his grip and said, "I'm sorry."

"I know you want to be with me. But we just can't. I need a break."

He eyed her incredulously. "You want to break up with me?"

She met his gaze and said, "It isn't your fault. It . . . it isn't anything you did."

"If you want to break up, you owe me some kind of explanation."

"Well, it's . . . it's just weird, that's all. We've always been like brother and sister. You've always thought of us like one of the guys."

He squeezed her hand and said, "You're not one of the guys now." He leaned in and kissed her again. "You're a woman. And I'm nuts about you."

She wiped away tears and said, "That's what makes it worse. I don't want to hurt you."

She tore off through the woods, and he ran to catch up.

"Come on, talk to me. I can help you, if you'll let me."

21

\* \* \*

Rudy and Wendy were having the opposite problem. She wanted some action, but he got bashful and started tossing rocks into the water. They just sat on the small section of the beach holding hands and talking instead.

"You're not too experienced in this department, are you?" she said.

He looked straight ahead and said nothing.

"It's okay. That's what I like about you. You're sweet. And you're not a phony like some of those muscle guys, if you know what I mean."

"They're a bunch of jerks, aren't they?" he said at last. "Come on, let's see what the others are up to."

Phillip walked hand in hand with Susan. He stopped and kissed her, but she pulled away.

"I want you to patch things up with Chad," she said.

"Huh?"

"I can't take much more. He didn't understand. Please go talk to him."

"But, Susy!"

"I'm not feeling well. I want to go back now."

"All right, but will you still be here if I talk to him?"

"I don't know. I'm sick of both of you. The way you've been acting all night, treating me like a trophy and staring at me all night, trying to get my attention. I'm not anybody's property! Please just tell him the way things are."

"Okay, I'm sorry. I love you, Susy."

She ran off. He hurried to catch up but lost sight of her. She found a rock by the brook and sat there thinking about the past few months. She was going to have to make a decision that would affect her life . . .

Michelle sat on the driver's seat and folded her arms.

Andy rolled his eyes and said, "Michelle."

"Susy wants to go back. She's feeling sick."

"But it's only nine thirty!"

Mary and Wendy got in back.

"Wendy?" It was Rudy this time.

"Mary," Chad whined.

Mary rolled down the window and stuck her head out to kiss Chad's cheek. "Maybe next time. When your mind isn't on someone else."

The car sped down the road with the girls in it. The boys looked at one another in disbelief.

"Way to go, Chad!" Rudy and Andy cried in unison.

Phillip emerged from the woods and gave them a puzzled look. "Where did they go?"

Andy shook his head and said, "Do you have to ask?"

"Susy wants me to have it out with you once and for all, Chad," Phillip said. "Come on, I've had enough of this shit. Let's get it over with."

They approached a clearing at the top of a hill and headed down toward the brook.

"What the hell is wrong with you?" Phillip asked.

"I'll tell you what's wrong! Susan doesn't love you."

"She wants me to tell you why she broke up with you."

"Because you stole her!"

"It wasn't like that. Things happened."

"Things?"

"Maybe it's better if she told you herself. It's not my business to say."

He slapped Phillip on the chest and said, "That's right, it's not your business at all to even be near her! You knew I loved her, and you stole her from me. After all those times we sat up talking into the night . . . you told me what to say and do, and all the time you were in love with her too . . . and now you stole her from me!"

"You've got it all wrong!"

Chad shoved him, and Phillip fell on his back. When he tried to get to his feet, Chad kicked dirt on his face. Phillip rose to his knees, and Chad knocked him down with his foot. Phillip pulled Chad toward him, and he landed on his chest. They thrashed on the ground and punched each other until their hands were bloody. Phillip got back on his feet and started to walk away when Chad got up and darted in front of him. He pushed Phillip with such a force that he fell and hit his head on a rock. Chad went over and looked down at him.

He ran his fingers through his hair and said, "Oh my god, Phillip. Are you okay, man?"

He tapped him with his right foot, but Phillip didn't stir.

"Oh my god. Phillip!"

When they got back to the campus, Michelle sat at the edge of Susan's bed and said, "Do you believe the nerve of those guys? Fighting over you like that."

"I'm getting sick of it. I wish they'd stop it. I don't think I can take much more of their constant bickering."

"It's a shame. They used to be such good friends."

"It's my fault."

"No, it isn't."

"They're fighting because of me."

"Do you want me to have a talk with Chad? Maybe I can make him understand."

"Please don't. I don't think there's anything you could say that would make him understand."

Michelle nodded and said, "He can be pigheaded at times."

"I probably won't get much sleep tonight, worrying about them."

Michelle patted Susan's arm and said, "That's like the third night in a row, isn't it?"

"I think so."

Michelle got up and went over to her desk. She pulled open a drawer and handed her a prescription bottle. She handed her a water bottle and a pill and said, "Here, it really helps me to go to sleep."

"Thanks, I don't know what I'd do without you."

"It'll take a few minutes to take effect. Will you be all right if I go back to the dance?"

Susan smiled and said, "Go ahead. Have a good time, okay."

"You'll feel better in the morning."

They hugged and Michelle was out the door.

"Good night," Susan called after her.

Michelle got into her car and drove toward the student center. She went past the building and drove down the same road she and her friends had been on earlier that evening . . .

\* \* \*

Andy and Rudy were waiting by the car, looking at their watches.
"What's taking them so long?"
"I don't know," Andy said. "I'll go see what's going on."
He darted into the woods, Rudy at his heels. They got separated.

Andy was sitting in the car when Rudy came back five minutes later. Chad staggered toward them ten minutes after that. He had a bloody nose and a cut on his face.
"What happened to you?" they asked in alarm.
"We got in a fight," he said out of breath. "It got pretty ugly. Then we punched each other. He fell and hit his head and then . . . and then I ran back here."
"Where's Phillip?" Andy asked.
Chad shrugged his shoulders and said, "I don't know. In the woods, I guess."
"Stay here and rest up." Andy motioned for Rudy to stay with Chad.
He ran into the woods and returned ten minutes later. Rudy waved the flashlight beam in his face. Andy's face appeared ashen in that lighting. His eyes looked wild, and he was speaking so fast they couldn't understand what he was saying. Chad tapped his shoulder and told him to slow down.
"What did you do, man?" Andy said.
"Did you find Phillip?" Rudy asked.
Andy nodded and was quiet all of a sudden.
"Andy man, what—?" was all Rudy managed to spit out.
Andy's tone was emotionless. "Chad, come on."
"What's wrong?" Rudy's voice cracked.
Andy could not talk. He was trembling. "Come with me."
They followed him into the woods. Andy pointed his flashlight at the ground and looked away.
When Rudy saw what Andy saw, he screeched, "Oh my god, it's Phil!"

Andy froze in his tracks, too stunned to respond. He stood there watching his friends go to him and could not move.

Rudy turned him over and felt his pulse. "Oh my god, he's dead! Phil's dead!"

Chad now grasped the seriousness of the situation. He needed to hear Rudy's panicked voice to confirm what he was not able to accept. Phillip Randal Bishop was dead. He was seventeen.

## Chapter 2

The boys were talking over each other. Chad tried to remain calm.

"You killed him, Chad," Andy said.

"Did I? Oh my god! I can't believe this is happening."

"We've got to do something," Rudy said quickly. "The girls went back . . . they'll know we were here. It's only a matter of time before—"

"Calm down, Rudy," Chad said slowly. "I'm the one in trouble. You guys go."

"No, they'll know we were here," Andy said. "We're in this together. We've got to stick together."

While Chad and Andy contemplated their next move, Rudy continued raving.

Chad looked from Andy to Rudy and said, "We've got to move the body."

Rudy's eyes bulged. "What? They'll just think he fell. We could go back and say that he wanted to be alone or that he had a lot to drink and fell and hit his head."

"That won't work," Chad said. "Everybody knows I was mad at him. People heard us arguing the other day. They'll take one look at me and think I did it. I look like shit!"

He felt beads of sweat moisten his shirt. It was cold and clammy. His neck was tight.

He took several deep breaths and regained his composure.

"What'll we do?" squeaked Rudy.

Chad dropped to his knees and stared at the stars. They sat there, too stunned for words.

"We'll have to move the body and shove his car into the water to make it look like an accident," Chad said at length. "Somebody will find the car in the water, and the police will say he was in a horrible accident."

"Couldn't he have fallen or hit his head on a rock?" Andy asked.

Chad shook his head and said, "No, they'll take one look at me and know we were in a fight. My face is all messed up. Do I have to put makeup on to cover it up? It'll be obvious. Andy, go get Phillip's car and drive it here."

"But he didn't—"

"We can say we went back to campus after the girls, and he must've come back in his own car."

"But that doesn't make sense," Andy said.

"Just do it!"

Rudy's voice reached an annoying, squeaking pitch. "What are we gonna do?"

Chad ran his fingers through his hair and said, "I'm not sure. Just get the car, and we'll think of something. Rudy, help me—Oh shit! You'll have to go together. Bring your car to the gate and walk to the dorm so nobody hears the car pulling in. Andy, go to my room and bring me back clean clothes. You guys better do the same thing. We'll have to do something with what we're wearing."

When they got back to campus, they saw people inside the student center as they went by.

Chad pulled down the lane that led to Hullien Hall and parked by the pond. Andy got out and darted toward the parking lot. When he got to the dorm, he crept into Phillip's room. He grabbed his keys and hastily stuffed clothes into a pillowcase. He went across the dark passageway, and the floor creaked as he rounded the bend.

Willy Brown looked out to see a shadowy figure slip around the corner about ten fifteen. He closed the door and went back to his desk. He heard a car door slam and looked out the window. He saw Phillip's red sports car, pulling out of the parking lot.

He continued studying and thought nothing more about it . . .

\* \* \*

Chad breathed heavily and said, "Heave-ho!"

They hoisted Phillip's body over to the edge of the embankment and rested a moment. Then they carried him to his car. Chad opened the door on the driver's side.

"Are you sure this will work?" Rudy asked Chad, out of breath.

"No, but we have to hope it does or I'm in deep shit."

"It seems to me that people would just think he fell."

"No, they won't! Now quit talking and put some muscle into it!"

Andy left the car in neutral, and they pushed the back end off the road. They stood there motionless, feeling their chests heave, as they watched it teeter over the edge and topple down the hill. Rudy waved his flashlight, and they watched it disappear from view around underbrush. All they could see was the front and back headlights rolling down the hill. Seconds later, they heard the deafening sounds of metal scraping against the rocks. Then there was a loud splash as the car hit the water. A twinge of paranoia came over Chad. For a moment, he was not sure he could trust them, but he knew they would comply.

"Andy, go check to see if it looks all right," Chad ordered.

Andy edged his way down the hill and aimed the flashlight beam toward the wrecked car. The front end was half submerged. The back end slanted on the hill. He pointed the flashlight toward the shrubbery and searched for the trail and scaled the hill.

"How does it look?" Chad asked him.

"It looks all right."

"You don't think anybody will suspect?"

"No, it looks like Phillip got into a really bad accident. Don't worry about it."

"Come on, we better get cleaned up," Chad said.

They followed him to the stream. He dunked his hands in the water and sponged off his face. Andy and Rudy did the same. They took out the clean clothes from the pillowcase and tossed their soiled ones as they disrobed. They got dressed quickly and gathered the dirty clothes together and put them in the pillowcase.

Andy looked at Chad and said, "They'll never suspect?"

"Never."

Rudy's voice rose a decibel. "I hope not or our goose is cooked."

Chad looked from Andy to Rudy and said, "We're in this together and nobody tells."

"We'll never tell," Rudy said. But he did not sound as enthusiastic.

"God, Rudy, you better be cool about this!" Andy cried. "Chad's in trouble. We're in it too. If people find out we moved—"

"I'm okay, guys." Rudy glanced at his hand and noticed it was bleeding. He wiped it off on his jacket.

"Let's get out of here," Chad said.

They arrived back on campus about eleven thirty. Chad wouldn't go inside. One look at his face and everybody would know that he had been in a fight. He leaned against his car and popped out his cell phone. He sent a friend from home a text message and closed the lid. A moment later, it rang and he pulled it out of his pocket. Chatting with Chuck was a nice distraction from his current problem. He would worry about what to do about the cut on his face later. He was just a shadow outside the window. Students could make out his figure and knew that it was him.

Andy and Rudy zipped up the jackets that had been stuffed in the pillowcase and went inside. No one knew they changed into other blue jeans. They grinned dumbly at couples on the dance floor as they made their way over to the food table. They shoved pop corn into plastic cups and sat at a booth away from the action. Fortunately, no one suspected anything was wrong. A few minutes later, they met Chad on the steps. They got back to their dorm five minutes before the midnight curfew and sneaked back to their rooms to avoid being caught by the dorm supervisor.

Andy and Rudy went into their rooms and got ready for bed. Chad went into their room and slipped them notes.

Rudy's read, "Remember Mrs. Bradshaw."

Andy's read, "Remember the Stallion."

Rudy's throat tightened. Chad went over to them, and they clasped hands.

"Just a simple reminder, in case you forget the oath you just made," he said. He slapped their shoulders and went back to his room. He knew he had better try to get a good night's sleep. It would be hell when the body was discovered.

**LOVE'S A CRIME**

\* \* \*

On Saturday morning, Chad bandaged his hand and put on a hooded sweatshirt. He pulled the hood up to conceal the cuts on his face and slipped on sunglasses. He went to breakfast and kept his shades on. If people noticed his face, they would think he had been in a fight. Fortunately, a lot of students slept in. The one's that were up at that hour were too wrapped up in their own little dramas to notice. He slopped down scrambled eggs and slipped out the side door that let out to the guest parking lot. He smiled and bowed his head when students went past him and walked hurriedly to Stewart Hall. He locked himself in his room for several hours. Andy brought him a sandwich and chips from the cafeteria.

Late that afternoon, there was a knock at his door. It was Headmaster MacPharlan.

*What was he doing here?*

Chad held the door open a crack and hid his face so the old man couldn't see the cuts.

"I just got a call from Phillip's parents," MacPharlan said. "They were expecting him home after the dance and he hasn't gotten there yet. They're getting worried."

"I haven't seen him since last night," Chad lied.

"Well, if you see him, let me know."

Chad grinned and said, "Okay."

He heaved a sigh of relief when the headmaster left. He peeked out the door and saw him go across the hall and knock on Rob and Butch's door. He heard him ask Butch the same question and locked himself back in the confines of his room.

He went to dinner at seven o'clock, figuring there wouldn't be a line at that point. He tucked the hood over his face and headed out without the shades this time. Gertie Vernon handed him a plate of spaghetti, and he put it on his tray. He turned to his right and saw Andy and Rudy sitting by the milk machine. He pulled up a chair and sat with his back to the crowd. They heard guys talking about the surprise visit from the headmaster. They hadn't seen Phillip since Friday night. His car wasn't in the parking lot.

Chad had no appetite. He got up, his meal half finished, and disposed of it. Then he slipped outside.

\* \* \*

Later that evening, Wendell Bishop called Jonas MacPharlan again. His voice sounded strained.

"Did you find out anything?"

"His car isn't in the parking lot," Jonas said. "Phillip must have forgotten to tell you where he was going."

"It isn't like him to do that. He always communicates with us."

"I'll call you back if I hear something."


Phillip's car was tucked away in the underbrush and went unnoticed. By Monday morning, it was still not in the parking lot, and Jonas MacPharlan wondered what was going on. After breakfast, he went over to the table where Chad, Andy, and Rudy were sitting.

"May I have a word with you, Mr. McAlpin?"

"Okay."

Chad exchanged nervous glances with his friends and followed the headmaster out of the cafeteria. Jonas pointed at the bandage on Chad's right hand and asked, "What happened to you?"

"Oh, I fell down jogging the other day."

"That must have hurt."

"It was okay."

They went into the headmaster's office, and Chad sat across from his desk. He folded his hands and stared at the old man's bald spot.

"Are you sure Phillip didn't mention where he was going this weekend?" the headmaster asked.

"Yes, sir."

"You're sure he wasn't here?"

"He wasn't on campus."

Jonas scratched his head and said, "That's odd. I wonder where he went."

"I haven't seen him since Friday night."

"Was he feeling okay?"

"I don't think so."

"What do you mean?"

Chad leaned forward and said, "He told me he wasn't feeling right, and I figured he had the bug that's been going around. In the morning, I got up to go jogging, and his car wasn't in the parking lot. I just figured he got up early to go home. Is there anything wrong, sir?"

"It isn't like him to leave without a word. Did he say anything at all to you lately? Was he unhappy with school?"

"No, sir. He was happy."

"Did he want to leave?"

"No."

"Well, it looks like Mr. Bishop has gone AWOL. We called his parents and—"

Chad shook his head and said, "I can't believe it!"

"I just wanted to let you know. You may go now."

"Will he get in trouble?"

"That depends. But it is not your concern, Mr. McAlpin."

Chad sprang to his feet and quickly left the room.

MacPharlan reached for the telephone and called the police.

"Hello, this is Jonas MacPharlan at Broad Meadow. I would like to report a missing person."

Chad saw Andy and Rudy walking toward Forrester Hall and ran to catch up. They stood on the sidewalk, and Chad waited until classmates were out of earshot before he started talking.

"We're dead! MacPharlan was talking to the police when I left his office."

Andy looked at him and rolled his eyes. "You mean you didn't think it would come to this?"

"I knew it would, but now it's happening."

"In a few minutes, the police will be here, and they'll be searching the area," Rudy whined. "They'll find the car and the body."

"And they'll think it was an accident," Andy said.

Chad chewed his fingernails, his eyes darting from Andy to Rudy. "Maybe."

"We'll stick together, remember?" Rudy said quickly.

"I can't let you guys do this," Chad insisted. "I'm in it up to my ass . . . there's still time to save yourselves."

"We faked the wreck," Andy reminded him. "We're just as guilty. We're in this to the end."

"There's still time to get out before you're in over your heads."

"We're already in over our heads."

"We'll help you," Rudy said.

"Okay, but this is your last chance to pull out. I was serious about the notes."

Doubting their loyalty, he knew he could count on them after providing little incentives to keep quiet. He removed the sunglasses and pointed to his face.

"It's nasty looking!" Andy cried.

Chad put them back on and said, "Tell me about it."

"Do you think they'll suspect?" Rudy wondered.

"Not if you keep your mouth zipped," Andy said.

They walked hurriedly toward Forrester Hall. It was a two-story brick building with white pillars at the front entrance and a clock tower sticking up from the roof.

They scrambled up the front steps and pushed through the double doors. They went into Mrs. Ferguson's calculus classroom and sat at their seats in back. She checked attendance and was surprised not to see Phillip there. Jonas was so busy talking to the police, and he didn't have time to tell the faculty about his absence.

By third period, a rumor was circulating that something fishy was going on. The physics teacher asked, "Has anyone seen Mr. Bishop?"

"He wasn't feeling right," Chad answered before Andy and Rudy could possibly slip up. "He got sick at the party and—" He froze, else not to slip up himself.

"And what, Mr. McAlpin?"

"He came back pretty early from the party . . . he was really sick."

"I'll call the infirmary and—"

"He went home early Saturday morning and wasn't here last night."

Michelle and Susan stared at him in astonishment. Butch Hughes glanced from the girls to Chad and said, "His car isn't in the parking lot."

The teacher marked Phillip Bishop's name on the absent grid.

## LOVE'S A CRIME

Chad glanced at Michelle. She scowled and said something under her breath. He knew she knew he was lying. For a moment, he was afraid she would tell Mr. Wriggley that Phillip was in tip-top health when she and the girls left them in the woods the other night. But she didn't. She just looked at him as if she knew what he was thinking. He hoped she had not heard him stammer. It was a dead giveaway that he was not being truthful. He prided himself on being calm and collected when he lied. She would wonder what was going on and ask questions. Then she would tell the girls. He could not afford that happening.

Rudy stirred from a peaceful slumber when Mr. Wriggley raised his voice. The teacher looked over at Andy, who was looking elsewhere. His mind was clearly not on physics. He went over to him and slammed a book near his face.

Andy stammered the response to a question he had not heard. It was a pretty damned good answer at that. The bell rendered other students out of trancelike dreams about boyfriends and girlfriends or cover-ups.

Andy, Chad, and Rudy filed out the door. Michelle struggled to keep up their pace.

"Hey guys, wait up!"

They darted toward the steps, and she lost them in the crowd.

At about one o'clock, a police car pulled into a parking space at Hullien Hall. Jonas MacPharlan met two uniformed officers at the door. They introduced themselves as Officers Lynch and Saunders.

"Did you find out anything?" MacPharlan asked.

"I'm afraid we have some bad news, sir," Officer Lynch said. "A car matching the description you gave us was spotted at the bottom of the ravine on Snake Turn Road."

MacPharlan squeezed the eagle emblem on his cane with his right hand. He pressed his left hand over his mouth and groaned. "How bad is it?"

"It was a red sports car. A male about eighteen years old was behind the wheel. He fits the description of your missing person. He must have been killed on impact. We'll need you to make a positive identification."

"I'll be there right away."

* * *

Jonas MacPharlan reluctantly lifted the cloth and held his hand over his nose so he didn't have to take a whiff of the three-day-old corpse. It smelled like rotten meat. Phillip's skin was a ghoulish color. Dried blood had oozed from a deep gash from his forehead down his right cheek. Blisters had started to form on his skin. His lips were pale, and his corneas looked cloudy.

Jonas swallowed hard to avoid vomiting. He looked away quickly and gasped, "It's him."

Officer Saunders asked him questions, but he was too flustered to answer them. Assistant Headmaster Tim Price did most of the talking. He was of medium build and in his midforties. He had thick dark hair and a mustache and beard.

The officer thanked him and went over to his colleagues. Tim listened while Jonas ranted about the car accident.

"I've been trying to get somebody to do something about this road for fifteen years, but no one listened," MacPharlan said. "We've tried to get kids not to come out here, haven't we?"

"All the time."

"I've warned them so many times, but they never listen."

"Kids think they're invincible," Price said.

"This is the last straw."

Tim tapped MacPharlan's shoulder and said, "Come on, Jonas, there isn't anything we can do now. Let the police handle it."

He sighed and said, "You're right, Tim."

"Do you want me to call his parents?"

"What would I do without you?"

"Come on, we should get back before the police call them. It would be better if they heard it from me first."

They went back to the car and looked back at the detectives investigating the scene.

"The highway department thinks there are more important things than fixing roads,"

MacPharlan grunted. "Now it is on their heads."

Tim slowly turned around the bend, headed back to campus.

# Chapter 3

Detective Frank Logan had always dreamed of becoming a cop just like his father, Francis, who was a Philadelphia legend. When Frank was twelve, his father was killed in the line of duty. Two years later, Frank's mother, Vera, died in a car accident. He went to live with his grandfather, whom he affectionately called Gramps.

Losing his parents at an early age hardened him to life's harsh realities. He was a straight arrow. While his friends partied, he studied and maintained good grades. After high school, he graduated from the police academy and was assigned to the same precinct as his father. As an officer, he dealt with problems like homicide, rape, incest, suicide, robbery, abortion, teen pregnancy, prostitution, and drug addiction. He worked hard, knowing his father would have been proud of him and made detective five years after joining the force. The stress took a toll on him, however, and he transferred to the rural community of Townsend. It was a small staff, and detectives often had to do the jobs that criminalists did in the city. Small-town life was a major adjustment, and he felt alienated from the people he was trying to serve. He knew he had to give it a chance. He knew he had no choice.

At thirty, he had a young-looking face and was often taken for a rookie. He could easily blend in with high school students, and they had no idea how old he was. Though he worked out on a regular basis and had the abs to show for it, his youthful appearance was one trait that annoyed him. He knew he had been a good police officer and had worked too hard to be treated like he was a new kid on the block.

He studied the blacktop and noticed there were no skid marks. Then he looked down on the wrecked vehicle and took extensive notes. Though the trees were bare, the car would have been difficult to see from the road. It was about a fifty-foot drop and was hidden by underbrush. He had to carefully edge his way down the hill to get a better look. From that angle, the back end was sticking up, and the headlights and hood were submerged. He waded into the stream to get a closer look and jotted down what the twisted metal looked like. A photographer in a rubber suit was waist deep in the water, shooting it from every conceivable angle.

Lieutenant Harry Winters looked inside the car and took notes. At forty-five, he was tall and trim, with a shaved head and a dark mustache. His eyes were cold and harsh, and there was a scar above his right eyebrow.

Logan looked at him and said, "When will kids ever learn? It's a crying shame."

"Tell me about it."

He pulled a flashlight from his coat pocket and aimed the light to take a better look. He opened his evidence collection kit case and removed a large fiberglass brush. He fluffed out the bristles with the palms of his hands, dipped the tip into the container of black powder until the fingerprint became more visible. He blew off excess powder and continued brushing it. Then he pressed a strip of clear tape onto the door handle. He lifted the tape and pressed it on a blank index card. He pulled out his pocketknife, cut the tape from the roll, and wrote down pertinent information on the card. He put it in a plastic evidence bag and labeled it.

Then he ran his fingers along the smashed windshield, peered through the window, and studied the distance from the front seat to the steering wheel and noted that the gearshift was in neutral.

"How tall would you say he was?"

"A little over six feet," Harry said.

"That's interesting."

"What?"

"Take a look at the front seat and tell me what you think."

Lieutenant Winters leaned down to examine it. He looked back at Logan and said, "The front seat is too close to the steering wheel."

"Exactly. It's as if someone shorter was driving. It looks like somebody faked the accident. Most people adjust their seats before they start the car. Unless he was driving somebody else's car at night and couldn't find the lever to adjust it. If you're as tall as this guy was, he wouldn't have been able to drive comfortably like that. Maybe that's why he got into the accident, but that's doubtful."

"I don't think this was an accident."

They scaled the hill and went over to Coroner Stan Green. He was a beefy man in his midfifties with thinning gray hair and a large round face.

"What do you have, Stan?" Logan asked him.

Stan lifted the sheet, and they looked at the victim's body. Phillip Bishop's forehead was caked in dried blood. There was a deep cut on his left cheek. His right knuckle looked swollen.

It looked like there was a bloodstain on the front of his shirt. There was a rip on the right shoulder area, and a piece was missing.

Stan turned Phillip's head to the side and said, "It looks like he fell and hit his head."

"Most people don't have injuries on the back of the head if they're in a car accident like this," Logan said. "He must have fallen on his head. And then somebody put him in the car and shoved it off the edge. That makes sense. Nobody drives in neutral."

"When do you think he died?" Lieutenant Winters asked.

"I'll let you know when I do the autopsy." He covered the body with a sheet and went back to talking in his tape recorder.

Logan went over to the edge of the road and watched the recovery crew pull the car up the hill. It was a slow and arduous process. The tow truck driver backed away, pulling with a winch the heavy wire cables that were attached to the car. When they got it over the embankment, he could take a better look at it. When the photographer finished taking pictures of it, Logan opened the driver's side door and dusted for prints on the rearview mirror.

Meanwhile, Tim Price wondered how to tell Phillip's parents about the death of their son over the telephone but knew it had to be done. He slowly dialed their number, rehearsing what he would say. Lois Bishop answered it on the fifth ring. Wendell got on another line.

"Hello, this is Assistant Headmaster Tim Price. I'm afraid I have some bad news, Mrs. Bishop. Is your husband there? I think you should both hear this."

"I'm here," he said.

"Have you heard from Phillip?" Her voice sounded strained.

"I don't know how to tell you this, Mrs. Bishop. Phillip was in a car accident. He ran his car off Snake Turn Road."

"Oh my god," Wendell said. "Is he all right?"

"I'm sorry, sir, the police said he died on impact."

Tim put his finger on the bridge of his nose when he heard her wailing in the background.

"God nooooo!" she shrieked.

Tim spent the next few minutes trying to console them.

"We'll be there as soon as we can," Wendell shouted to be heard over his wife's wailing. "Thank you for calling, Mr. Price."

"I just didn't want you to hear it from a police officer," Tim said. "If there is anything I can do, please don't hesitate to give me a call."


The telephone receiver shook in Wendell's hand. He slowly hung up and went over to his wife. She collapsed in his arms, her body trembling. He squeezed her tight and wept with her. Her tears soaked through his shirt.

They both felt like they had been punched in the stomach. They hoped, against hope that it was a mistake. Maybe Tim Price would call them back and tell them the police made a mistake. Or maybe they were just stuck in a horrible nightmare. When they awoke, Phillip would be okay. Unfortunately, it was true, and there was nothing they could do to change it.

A few minutes later, Wendell left word with a coworker that he would not be attending a meeting that afternoon. He went back to his wife, and they sat at the kitchen table, hugging each other.


At one o'clock, Tim knocked on Jonas MacPharlan's office door. He stuck his head in and said, "I just called the Bishops, sir. They're on their way."

"Thank you, Tim. I just didn't know how to tell them."

"It's never easy, sir."

Jonas rose slowly and went over to the coatrack by the door. He put on his cap, and Tim followed him outside. They pushed through the crowd gathered in front of Forrester Hall and climbed the front steps.

Jonas looked solemnly at the students and fought back tears. "I have some bad news," he said. "This weekend, Phillip Bishop was killed in a car accident off Snake Turn Road."

"Noooo!" students shouted in unison.

The sound of shrill wailing echoed across the sidewalk. Students wept uncontrollably, their bodies rocking as they consoled each other.

Michelle wrapped her arms around Susan and felt her body tremble. Susan wiped tears away with her hands and breathed heavily.

Students were so lost in their sorrow, MacPharlan's speech did not sink in.

"From now on, Snake Turn Road is off-limits," MacPharlan continued. "If you are caught within a one-mile radius, you will receive a three-day suspension. If it happens again, you will be expelled, no questions asked."

Chad looked at Susan and then at his shoes. He did not know what to do. He wanted to put his arms around her, but he knew she was mad at him. He bit his lip and tried not to give himself away. He glanced over at Andy and Rudy, and they refused to make eye contact. He imagined they were just as nervous as he was. They watched the headmaster's lips move but were too busy thinking about the reality of the situation. It was only a matter of time before the police started asking questions. From now on, they would have to watch what they said.

Jonas MacPharlan stared down at the students and asked, "Does anyone have questions? I hope I have made myself clear. I'll be glad to answer your questions in detail if need be. Remember, you have all been warned."

He told everyone to bow their heads and said a prayer for Phillip.

"Tonight, there will be a mandatory memorial service at the chapel," he said after a long silence. He canceled classes for the rest of the afternoon and drew the meeting to a close.

Students filed toward their dorms, deadly quiet for once. They were like spirits who wander the earth silent and invisible.

Coach Reynolds went over to Susan and Michelle and said, "I'm so sorry about Phillip."

Susan looked down and wiped her tears. "Thank you."

"If there's anything I can do, just give me a call."

Susan's breathing was heavy. She was too upset to respond.

"Thank you," Michelle answered for her.

JOSEPH REDDEN

The coach met Susan's gaze. "Will you be all right?"

Susan nodded her head and wiped away tears.

The coach went over to some other students and offered his condolences. Then John Fletcher went up to make sure they were okay.

"It's such a tragedy," he said. "If you ever need to talk, I'm a really good listener."

"Thanks," Michelle said. "It's too overwhelming right now, but I'm sure she'll take you up on it later."

His eyes flashed concern as he turned his focus on Michelle. "How are you holding up?"

"It probably won't hit me till later, but thanks for asking."

"You know where I am." He reached over and gave them a group hug. Then he merged with the crowd.

Susan leaned toward Michelle and held onto her hands for dear life. "Are you okay?"

Susan closed her eyes, her head tilting forward. "I feel dizzy."

Chad watched Michelle walk Susan over to the nurse and heard her say, "Susan isn't right, Mrs. Grier."

The nurse wrapped her arm around Susan and said, "Come lie down in the infirmary, honey."

"I feel lightheaded and—and everything's spinning," Susan managed through her tears.

She put her arm around Michelle's shoulder, and they helped her up the front steps. Chad watched them enter the building. Then the door closed, and he looked at his shoes.

Andy patted his shoulder and said, "Are you all right?"

"I wish there was something more I could do for her."

"She'll be okay. Come on, you better get some rest too. Let's go back to the dorm."

Reality sank in, and it didn't take Chad long to get back to normal. He called Andy and Rudy together for another meeting to discuss their situation.

"One of the girls will probably let it slip that we were all there," Chad said. "They know we were there. We came back a few minutes after they did. You guys went back to the dance, and people saw me outside the student center, remember?"

"Yeah, that's right," Andy said.

"Phillip went back to his dorm, and we got back just before curfew, right?"

"Yeah," Rudy said.

"I don't remember seeing Phillip's car here on Saturday morning, do you?"

"No," Andy said. "He said something about getting up really early to go home for the weekend, didn't he?"

"Yeah," Chad said. "You got it, Rudy?"

He nodded and met Andy's gaze.

"We've got to get our stories straight or the cops will be on to us," Chad said. "If the truth comes out, I'm in big trouble."

"They'll never know what happened," Andy said.

Officer Lenny Sherman went over to Lieutenant Winters and said, "We found something, sir. I think you had better take a look at it."

They followed him through the woods. The trail wound around like a labyrinth. Logan's eyes trained on footprints that were heading toward the road. They were about six feet apart and set deep in the ground. Another set appeared to the left of them. At some point, the ones in back and at the side appeared to have switched places. A few feet away, prints went in opposite directions. There were multiple marks of all sizes and styles. Some of them were on top of each other, as if people had been going up and down the path. The impressions were deep. Many were spaced far apart, as if they had been running. High heel marks were among the men's footprints, which meant that couples had been there recently. When they reached a clearing, the footprints were more sporadic.

Logan studied pine needles strewn on the dirt. The pattern was disrupted, as if there had been a struggle. Dried leaves were in the mix. He knelt down to examine the rocks and said, "There appears to be blood on a rock. It looks like a definite sign that a fight occurred here."

He photographed the scene, then put the rock in an evidence bag. He collected leaf samples and put them in separate bags. When he was finished, he wrote down pertinent information, initialed, and dated them.

They followed Logan back to the site where Officer Sherman saw the footprints and photographed each set. Criminalist Bonnie Draper sprayed them with a can of aerosol spray and placed wooden frames around them. Officer Sherman went down to the stream to collect water in a bucket and came back a few minutes later. Bonnie removed a bag of plaster from her evidence collection kit and dumped the powder into the bucket. She stirred it with a mixing stick until it was the right texture and poured it into the frame and reinforced the plaster with Popsicle sticks. She wrote her initials, the date, and the case number on back. Then she went on to do the other ones.

Meanwhile, Logan and his colleagues examined bushes and tree limbs on the footprint trail that led to the road. Logan saw something white entangled on a tree limb. It was about one inch in diameter and looked like the material that ripped off Phillip Bishop's shirt. He photographed it and put it in an evidence bag. He jotted down where he found it, dated, and initialed it.

At that point, he decided to go to Broad Meadow to talk to the students. He drove slowly around the twists and turns and decided it was appropriately named Snake Turn Road. He saw the rushing water below out of the corner of his eye, but concentrated on the wheel for fear of his life. Two burned-out stone buildings jutted out on opposite sides as he approached a bend. It was just the shell of a home probably built in the 1700s that was set at the top of the hill. Moss was on the walls. Graffiti was splattered on the stones in bright colors. For many decades, lovers scrawled their initials on the stones to announce their love for each other. Names were painted over and replaced with a new crop of lovebirds who advertised their love for each other. Modern lovers used more colorful adjectives and profanities to express their feelings for each other. In large pink letters, Logan was assured that Chris 'N Jack were an item. He wasn't sure if Chris was male or female. These days, it could be either way. He stopped and honked the horn to warn a possible oncoming motorist that he was approaching and proceeded with caution as he drove toward Broad Meadow.

# Chapter 4

Logan got a sense of how old the school was when he drove down the entrance road at two o'clock. On his right, there was an Episcopal church with a tall steeple and massive stained glass windows. He imagined the colored glass looked spectacular from inside. At his left, there was a stone archway with a cobblestone walkway tucked under trees. About fifteen feet behind it, there was a one-story brick building with a steeple on top. There was a sign in large red letters that read Student Center. At one time, it must have either been a church or a one-room schoolhouse. He reached a stop sign at Broad Meadow Road and saw girls walking into a Victorian house across the street from the church. It was painted yellow and had lattice trim at the bottom. There were bay windows on the first and second floors. He whistled when he read the sign by the road that read, Broad Meadow, 1885.

He turned left onto Broad Meadow, which was a back road parallel to Highway 558. He drove past the soccer field and made a right onto a tree-lined lane that led to Hullien Hall. A boy zipped by on his skateboard. He was leaning down in a hunched position and talking on a cell phone, oblivious to motorists. Logan pulled into a guest parking spot and went inside. He saw a sign for the headmaster's office and walked down a long corridor. The carpet was bright red and annoying to the eyes. There was the pungent aroma of mold typical of old buildings. Students brushed past him and skipped up creaky wooden stairs. He heard their voices echo in the stairwell. Others hurriedly made their way downstairs.

He went to the end of the hall and saw the headmaster's name on a plaque by the door. He went inside and saw a heavyset woman with stringy white hair at a computer. Behind her, there were French doors with white lace curtains on the windows. She told him that Mr. MacPharlan was on the phone, and he sat on a wooden chair with the school's insignia painted on it. Ten minutes later, the doors opened and Jonas waved.

Logan figured he was the mild-mannered type with a blue bow tie and glasses. He had on a white button-down shirt and tweed jacket, gray pants, and black loafers.

Logan followed him inside and watched his back hump as he leaned on his cane. With effort, he slowly eased onto his swivel chair and was dwarfed by the mahogany desk.

MacPharlan looked at the detective for a moment with his left eyebrow raised. Logan had seen that look before. The headmaster was probably thinking that he was too young to be a detective.

Jonas MacPharlan drew a deep breath and said, "I've warned those kids for so many years. This will be the last time. Parents will have to be notified. It's the highway department's fault for not barricading that curve. How many lives have to be lost before anything is done?"

"Calm down, sir. We don't think it was an automobile accident."

"What did you say?"

"We believe the vehicle he was in was pushed off the road."

"Surely, you must be joking."

"I'm afraid not, sir. The car was in neutral. That means he was either unconscious or already dead before he was moved. More than one person was involved. It would take somebody with incredible strength to move the body and push the car down the hill alone."

MacPharlan glowered at him and said, "Stop this nonsense! I don't want to hear it!"

"I know it's hard, but I need to ask these questions."

"I don't like you accusing my students of—"

"I haven't accused anyone, sir."

"Do you have fingerprints? Are there any marks on the body?"

"Yes, his face was cut up pretty bad. It looked like he had been in a struggle. He did have money in his wallet, though. Maybe he tried to stop somebody from mugging him. Have you had any problems like that in the past?"

"Yes, over the years a lot of weirdos have wandered the streets in town. It isn't safe for people to go anywhere now."

"I know what you mean. Can you think of anyone who might have wanted to harm Phillip?"

MacPharlan leaned back in his chair, lost in thought. Logan glanced at the Scottish memorabilia on the wall behind him, then at the antique furniture around the room. He looked back at the headmaster and waited for him to say something. Then their eyes met.

"Terry Dawson had a grudge against Phillip."

Logan jotted the name on his pad and asked, "Who is he?"

"He's a nasty young man. He was such a good student. But then he got mixed up in selling drugs last year and got expelled. Phillip found out about it and turned him in. You can ask anyone here and they'll all agree. Terry Dawson had motive. He wanted revenge because Phillip got him in trouble."

"Were other people involved?"

Jonas nodded and sighed. "A teacher named Graham Humphries started it. Graham ruined this school's academic reputation. I didn't screen him well enough, I'm sorry to say. That won't happen again."

"What happened?"

Jonas removed his glasses and rubbed his eyes. "Humphries was involved in a drug operation. Terry was an excellent student but got dragged down to their level. It was a lapse of judgment. Somehow, Phillip got wind of it and stepped forward. Graham was fired, and Terry was kicked out."

"Are there any teachers still working here who were involved in it?"

"They wouldn't be here long if that were the case."

"Did Phillip use drugs?"

"No, he was a straight arrow."

"Are you sure?"

MacPharlan laid his glasses on the desk and said, "Now look. Phillip was a decent young man, and I resent you besmirching his reputation. He was an honor student, well liked. He was a hero. His parents will be arriving from Princeton soon. It's going to be hell. I don't like what you are implying, that he was involved with drugs or any other illicit activity. You are leading up to something. You're going to tell me that he was on drugs. He was a good kid."

"Calm down."

"I won't calm down!" The veins in his neck bulged. "Detective Logan, this is one of the leading college prep schools in the state. We have already had bad press because of the drug incident. We don't need another scandal! Now, if you'll excuse me, I need to attend to some pressing issues."

Logan rose and said, "I'm sorry I upset you."

Jonas escorted him into the outer office and sat back at his desk. He picked up the telephone and dialed. "Hello, this is Jonas MacPharlan. We're in big trouble."

---

Logan leafed through old yearbooks to learn as much about Phillip Bishop as he could. The librarian was busily restocking shelves behind him. She was about fifty, plump, with short frosted hair. Glasses were attached to a chain around her neck.

He flipped a page and laughed at the corny captions that were similar to the ones in his old yearbooks. He glanced at the senior portraits and read their comments. One girl had been involved in so many activities that her blurb had to be printed in a smaller font size.

"She's a nice-looking girl," he said.

Mrs. Henley leaned over his shoulder and said, "She was a beauty, that's for sure."

"I'll bet she'll go places."

She shoved a book in its slot and said, "It's a shame what happened to her."

"What happened?"

Her eyes darted around the room. Then she lowered her voice and said, "It happens to kids once in a while. She was trying to do so much and burned out."

"That's too bad."

"She didn't finish up here, the poor thing. But she's feeling much better now."

He continued flipping pages and said, "Phillip kept busy. He was an athlete, a scholar, and an honor student."

"He might have been class valedictorian if—I can't believe he was murdered like you said. He was a popular young man."

"He apparently wasn't that popular."

Mrs. Henley shook her head and said, "You're wrong. He was so kind. He always looked out for people. That's rare these days."

"I know this is hard for you, ma'am, but I believe somebody tried to make it look like an accident."

Her eyes widened. "Are you sure?"

"I'm afraid so."

"Detective, we are a close-knit community here. We know each other's business—good or bad. We would know if something wasn't right. I can't imagine anybody around here doing such a thing."

"How about Graham Humphries or Terry Dawson?"

She shuttered and said, "Not even them. Sure, they had reason to hate him, but they wouldn't do anything like that."

"You're too trusting."

"I know. I always look for the good in people even if they are truly wicked."

"I don't work that way, ma'am."

"No, perhaps not." She checked the number on a bookbinding and shoved it in a slot three shelves down. "You should know something about Graham, though. He couldn't have done it. He's been in rehab for several months."

She told him the name of the clinic, and he jotted it in his pad. His eyes trained on a photograph of Phillip and Terry in their football uniforms.

"I bet Terry Dawson could have gone places," he said.

"If it hadn't been for his lapse in judgment." She went across the room and continued stacking shelves.

Logan flipped a page and saw a group shot of Phillip and his friends. The caption read, "The gang's all here: Susan, Chad, Michelle, and Phillip ham it up for the camera." A short time later, he handed the yearbooks to Mrs. Henley and asked her directions to Phillip's dorm.

"Thank you for your time, Mrs. Henley." He whistled on his way out the door.

The dorm supervisor unlocked Phillip's bedroom door, and Logan looked around. It was a small room with dark blue cinder block walls. Clothes were neatly folded in plastic bins, and nothing appeared out of place. Above his desk, there was a bulletin board with Tigers banners and snapshots of athletic events. A lot of newspaper photos were pinned to it. There were several pictures of Phillip clowning around with girls. He recognized their faces from yearbook photos. A laptop computer and printer were on the desk. An iPod was next to it. Video games and CDs were on a rack by the door.

He opened desk drawers and sifted through papers placed in a neat stack. He looked under Phillip's bed and pulled out a shoe box. He pried off the lid and saw a stack of printed e-mails and actual handwritten letters. He sifted through them and stopped when he saw a pink card with a heart drawing on it dated October 15, over a year ago, that read,

> Dear Phillip,
>
> It's hard for me to tell you how I feel in person. The other night when we kissed, I felt alive for the first time in my life. I wondered if you felt it too. Please talk to me.
>
> Love,
> Michelle

Logan sifted through the stack, then his eyes fell on a note that was still in the envelope that read,

> Dear Phillip,
>
> Thank you so much for the cards. I'm sorry it has taken me so long to write. You'll probably be reading this when I return. You're so kind. I'm sorry for scaring everybody. I can't explain how I was feeling. Maybe in time you'll know why. Thanks again for being so understanding.
>
> Love,
> Susan

He checked the envelope and grunted. The name of a psychiatric hospital in Chicago was on the return address. January 11 was stamped on it. A year ago, Susan had written a lot of notes from there. He finished looking through the stack and shoved the shoe box under the bed.

Then he pulled out his pad and wrote, "Ask Phillip's parents what his password is."

Chad was studying when he heard a knock at the door. "Who is it?"

Logan pushed the door open a crack and introduced himself. "I need to ask you some questions regarding Phillip Bishop. I understand that you were friends."

"Come in."

When Logan entered the room, he saw him sitting at his desk. He had on blue jeans and a dark green sweat shirt. Logan looked to his left and saw trophies and metals displayed prominently on a bookshelf. He went over to a chair next to a small white desk by the window and glanced at an open history textbook. Chad removed a pile of clothes on the chair and laid them on the floor. He sat at the edge of the bed and looked intently at the detective.

Logan looked at the bandage and asked, "How did you hurt your hand?"

Chad laughed and said, "I slipped and skinned it when I went jogging the other day."

"Hmm, that must've hurt."

"I've had worse scrapes at basketball practice."

"It can get rough at times," Logan agreed. He pointed to the bruise over his left eye and said, "I guess that's how you got the shiner too."

"Uh-huh."

"But anyway, I didn't come here to talk about your injuries. I was hoping you could tell me some things about Phillip. Was he depressed?"

"No, he was happy. He told me it was the first time he had been happy in a long time."

"He wasn't before?"

"His folks were having troubles. That's why he came here, at least that's what he said. They sent him to boarding school to get rid of him . . . they didn't want him to be around when they were fighting. I understood exactly how he felt because I wasn't getting along with my family either.

Phillip and I helped each other through rough times. His folks seem to be getting along better now, though."

"You were close?"

He held his hands together and said, "Tight."

"Were you jealous of his athletic abilities?"

Chad bristled and said, "No."

"I'd be jealous."

"I wasn't jealous!" he snapped.

"It's okay to be envious. Was he dating anyone?"

"Yes," Chad said through clenched teeth.

"Who?"

"Susan Williams."

"For how long?"

"A while."

"I sense some hostility here. You liked her, didn't you?"

"I still do."

"Were they serious?"

He huffed and said, "Yes."

"Do you have a girlfriend?"

"A few to pick from."

"I'm surprised you don't have a girlfriend."

"What business is it of yours?"

"None at all."

Chad apologized and tried to remain calm so the detective would not catch him off guard.

Logan glanced over at the bulletin board and saw a snapshot of Susan on Chad's lap. "I take it you were all good friends."

"In a manner of speaking."

"Did you have a falling out with him?"

"It's the talk around campus."

"Were you angry because he stole your girlfriend?"

He glared at him and said, "You're way off base, sir."

"Why are you so hot under the collar? I struck a nerve, didn't I? When was the last time you saw him?"

"We went to a dance at the student center, then we went to the woods."

"The woods where Phillip died?"

Chad waved his hands and said, "I was with friends. They can vouch for me. Wait a minute, Phillip drove his car off the road."

"That's what somebody wanted people to think, but I know otherwise. I know for a fact that he was murdered."

"How?"

"I can't say at the moment. Right now, I'm trying to put the pieces together. When did you go to the woods?"

"About eight o'clock."

"How long were you there?"

"About an hour and a half or so. We would've stayed longer, but the girls got mad at us and drove back to their dorms in Michelle Martin's car. Susan had a headache, or so she claimed. We went back right after they did."

"Can anybody verify that?"

"Yeah, people at the dance can. They must've seen us driving back on campus, but I can't remember the exact time. We dropped Phillip off at the dorm and went back to the dance. He stayed there. He was in a bad mood."

"What was he mad about?"

"I don't know, I didn't ask. He probably got into a fight with Susy."

"Did anybody else see him there?"

"I don't know, I was in my room. And then I went back to the dance."

"Did anyone see you there?"

"I'm sure they did."

"What does that mean?"

"Well, I started to go into the student center but got a call on my cell phone. I sat on the steps talking for about a half an hour or so."

"Who called you?"

"I don't think that's any of your business."

"I know, but it couldn't hurt. Who were you talking to?"

"A friend from home. We went to grammar school together, all right?"

"What's your friend's name?"

Chad rolled his eyes and gave him the name and telephone number of his friend.

## JOSEPH REDDEN

"What time did you leave the dance?"

"About midnight. I didn't want the dorm supervisor to get mad at me. The curfew is midnight, you see."

"Was Phillip there when you got back?"

He looked Logan square in the eye and said, "I don't know. It was late and I was so tired, I didn't think about it. I got in bed and woke up early Saturday morning to go jogging. His car wasn't in the parking lot when I got back, and I figured he must have gone to his parents' house for the weekend. I went home after breakfast and got back Sunday night in time for curfew. A friend and I spent the night studying for an exam. I don't think Phillip's bedroom light was on. It does seem a little strange now that I think about it. It was an important test, and he always studied in his room."

"Did he ever go off campus alone at night?"

"Yeah, I guess. He used to go to the woods to think a lot. We always blew off steam, but we were tight."

"Did he have enemies?"

He told him about Terry Dawson and Mr. Humphries.

"Did anybody else have it in for him?"

"Coach Reynolds was pretty hard on him after the basketball game. I can't think of anybody else at the moment."

"Why was the coach so mad at him?"

"You'll have to ask him yourself. I have no idea."

"Who is Michelle?"

"She used to go out with Phillip."

"Why did they break up?"

Chad waved his hand and said, "I don't know. Some things are nobody's business, but you probably wouldn't understand that."

"No, I probably wouldn't. Do you know why Susan was in a psychiatric hospital in Chicago?"

Chad hung his head and looked down. "She was really sick," he said in a hushed tone. "I heard that she had a nervous breakdown, but she wouldn't talk about it."

"Hmm, that's too bad."

"When she came back, she and Phillip got real chummy, if you know what I mean."

"Is there anything else I should know about?"

Chad shrugged his shoulders and said, "I don't think so, but I'll let you know if I remember anything."

Logan thanked him and showed himself out.

Chad went into Andy and Rudy's room without knocking. They were lying on their bunk beds, doing homework before basketball practice. He pulled a chair toward the bunks and said, "That guy grilled me pretty good. I have a feeling he's onto me."

"I don't see what the big deal is," Rudy said. "We were pretty out of it at the time—we weren't thinking clearly. Why can't we just say he hit his head and we panicked?"

"Because people saw us arguing, that's why! We need to stick together."

Andy looked at Rudy and said, "We need to say the same things."

"One slip and he'll be on to us," Rudy mumbled.

"Rudy, we told you if you wanted to back out, you could do it," Chad said. "It's too late now."

"I know, but there's got to be something else we can do."

"Transfer," Andy suggested.

"Or think of a way to shut that Logan guy up," Chad said.

Rudy's jaw dropped. "You mean—?"

"No, not kill him," Chad said. "Maybe we could just put him on a wild goose chase."

Rudy's voice rose, and he started speaking rapidly, "It'll never work. We'll trip ourselves up. He's got years of experience and—"

"Do you have any other ideas?" Chad asked sarcastically.

Rudy shook his head. He had no ideas at all.

"We have to think of something and fast," Chad said.

They looked from one to the other and didn't say a word. A knock on the door cut through the silence. Tom opened the door and said, "Hey, Rudy, you've got a phone call."

Rudy darted over to the door, and Chad said, "Rudy, remember Mrs. Bradshaw?"

Rudy stopped dead in his tracks, his eyes bulging. He looked back at Chad and said, "You can't threaten me!" Then he tore out of the room.

Andy swallowed hard and said, "He's going to be a problem. It's only a matter of time before he slips up and tells the police everything."

"You're right, so we need to do something."

"What?" Andy was concerned about his friend. "What's this about Mrs. Bradshaw?"

"I'll tell you later," he lied.

Rudy held the receiver with trembling hands.

"Hello?" he squeaked.

It was his mother. She recognized that whiny tone and knew he was upset. "What's wrong?"

"Nothing."

"I've been trying to get a hold of you. You keep leaving your cell phone off. And you don't check your e-mails."

"I'm sorry. I've been really busy."

"We're coming this weekend. Maybe we could go to a movie or something."

"It sounds good." But he did not sound enthusiastic.

"Rudy, are you sure there isn't something wrong?"

He insisted nothing was wrong but spoke so fast that she knew something was definitely not right. His hands shook as he held the receiver.

"I'm okay—there was a party Friday night and we got in real late. Oh well, but—"

"I also want to ask—"

"I've gotta go now, bye!" He hung up quickly and knocked against the receiver on his way down the hall. It fell off the hook and was left dangling.

## Chapter 5

Rudy spoke with the same high-pitched nasal tone that he did when he got nervous.

Logan figured he must be an excellent basketball player. He seemed to have an overabundance of energy.

"I don't know anything," he said quickly. "I don't know why you should ask."

"Calm down," Logan said slowly. "I just want to get some things cleared up. You were one of Phillip Bishop's best friends. You probably know a lot about his habits, his loves, his secrets. I know Susan broke up with Chad and started seeing him. Did he feel threatened by Chad's presence?"

Rudy chewed his nails and said, "Yeah, I guess you might say that. Chad was always trying to get her back."

"Susan was a sore spot between them."

"It's all people have been talking about lately. It took a toll on Susy, that's for sure."

"How so?"

"Rumor has it, that she—" He fell silent.

Logan leaned forward and asked, "What?"

"It's not my place to say."

"You brought it up."

"People said Susy had a nervous breakdown last year. It happened way before she started dating Phillip. But you know how rumors are. I'm sure it got blown way out of proportion."

"Was it before or after she broke up with Chad?"

"Before, I think. I can't remember. So much happens in a year by way of the grapevine."

"Do you know what happened?"

"Susy went to a hospital for a month or so."

"That explains the letters she wrote to him."

"What?"

"She wrote letters to him from the hospital. Anyway, you were saying?"

"I don't think she wanted to come back, but her parents forced her to. They thought it would be good for her to be here with her friends. I'm not really sure. Michelle and Phillip really came through for her, though. She's got guts. I wouldn't have come back if I were her."

"What about Chad?"

"She alienated him or he alienated her. He wasn't at all sympathetic. In fact, he was pretty nasty. He cared more about how it affected his ego than how she was feeling. I think that's why they broke up. Chad got really upset when he saw Phillip hanging around her so much. I can't blame him. They seemed really close."

"Do you know what caused her breakdown?"

"No." He thought carefully a moment and said, "Her folks split. She's an overachiever. She worked too hard."

"Are there any other rumors that circulated from the years you've been here?"

"A few, but they're all fuzzy. There's so much gossip, all the rumors blend together after a while, if you know what I mean."

Logan nodded and said, "So true."

"Sometimes I just don't know how they get started."

"Me neither. Now, can you tell me what happened the night of the dance, when you were with Phillip?"

"It's a blur," Rudy mumbled.

"Do the best you can."

Logan watched him squirm. Throughout the conversation, he had changed seating positions several times. He moved his legs in and out, tapped his feet, and bit his nails. By nature, Rudy was the nervous type. He had a good reason to be nervous. It was not easy answering the questions about his friend's "accident." Logan suspected he knew more than he was letting on.

Rudy's voice rose as he relayed the events that unfolded that night. "We went to the woods. Chad and Phillip's feud killed the mood. The girls got pissed off and left. Susy wasn't feeling well, and the girls were mad. We went back to the dance a few minutes after that."

"What time was that?"

"About eleven o'clock."

"Where was Chad?"

"He was with us. But he spent most of the time outside, talking on his cell phone."

"Where was Phillip?"

"In his room, I guess."

"When you got back to your room, did you see a car going off campus?"

"Not that I can think of."

"You're sure?"

"I'm sure. Headlights are noticeable, especially when they're heading in and out of campus after curfew. Sometimes I lie in bed at night and watch the lights go around the wall after curfew and wonder who's going to get in trouble."

"Do you know anybody who would have wanted to kill Phillip?"

Rudy sprang forward and cried, "God no, it was an accident!"

"That's what somebody tried to make it look like."

Rudy's eyes widened. "What do you mean?"

"I can't tell you at the moment." He thanked him and Rudy left the room.

Andy came in a couple minutes later. Logan introduced himself and told him the reason for his visit. He thought Logan could have been the same age as his older brother. Logan thought Andy was in desperate need of a shave. He took note of his bulging biceps and figured he was probably always working out at the gym. His face and hair seemed oily. At once, he realized how strikingly different the two boys were. While Rudy was wound like a top ready to fly off, Andy appeared cool and introspective. He thought carefully before answering questions. He sat at the edge of the bed and looked intently at the detective.

"What can you tell me about Phillip Bishop?" Logan asked.

"He was a great guy," Andy said. "I'm gonna miss him. I can't believe it happened."

When he told him it wasn't an accident, Andy had the same shocked reaction. Logan asked him the same kinds of questions and got similar answers.

"Did you see or hear anyone threaten him?"

"Yeah, it happened last week," Andy said. "After the basketball game, I heard Coach Reynolds yelling at him."

"What about?"

"He was mad at him because he made mistakes on the court. He was totally off base. We all thought Phillip played well."

"Why was the coach so upset?"

"He said Phillip was too busy flirting with the girls and not paying attention to what he was doing on the basketball court."

"Were they fighting over Susan?"

"Yeah. Phillip did make some careless mistakes during the game. Maybe Susan was a distraction and maybe the coach called him on it. I don't know. When I stuck up for him, the coach told me to mind my own business and went back to his office. I think he was being totally unreasonable."

"It does sound pretty bad."

"The coach is a good guy, but he just has a short fuse. He's so obsessed with winning. He blows into anybody that does the slightest thing wrong. I figured he'd blow off steam and forget about it later."

"Did he?"

"Yeah. The next day, he apologized and that was that."

When Logan asked him if anybody else was upset with Phillip, Andy told him what the others had told him earlier. Terry Dawson was angry that Phillip turned him into the police and threatened him in the gymnasium lobby after the basketball game, in front of several witnesses.

When he asked him about what happened the night Phillip died, he repeated what Chad and Rudy said.

"We went back to the dance. There was still not much action, so we went back to the dorm before curfew."

"When was the last time you saw Phillip?"

"When we dropped him off at the dorm—after we were in the woods. We went back to the dance, and when we came back, I didn't see him."

"Was his car in the parking lot?"

"I don't remember."

"Maybe he went out after you got back."

"He must have. Because I didn't see it there on Saturday."

Logan grunted and said, "It seems funny, though. Why would he drive his car in neutral?"

Andy gulped and said, "I don't know. It does sound strange."

"I know. It's really hard driving that way." He thanked him and showed himself out.

Andy was changing into his basketball uniform when Rudy came back in. He went over to the closet and reached for his jersey. He peeled off his shirt and slipped it on in its place.

"Well?" Andy asked.

"It was okay."

"Did you crack?"

"No, I was fine."

"You better hope so. If not we're up a creek!"

Logan approached a lounge at the other end of the hall and heard loud, explosion sounds. When he entered the room, he saw two boys in sweats pounding the life out of their joysticks. One was lanky, with red hair and freckles. His friend was heavyset with a blond crew cut. Logan walked by in time to see a monster explode on the TV screen.

"Oh man!" squealed the tall boy.

"He's toast!" the other one exclaimed.

Logan went over to a boy who was sprawled on a worn-out-looking sofa in front of the window. He had long blond hair and needed a shave. A large textbook was lying on his chest, and he held it up with both hands. Logan leaned down and tapped his shoulder to get his attention. He looked up at him and removed his iPod earplugs and sat up straight.

Logan asked him a few questions and didn't find out anything new. Other Stewart Hall residents told him basically the same thing. Half had gone away for the weekend. The rest were at the dance on Friday night and weren't paying attention to what time people came and went. They all figured he went home for the weekend because his car wasn't in the parking lot.

He started to go out when a scrawny boy came toward him, carrying so many books that his back arched as he maneuvered down the hall. He had on large glasses that covered most of his face. He was wearing brown corduroys and a red checkered shirt with pencils hanging out of the pocket. He had a ruddy complexion and neatly combed red hair.

He reached up to shake the detective's hand and introduced himself as Willy Brown. Logan towered over him like a giant.

"Did you go to the dance on Friday night?" Logan asked him.

"No, I was studying all night."

"Did you see or hear anything unusual?"

Willy adjusted his glasses and said, "Somebody pulled out of the parking lot about ten thirty, but I didn't see who it was."

Logan handed him a business card and said, "Well, if you remember anything else, give me a call."

At four fifteen, Logan went to the girls' dorm that was a short walk from Forrester Hall. It was the same architectural style as the building he had just been in. He went inside and cupped his ears to drown out the blaring music as he wandered down the hall. He checked the room number and knocked. The door opened, and he saw a tall girl with auburn hair stick her head out.

"Miss Williams?"

"I'm her roommate Michelle." Her tone sounded icy.

She let him in, and he saw a girl with long blonde hair reading in bed. Her eyes had a vacant look about them. The room seemed a lot more cheerful than the boys' rooms. There was more window light, and the walls were not cinder blocks. They were painted in a powder blue color. Logan looked at pictures on the bulletin board. Susan and Chad as Homecoming King and Queen. Susan and Michelle dressed in Halloween costumes. Or maybe they were at a costume party. Susan was a mouse. Michelle was a cat. Maybe they were dressed as Tom and Jerry. Next to it, there was a picture of Michelle on a horse. Red and blue ribbons were under it.

"Miss Williams?" he asked.

Susan looked up and hesitated before responding, "Yes?"

He introduced himself and said, "I need to ask you some questions about Phillip."

"Okay."

Michelle folded her arms and cast a cold look in Logan's direction. "She's been through a lot, sir. This isn't the time."

"That's okay," Susan said. She put the book down and sat at the edge of the bed.

Michelle scowled at the detective and marched out of the room.

Logan pulled a chair close to Susan and said, "Did Phillip seem upset about anything before the dance?"

She sighed and said, "Yeah." Her answer was barely audible.

"You can trust me. Come on, I want to help you."

She sat with her arms wrapped around her knees and slowly rocked her body to and fro. "He was angry because Chad kept hanging around me."

"What did he do?"

"He yelled at him. It was horrible."

"Was the fight about you?"

"Yes." Tears trickled down her cheeks, and she started sobbing. "Chad and I talked at lunch a few days before the dance. I told him off. Phillip told me he was looking out his dorm window after lunch and saw us. He didn't know I was giving Chad the brush-off. I found out later that they got into a shouting match in the dorm."

Her sobbing was uncontrollable. She reached for the Kleenex box by her side and pulled a tissue out. She rubbed her eyes and wept.

"It'll be okay." His voice was calm and gentle.

She trembled and said, "I thought they were okay at the dance. We went to the woods. I just wanted them to patch things up, once and for all."

"Did they?"

She wiped her tears with the palms of her hands and said, "I don't know. Chad won't talk about it. I came back with the girls. I wasn't feeling well. I just wanted to get away from them."

"Did he tell you what happened when they came back from the woods?"

She sniffled and said, "No."

"Do you remember anything else?"

She shook her head.

"Did the girls stay in the dorm?"

"No, they went back to the dance . . . well actually, Michelle joined them later. She drove me back to the dorm. When I got back to my room, I took a sleeping pill. I have insomnia, you see. I guess with all that's been happening lately, I've been a bundle of nerves. I was really upset and she helped me so much. After I took the sleeping pill, we talked until I felt drowsy, and then she left to go back to the dance."

"What time was that?"

"About ten o'clock."

"You always confide in each other?"

"Always."

"I found a letter you wrote to Phillip from the Chicago hospital."

She folded her arms and rocked to and fro.

"I'm sorry to have to ask you this, but I have to do it. I was told that you had a nervous breakdown. Is that true?"

She blubbered and looked away.

"You can tell me," he said softly.

After another moment's hesitation, she said, "It's true."

"What happened?"

"I can't talk about it!" She leapt off the bed and darted out of the room.

"I'm sorry!" he shouted after her.

Michelle came back into the room and glared at him. "What did you say to her? She's extremely upset. You're so cold and unfeeling!"

"Calm down, Miss Martin."

She flapped her arms and cried, "I won't calm down! She's upset as it is, and you come in here and make things worse! Get away from me!"

"Shh, it's okay. Calm down."

She looked up into his dark eyes, then at his face. It was a kind face. There was something about him. Something she could not figure out. For some reason, she knew she could trust him. She sensed that he was on her side.

"I want to help her," Logan said softly. "I can see she's very upset. Maybe you can help me."

Michelle changed her tone. "I'm sorry. I'm just overly concerned about her."

"I can understand. You two are really close."

She sat on the bed and said, "That's for sure."

"I bet you confided in each other a lot."

"All the time."

"Last year, did she say or do anything unusual prior to her nervous breakdown?"

"I know she was unhappy."

"About what?"

"Her parents were fighting. She went home on weekends and got in the middle of their squabbles. She blamed herself for their breakup. That's probably why she broke up with Chad. She thought she wouldn't be able to hold onto a relationship because of her parents' problems. That's probably why she got along so well with Phillip. His parents were having a rough time of it too."

"Is there anything else you can remember?"

"No, she just seemed really withdrawn and lonely. I tried to cheer her up, but it didn't do any good. We all tried to help her, but she wouldn't let us in."

"She seems withdrawn and lonely now. But that's perfectly understandable. She just lost a close friend."

"It isn't nearly as bad as it was a year ago. I hope this doesn't make things worse."

"Chad and Phillip were fighting over her?"

"That's an understatement! Chad was incensed whenever he saw Phillip with her. And vice versa."

"I looked around in Phillip's room and found a note you wrote to him. Were you in love with him?"

Her face glowed. "I can't believe he actually kept it. How sweet. That's the kind of guy he was. Yeah, we went out a few times, but he always loved her. I guess you'd say I loved him from a distance."

"Were you jealous that he loved Susan?"

"A little bit."

"I don't believe it was an accident. Maybe you were so jealous that you went back to finish him off."

Her eyes flashed with rage. "How dare you say such a thing!"

When he asked her what happened the night Phillip died, she repeated what the others told him before. "I was so fed up with them bickering over Susan that I got in my car and drove the girls back here."

"How was she feeling?"

"It was the worst I'd seen her in a really long time. She was so uptight, I gave her a sleeping pill. I know you're not supposed to give other people your pills, but she was so upset. I thought it would help her get to sleep."

"What time was that?"

"We got back here about quarter of ten. Susy and I talked for little while, and I waited for the pill to take effect. And then I went back to the dance."

"What time was it when you got back there?"

"About quarter after ten."

"All right, thanks, Michelle. I'm sorry I upset Susan."

"I'm sorry I got so upset. I know you're trying to help her. Maybe it's good for her to talk about it."

He smiled and said, "I think so. Thanks for taking the time to talk to me."

Logan felt hot, penetrating gazes on him as he entered the girls' lounge. They silently checked out his rock-hard abs and rippling muscles and snickered. He flashed a big grin at a pretty brunette and said, "I'm looking for Mary and Wendy. Has anyone seen them?"

Mary waved and said, "Over here."

She was an attractive girl, with wavy blonde hair and a light complexion. Wendy was pencil thin, with mousy brown hair and large blue eyes.

They were watching a soap opera and had spiral notebooks on their laps. He went over to them and introduced himself. They confirmed what he already knew.

"Michelle dropped us off at the student center about nine thirty and took Susy back to the dorm," Wendy said. "Then she drove back to the dance."

"What time did she come back?"

"About eleven o'clock," Mary said.

"Was she at the dorm the whole time?"

"Susan was really upset, and I think they were talking," Wendy said.

"Thanks."

The girls looked up from their notes as he headed out of the room and gasped a collective "That guy's really cute" when they thought he was out of earshot and went back to what they were doing. He heard them and chuckled.

Then he went to ask other girls what they knew. Tanya Lowell spent that night studying in her room. She was plump with a pasty complexion and glasses.

"I didn't see anybody all night," she said. "I was quite ill. But I did see someone drive off campus."

"What time was that?" Logan asked.

"About ten."

"Thanks," he said on his way out.


The sun was setting when Logan left the girls' dorm. He wandered toward Hullien Hall and asked a girl for directions to the gym. She pointed to the building across from the entrance road. He started to go to his car but decided to walk instead. It would give him time to think about what he had learned so far. He whistled and strolled down the lane, past the small stone bridge where students probably fished on warm spring days. He gazed across the pond and saw a sprawling oak tree across the way. It was sandwiched between the pond and a field with dried-up cornstalks. Students were sitting on a bench by the tree. Others were walking up and down a path and disappeared from view around the pine trees. By now, the pond reflected the glowing pinks and oranges from the setting sun.

He stood at the gym parking lot and looked across the soccer field that was parallel to the road he turned on to drive into the school. He saw the student center through the trees in the distance. He reached in his pocket for his notebook and scribbled, "It's about a ten minute walk from the girls' dorm to the student center. It wouldn't have taken long for her to drive there. Michelle said she dropped Susan off and went back to the dance; why did it take her almost an hour to get there?"

He went inside and followed the sign for the men's locker room. The boys were loud and crude and telling dirty jokes. They were laughing hysterically. He peered around the corner and saw Chad, Andy, and Rudy standing at their lockers with towels around their waists. He went two rows behind them and waited till they were gone. He saw them go out the door and went back to their lockers. He whipped out his notebook again, and wrote down their locker numbers. Then he made a note to just the handles, for prints later.

He went through double doors and stopped when he saw an office to his right. He knocked and stuck his head in the door. He saw a man with a buzz cut doing paperwork.

"Ian Reynolds?"

He looked up at him and said, "Yeah?"

"I'm Detective Logan. I need to ask you some questions about Phillip Bishop."

He gestured for him to have a seat. "Shoot."

The coach looked shocked when Logan said he believed Phillip was murdered.

"Word has it, you laid pretty heavily into Phillip a few days before the dance."

"Yeah, so what about it? He was too busy flirting with his girlfriend and made some careless mistakes. So I called him on it. I lay into everybody. I've gotta whip the team into shape. I'm competitive and I like to win."

"There's nothing wrong with that."

"The harder I push, the more potential my men will have. It builds character."

Logan took note of the marine insignia tattoo that stuck out from Reynolds's left shirtsleeve. "When were you in the marines?"

"It shows?" he said, grinning. "Ten years ago. I went straight from high school, to the service, to college, to here."

"Oh?"

"Yep, I got married, and we have three beautiful children. This is a great place to raise a family. I live just down the road."

"It sure beats the hubbub of city life," Logan agreed. He glanced at the photo cube on his desk. There were pictures of his wife and three small children.

"Oh, you're from the city?"

"I transferred here from Philly six months ago. I'm still having trouble with roads, though. They're so windy and narrow."

"Especially on farm roads! Just watch out for horse and buggies. They're all over the place."

He rolled his eyes and said, "I know."

"This stretch of land isn't so bad. Have you had a chance to look around?"

"A little bit."

"It's a beautiful campus."

Logan smiled and said, "I was just thinking that myself."

"It's a great place for jogging. Do you jog?"

"Not as much as I used to when I was in training."

"Same here. But I try to keep at it though. And I try to get a good work out at least every other day. We have excellent equipment here."

"Mind if I try it sometime? It's been a while."

"I figured," he said, grinning. He looked down at Logan's chest and abs and added, "But it hasn't been too long—you look like you're in good shape."

Logan thanked him for the compliment and said, "I like to work out, but I just haven't had time since I transferred here. I've been bogged down with so much paperwork, I haven't had time to exercise."

"Well, you can do it now. Come on."

He followed Coach Reynolds through the gymnasium. There was a stage at the other end of the room with steps on opposite ends.

"I guess you have plays in here too."

"And graduations when it's raining," Reynolds said.

The coach went through a door to the right of the stage and turned on a light switch. Logan followed him through a hallway and trotted down basement steps after him. There was a pungent mildew smell as they entered the weight room. Reynolds turned on the fluorescent lights and went over to a weight lifting stand, Logan at his heels. Logan laid on the bench, and Ian hoisted the bars to spot him.

Logan reached his arms up to grip the bar and said, "Why did you get mad at Phillip for mistakes he made during the game? The guys thought Phillip played better that night than he had in a long time. Why did you yell at him? What did he do to you? Did you have a grudge?"

"Locker room talk is mostly BS. You should know that."

"I know." He did a set of ten and breathed heavily.

"I've made my share of mistakes, and I've learned my lessons the hard way."

"Were any of your athletes on drugs?"

"I don't know," Ian said through clenched teeth.

He laid the bar on the stand and watched Logan wipe his face with a towel. He looked up at Reynolds and said, "I'm sure I would have noticed something was wrong if they were stoned."

"To my knowledge, no one was on drugs."

"What about Terry Dawson?"

"He was a good kid gone bad. He was a fine athlete."

"He was seen arguing with Jonas MacPharlan at a game a few days before Phillip died. After the game, he threatened him."

"That's because Phillip turned him in. Dawson was dealing drugs, and Phillip found out about it somehow."

"How did he find out?"

"I don't know. He must have overheard a conversation or something. It's hard to say. It's not hard to find out about things around here."

"Did Dawson do drugs when he was on the basketball team?"

"He was on the football team, actually. I don't know if he was on drugs then. I didn't want to know. He was my fastest runner at that time. He could have gone places."

"So I suppose he had a real good motive for wanting to kill Phillip."

"I guess so."

The coach hoisted the bar into Logan's hands, and the detective bench-pressed another set of ten. Reynolds took the barbell from his hands and placed it on the rack. Logan wiped his face with the towel and looked back up at him. "Was there a serious drug problem on campus?"

"Yeah, but what campus in the country hasn't had problems like that? It gets to a point where teachers turn their heads the other way. We can't do anything. The kid gets expelled and another one takes his or her place."

"What would you do if you caught a player on drugs?"

"I'd kick his ass off the team so fast he wouldn't know what hit him."

"Have other kids been kicked out for illegal drug use?"

"A few, but they're more than likely repeat offenders. They get warnings, once or twice. They're off the team if they get caught more than that."

Logan rested after another set and asked, "Where were you between nine and ten o'clock on the night Phillip died?"

"I left the dance about ten and came here to work out. I always work out at night. It's quiet and nobody's around to bother me."

"Did anyone see you?"

"The custodian."

"Thanks, Coach. You've been a lot of help."

"Anytime. If there's anything else I can do, you know where you can find me."

"Thanks," he said on his way out.

## Chapter 6

Logan felt like he was on vacation the first week he started working in Townsend. It took a while to get used to the slow pace. He couldn't get over how quiet it was there. Philadelphia streets were loud, and there was always something happening. On a daily basis, overworked cops handled their share of murder investigations. Street hookers were arrested and released to ply their trade all over again. Addicts overdosed like clockwork.

No one had been murdered in Townsend for quite a while, which was a good thing. Even prostitutes were bored. People knew each other's business. Husbands and boyfriends couldn't cheat on their spouses or girlfriends with a prostitute without residents knowing about it. Men and women had anonymity in Philly.

Over the years, farmers began selling their land in neighboring towns. As a result, a surge of housing developments cropped up. Wealthy Philly residents began building mansions on what used to be fertile farmland. The mixture of rich and middle-class citizens created tension. It would only be a matter of time before the crime rate escalated.

The police station was a block from everything. There were never high-speed chases here. It was a small staff and detectives often did the jobs that the crime scene unit did in the city. Often the only excitement came when a cop handed out a speeding ticket.

Logan got a meatball sandwich at the only deli in town. It was in between a Laundromat that wasn't open all night and Sammy & Sons Hardware Store, which had been there for fifty-four years.

He felt a blast of cold air shoot down his spine as he walked to the police station. Eighty-degree weather gave way to frigid temperatures, and he didn't like it one bit. It was a major shock to the system. About seven o'clock, he sat at his desk and caught up on paperwork while he ate. Night-shift officers were out on patrol, and it was quiet. He could work alone without distractions and review his notes on the Phillip Bishop case.

About an hour later, Lieutenant Winters went over to his desk and said, "Working late again, Frank?"

"Yep. I think Chad McAlpin and his buddies are lying."

Harry grunted and said, "Nobody ever tells the truth."

Frank handed him an outline of the time line. Harry read it and asked, "So what do you think?"

"The boys are covering for each other. I was so close. That Preston kid was all wound up. He's the nervous type. He's not a cool one like McAlpin. I'll bet he'll be the one that slips up and tells me what I want to know."

"That might be true, but never underestimate the human mind. Anything's possible."

"I think Rudy Preston is involved and knows too much. His conscience is eating away at him. All we have to do is set up the bait and let him unravel. At least we can catch him saying something that doesn't go with what he said before."

"They're definitely helping McAlpin cover it up."

"I agree. I think Chad and Phillip got into an argument and started hitting each other. Chad probably panicked when Phillip fell and hit his head. Maybe he was just unconscious and Chad thought he was dead. Stan should have the autopsy results soon, so we'll know more then."

"There's not much we can do about it tonight. Why don't you call it a night? You look exhausted."

Logan rubbed his eyes and said, "You're probably right."

"Well, I'm gonna get going or my wife will wonder where I am."

"Good night."

The telephone rang at about eight thirty. The dispatcher told him Warren and Lois Bishop were there to get information about their son's automobile accident. Logan looked up to see him escort them into the office. They were both tall like Phillip. Warren was almost a mirror image of Phillip, except for his expanding waist and thinning red hair. Lois had short strawberry blonde hair and high cheekbones. Her eyes were red, and her face was puffy.

Logan pushed a couple of chairs toward his desk, and they sat down. She cried uncontrollably, drowning out his words of comfort. Consoling grieving parents was the worst part of the job.

"Phillip was a star athlete, did you know that?" Warren asked.

"That's what I've been told," Logan replied with a soothing tone.

"He was a handsome boy," Lois said. "Why would someone do this to him? He never bothered anyone. He always tried to help people."

"I don't know why it happened, Mrs. Bishop, but I can assure you I will do everything possible to find out who was responsible."

He avoided making promises for fear that the murderer would get off on a technicality. That was the unfortunate reality of police work. He asked them things he thought were pertinent to the case, then jotted down Phillip's Internet password. An hour later, they thanked him and went to look for a motel. He checked Phillip's e-mails on his laptop and read notes from Susan. Classmates sent him jokes, but he didn't take time to read them. The coach sent notes about the basketball team. Andy sent him a lot of pictures of nude women. There were no death threats posted after he died, which meant everybody knew what happened. If he received any, he would have deleted them. A few minutes later, he signed off and called it a night.


Chad was half listening to the science teacher. He was thinking about all those questions Detective Logan asked him. He didn't think it was an accident. They didn't do good enough a job making it look that way.

Mr. Wriggley was in the middle of a lecture about black holes when Detective Logan appeared in the doorway. Chad, Andy, and Rudy exchanged nervous looks.

"Can I help you? We're in the middle of class here."

Logan looked coldly at Chad and pointed to him. "I need to speak to Chad McAlpin."

"Can't it wait?"

"No, it can't."

Chad rose and said, "Why do you want to talk to me? I told you everything I know."

He went begrudgingly with the detective. But they did not just go in the hall to talk. Logan took him to the police station, and Criminalist

Bonnie Draper got a blood sample from him. Then Logan took him back to school.

Chad met with Andy and Rudy between classes. They met at the front steps of Forrester Hall, and he told them what happened.

"They took you out of class for that?" Rudy's voice sounded as high-pitched and whiny as ever.

"Yeah, so that means Logan's onto me. He thinks I did it."

Andy eyed him suspiciously. "What are we going to do? If he does a little more digging, he might get us too."

"We'll have to think of something and fast or we'll end up in jail!"


Logan was drinking his second cup of coffee when Stan called to tell him the autopsy was completed. It was too early in the morning to contend with going to the morgue. It was never really the right time of day to go there, but it had to be done. He entered the room and grimaced when he saw Phillip Bishop's corpse on the autopsy table.

"What did you find out?" he asked.

Stan pointed to Phillip's forehead and said, "The victim's wounds are consistent with blunt force trauma. Someone hit him with such force, it caused a massive hemorrhage that destroyed brain tissue. I found an object smaller than a pebble embedded in the area of the impact site. I examined it under a microscope and determined that it came from a rock. It must have chipped off upon impact with his skull."

"So he was dead before he got in the car."

"It looks that way."

Logan looked at Phillip Bishop's face and said, "It looks like he was in a fistfight or something. And the other person must have pushed him down."

"Precisely." Stan turned over the body and pointed to the back of his head. "He received a soft tissue injury on the back of his head when he fell."

"Can you tell if he was moved?"

"The results were inconclusive. Normally, lividity sets in after about four to eight hours. If he died lying on his back, the blood would have settled on his back and would have started staining his skin. The stains would shift if the body had been moved. But there is no evidence that that happened in this case."

"What does that mean?"

"It doesn't look like the blood settled, which indicates that he died about an hour or so before he wound up in the car. It wouldn't have been enough time for lividity to set in, or become fixed."

"The kids got to the woods about eight o'clock, and the girls left about nine thirty," Logan said. "The boys said they went back right after them. Chad McAlpin told me Phillip must have driven back down Snake Turn Road later that night."

"If he said that, he's lying. When was the last time you saw a corpse drive a car?"

"That would be never."

"The time line would be about right. If the boys were seen at the dance about eleven o'clock, that would have been about an hour and a half after the girls said they went back to campus."

"McAlpin looked like he was on the receiving end of a fistfight himself. So he must've gotten into the fight right after the girls left."

"And then they must have gone back to campus to get Phillip's car."

"That sounds right. After they pushed it off the road, they went back to the dance to have an alibi. All I need to do now is to find the rock."

"If the killer didn't get rid of it."

"Thanks, Stan, you've been a real help."

"Anytime. You know where I'll be."

Logan signed the death certificate, and Stan handed him a copy of the autopsy report. Then Logan assembled a team to look for the rock in the woods.

The team scoured every square inch of woods near the site where they believed the fight occurred. About two hours later, Officer Lenny Sherman yelled, "Detective Logan, I found something. A rock was tossed under this thorn bush."

Logan got on his knees, and patted the dirt. He held a branch up with his right hand to sift through the underbrush. He felt a sharp object and pushed dried leaves out of the way. Clusters of leaves were sticking to what looked like blood. He photographed the scene, then carefully stuck the rock in an evidence bag. He collected the leaf samples and put them in separate bags. Then he wrote down pertinent information, initialed, and dated them.

"Good work, Lenny," he said.

The samples were taken to the forensics lab for analysis. When the test results were completed, Stan discussed them with Logan.

"DNA tests indicated that the rock found hidden under the thorn bush, and the splotches found on the leaves near the site both belonged to the victim."

"What about the blood sample we found on the leaves near the rock he hit his head on?"

"It was the same as the ones found in the bushes," Stan said. "The penny-sized splotch found at the site where Phillip Bishop fell matched the blood on his shirt."

Logan whistled and said, "Were you able to figure out who it belongs to?"

"We tested the sample of Chad McAlpin's blood that you gave us, and it came back positive."

"That's great news! Now there's sufficient evidence to link him to the crime. Thanks, Stan."

Chad's troubles didn't end with the trip to the police station. After school, Logan appeared at his doorway holding a warrant to search his shoes.

Chad rolled his eyes and said, "Is this really necessary?"

Logan wasn't in the mood to be chatty. He concentrated his search of Chad's closet, then looked under his bed.

Chad glared angrily at the detective. Then his face twitched when Logan examined the shoes he wore that night in the woods. He quietly kicked himself for not getting rid of them. How stupid was that? He hoped Logan didn't notice.

Nothing ever seemed to escape Logan's attention. He held the right shoe next to a color print and grunted. He stuck the shoes in an evidence bag and left without saying a word.

When he was gone, Chad sat on his bed and shook his head in disbelief.

About twelve thirty the next day, Logan made a beeline for the cafeteria. He saw Chad sitting with Rudy and Andy and went over to them.

"Good afternoon, gentlemen. May I have a word with you, Chad?"

Chad groaned and said, "All right." He followed him outside and said, "What is it, Detective Logan? Make it quick, class starts in a few minutes."

"I think you'll make the time for what I have to tell you."

Chad looked over at Andy and Rudy, and they looked wide-eyed at each other. He and Logan went out the front door and sat on a bench under an oak tree. Logan reached in his coat pocket and removed an evidence bag with an index card in it. "Chad McAlpin's right handprints" was typed on it with capital letters. He held up another evidence bag that read, "Blood sample from Phillip Bishop's shirt."

"It's an exact match," Logan said. "The DNA results prove that you dripped blood in the woods, a few feet from where Phillip hit his head on the rock. I think you got so angry that you had it out with him. I think he slipped and hit his head and you panicked."

"You're wrong!"

"Am I?"

"I didn't do it," Chad said with a wave of the hand.

"The evidence proves otherwise. Do you have a logical explanation for how your blood was found at the crime scene?"

Chad fell silent.

"I didn't think so. You were seen arguing with Phillip just before he was killed. Witnesses heard you threaten him. The bloodstain on his shirt has your DNA all over it. And your fingerprint is on the trunk of the car when you pushed it off the road."

"It doesn't prove—"

"I'm sorry, Chad, but you're under arrest."

Andy and Rudy stood on the front steps of Hullien Hall, watching dumfounded, as their friend was being handcuffed. Students watched in horror as the events unfolded before them. When Logan finished reading him his rights, he pushed him toward the parking lot. They walked hurriedly after them and watched Chad get into the back seat of Logan's vehicle.

Rudy felt a cold chill shoot down his spine as he locked eyes with Chad. His blue eyes were the last thing he saw before the car pulled away.

"I can't believe this is happening," Andy said.

"It's like a nightmare!" Rudy's voice cracked. "Now what are we going to do?"

Andy didn't say a word.

## Chapter 7

After Chad was processed, Logan led him into an interrogation room and went over the evidence that linked him to the crime.

"I'm not telling you anything without my dad here," Chad said. "His lawyer will destroy you!"

"It will be hard to do that when I have proof that you were involved in the death of Phillip Bishop."

Chad folded his arms in defiance. "I want my phone call, now!"

"All right, I'm sure something can be arranged."

He went out to the office and came back ten minutes later.

"It took you long enough!" Chad cried.

"Come on." He led him back into the office and pointed to a pay phone on the wall.

Chad's fingers trembled as he dialed his parents' telephone number. He rehearsed what he was going to say but lost his cool when he heard his father's voice.

"Dad, I'm in trouble. I need your help."

"What's wrong?"

"I'm in jail. They think I killed Phillip!"

"Oh my god, are you all right?"

"I don't know." He told him that he got into the fight with Phillip in the woods but left out details about pushing the car off the road. "The detective has been asking me a lot of questions. I didn't do it."

"How could you have done such a stupid thing? You should know better? Fighting over a girl? You should have quietly accepted the breakup with Susan and moved on."

"This isn't the time for a lecture! I need your help! Please hurry."
"All right."
"Hurry up!"
"We're on our way. Just hold tight. And don't say a word until our lawyer gets there."

A guard slammed the cell door, and Chad shouted, "Let me out of here! I didn't do it! Why won't anybody listen? I've been framed, damn it! Let me out of here!"

"Poor pampered little rich kid. I guess you're used to getting your own way. If you're smart, you'll let your lawyer do the talking."

He walked down the hall, whistling. Chad screamed till his throat was sore. The guard went over to him and slapped a nightstick across his fingers.

"Next time, I'll break open your skull."

Chad plopped on a cot, and tears trickled down his cheeks.

William and Ellen McAlpin walked hurriedly into the police station about two o'clock. They were just as blond and good-looking as Chad. At one time, William was Broad Meadow's star athlete and was popular with the girls. He lettered in as many sports as was possible and helped the football team to victory three years in a row. He also achieved great success in his academic studies. He was the class valedictorian and got a football scholarship to play at Penn State. Many Ivy League university recruiters were eager to have him play for them.

He now had a receding hairline and wore wire-rimmed glasses. The battle to stay fit was difficult. Years of attending important dinners had added a lot more pounds to his waistline. He tried to jog at least four times a week and had to get up at 4:00 a.m. to do it. He got to his office by six o'clock and tried to use the treadmill during his lunch hour, if he wasn't in a meeting. He met Ellen at college. She was also a high achiever. She was a social butterfly but also maintained excellent grades. Time had been kind to her. She spent a lot of time at spas and exercised daily and looked like she was in her late thirties.

William leaned on the front desk and said, "I want to see my son, Chad McAlpin."

The woman behind the counter said, "I'm sorry, once someone's in custody, there is no contact with the public."

"But we came all the way here to see him," Ellen snapped.

"You can watch him through a two way mirror outside the interrogation room."

William was allowed to sit in on the interrogation, because Chad was seventeen.

Logan unlocked the door and took Chad into the interrogation room. William McAlpin came in with his lawyer, Tony Mancini. He was a large man in a pin-striped suit with pudgy hands and fingers. His hair was jet-black, obviously dyed and meticulously combed. Traces of gray showed up in his mustache and beard.

Chad's hair was sticking up and his eyes looked dull and lifeless, William suspected he had been crying, but Chad would never admit it surely, it was not the image of a star athlete.

Logan placed the index card with Chad's fingerprint on the table next to the one he lifted from the car trunk and said, "What do you know? They're a perfect match."

Mancini glared at him and said, "So what? It doesn't prove anything. It could have been there before that."

"He pushed Phillip's car off the road, and I've got the evidence to prove it."

"Why would I go to that much trouble?"

"To cover up your crime." He placed a photograph on the table. It was a close-up shot of the bloodstain on Phillip's shirt. "Sometimes it's really amazing what you can find out in this line of work. The autopsy report proves that Phillip Bishop died in the woods, not in the car. A DNA test confirmed that your blood got on Phillip's shirt."

"It was a car accident," Chad said.

"That's what you wanted the police to think, but I know otherwise."

"What are you talking about?"

"Why was Phillip driving in neutral?"

"It's an easy mistake. He probably couldn't see the gearshift in the dark."

"That theory won't fly with jurors. It wouldn't have taken him long to realize he was driving in neutral. He would have switched gears. Here's what I think happened. You got into a fistfight with him in the woods. When he fell and hit his head, you panicked and went back to campus to get his car. But you couldn't have gotten back to your dorm, so you had to drive two cars. So you had to get Andy and Rudy to help you. I'm sure they will be more than glad to fill in the missing pieces."

"It was an accident!" Chad insisted.

Logan laid the plaster cast of the footprint found in the woods on the table, then Chad's shoes. Then he put the fabric from Phillip's shirt next to it.

"The footprint places you on the trail leading to the road that night. And this little piece of material came from Phillip's shirt. I found it stuck in a tree branch. It proves that he ripped his shirt as you carried him through the woods. Do you want to know about the rock we found under a bush?"

Chad grimaced and said, "What rock?"

"A bloody rock. You hit him on the head with it."

"You never mentioned anything about a rock. I swear I didn't hit him on the head with it."

Logan produced another close-up photograph of the rock in discussion.

"I think you got so angry that you hit him on the head with it. Then you panicked and hid it under the thorn bush."

Chad shook his head and said, "I didn't do it."

"There's no way you're getting out of this one with a lie. Just admit it."

Chad looked at his father, who sat silently listening. Mancini urged him to not say a word. Logan was pushing him into confessing.

"There's no way you're going to get around this, Chad," Logan said. "You cut your hand during the fistfight and it got on Phillip's shirt. DNA doesn't lie, McAlpin. Just make it easy. Admit that you caused Phillip to hit his head on the rock and we can start working on your case. Maybe you could get a reduced sentence. It was clearly an accident."

"Don't do it, Chad," Mancini said. "It's a trick."

Chad looked at his father, then back at Logan. "But it's true. We got into a fight, and he fell and hit his head. I panicked and tore through the woods. I went back to meet Andy and Rudy and just wanted to leave him there, but they insisted that we go back to help him. He met us a few minutes later—and yes, he was very much alive when we went back to campus. He must've gone back there later on and met up with somebody. He was talking on his cell phone when I left the dorm."

Logan eyed him skeptically. "Who was he talking to?"

"It sounded like he was talking to Terry Dawson. But I'm not sure." Logan jotted it down on his pad and looked back up at him. "It's funny how a dead guy can make a phone call like that."

"For the millionth time, he did ride back with us!" Chad shouted. "And I swear I didn't hit him on the head with the rock."

"Give it up. The evidence proves otherwise."

"Was a blood test done on the rock found under the bush?" Mancini asked.

Logan nodded and said, "It belonged to Phillip."

"Was Chad's blood found on the rock used to kill him?"

"No."

"Were Chad's fingerprints found on it?"

Logan shook his head. "It's difficult to get fingerprints off a rock."

Mancini laughed and said, "So what you're saying is that you have no tangible evidence linking Chad to the murder. His blood wasn't on the rock. And there were no fingerprints. It's circumstantial evidence. And I'm sure jurors will agree."

"The blood splotches on Phillip's shirt belonged to Chad, remember?"

"This isn't getting us anywhere," Mancini said. "Can I have a moment alone with my client?"

"Feel free," Logan said. He got up and left them alone.

Chad looked at Mancini and said, "How much trouble am I in?"

"You're in it pretty deep," he answered cooly.

"There goes your shot at college," William said.

Chad avoided eye contact. "I'm sorry, Dad."

"Let's not worry about that right now," Mancini said. "We need to concentrate on getting you off, Chad. You say you don't remember anything about the rock that was used to kill Phillip Bishop?"

"I didn't hit him with a rock. I used my fist. I pushed him down and left him there. A few minutes later, he shows up at the car, and we all went back to campus."

Mancini glanced at the evidence, then at Chad. "With all this evidence, are you sure that's the way events transpired."

Chad looked him square in the eye and said, "Yes."

"You had better be telling the truth," Mancini said. "A perjury charge will make matters a lot worse."

William sat there studying his son's behavior. Chad could bluff better than the most experienced poker player. That's what made him so good at it. He hated to think that he had raised a young man who had no conscience. He gazed into Chad's eyes, hoping to see the boy who had a heart. At the moment, he was sad to think that Chad didn't seem to have one.

"Chad, you had better not be lying," he told his son. "Your mother and I didn't raise you to be out for yourself. We can help you, but you need to level with us. If you're lying, we won't be able to do anything."

Chad looked at his father and said, "I didn't do it, Dad."

William folded his hands and heaved a deep breath. "Okay, I believe you." He looked over at Tony Mancini and asked, "What should he do?"

"The evidence links him to the fistfight, not to the murder. He pushed him down in the heat of the moment, which means the murder charge can probably be reduced to voluntary manslaughter, and you can be let out on bail."

"But if I do that, it's basically admitting that I did it," Chad said.

"You want to get out on bail, don't you?"

"Of course I do."

"If we don't do this, you'll stay in jail with the murder charge. You don't want that, do you?"

"No."

"You might not like it, but it's a start. We can lay out the groundwork for you defense when you get out. Since no prints were found on the rock, they can't prove that you did it. After he fell and hit his head, you ran back to meet Andy and Rudy, correct?"

"Yeah."

"Someone else could have gone over to his body after you left, and hit him on the head with the rock. At least, that's what I hope I can get jurors to believe. As far as the other evidence is concerned, I don't see how it would hold up in court. So what if they found your footprint in the woods. It doesn't prove you helped carry his body to Snake Turn Road. Phillip Bishop could have ripped his shirt on the tree branch before you two got into the fight. And as far as the print on the car, you could have touched it before that."

"Do you think it will work? Will I go to jail?"

"I don't know," Mancini admitted.

William leaned his head on his hand and looked down. He let out a deep breath and looked sadly at his son. When Logan returned, Mancini did all the talking. In a written confession, Chad admitted to getting into the fistfight with Phillip. He signed it, and then Logan led him through the station. William was not allowed to have contact with his son now.

Tears streaked down Ellen's cheeks, and William wiped them with his hands. He put his arms around her and followed Tony Mancini out of the office.

Logan hated to admit that Tony Mancini might be right. Chad could walk because there were no prints on the rock used to kill Phillip Bishop. He could have done it. Or maybe it could have been Andy or Rudy. Or maybe someone else was in the woods that night. If that was the case, he needed to do some more digging.

At about ten o'clock that night, he went to the gym to talk to the janitor. There was a light on in the coach's office. He turned the knob, and the custodian flinched. He was a thin man in his late fifties, with a scraggly white beard and rough looking hands.

"Who are you and what are you doing here?" he asked in alarm.

"I'm sorry." Logan held up his badge and said, "I'm investigating the death of Phillip Bishop. Did you know him?"

"Vaguely. You see one ball player, you see them all. I just heard that he was killed in a car accident."

"It's a shame. Were you working here that night?"

He leaned on the broom and said, "Yes."

"Did you see or hear anything suspicious that night?"

"Not that I can think of."

"Was there anyone else here that night?"

"Coach Reynolds came in for a late-night workout."

"What time did he get here?"

"About nine or nine thirty."

"Is it unusual for him to work out this late at night?"

He continued sweeping. "Not really. Sometimes he comes in at ten or ten thirty. He always works out after games to relieve tension."

"I understand that."

Logan glanced across the room at an eight-by-ten-inch framed color photograph of the coach with Phillip, Michelle, Susan, and Chad. They were all grinning and looked happy.

"Do you mind if I look around?"

"Go ahead, but just don't hang around too long down there. The mildew smell is terrible!"

He smiled and said, "I won't, thanks."

Logan went to the weight room and opened the exit door. There were steps that went up to the parking lot. He looked back at the equipment, deep in thought. He turned on the Stair Master and did a set for fifteen minutes. When he went back upstairs, the custodian was mopping the locker room floor. Logan slipped into the dark hallway and knocked over a can of Lysol foam.

The custodian turned on the lights and asked, "Who's there?"

"It's Detective Logan, again. I'm sorry about that. I didn't see it."

"You were so quiet. Don't sneak up on me like that again! You could give somebody a heart attack!"

"I was just on my way out."

"Well, you know where the door is. Use it!"

"Thanks for letting me look around."

He continued mopping, and Logan heard his whistles echo across the lonely stadium as he left the building.


William and Ellen McAlpin checked into a motel and spent a sleepless night, worrying about their son. Chad didn't get any sleep in the cell either.

At eight o'clock a.m., Ellen brought Chad's best-looking suit to the police station. About thirty minutes later, Tony led him to the front steps where William and Ellen were waiting. She looked at Chad and said, "You look tired. Did you get any sleep?"

He scratched his head and groaned. "Not really."

"We didn't either." She handed the suit to a policeman and waited upstairs for him to get dressed.

Tony escorted them to the courthouse. It was three blocks away, just before you got to the circle. They were expecting a much larger building.

The courtroom was small, as well. Pictures of past judges hung on opposite walls. An American flag and a state flag were in stands on opposite ends. A stern-looking judge entered from a door to the left and sat behind the bench. He was probably in his midsixties with sagging jowls and droopy eyes. He had a pallid complexion and pale blue eyes.

The McAlpins waited for almost an hour before Chad's case was called. The court clerk went over the details of the Phillip Bishop case. Tony Mancini managed to get the murder charge reduced to manslaughter, because Detective Logan wasn't able to prove that Chad actually hit Phillip Bishop on the head with the rock.

Judge Griffen set the bail and released him into his parents' custody. He ordered Chad to attend all court proceedings. Chad waited in the holding cell while his father arranged for bail. In ten days, he would go to the preliminary hearing in the court of common pleas and plead not guilty.

Time dragged. Where were they? How long would he have to stay in that horrible cell?

He lay on the cot with his arms wrapped around his legs. A feeling of dread came over him. He had not been so dependent on his parents since he was a child.

"What's taking so long?" he moaned.

About two thirty, the guard unlocked the door and escorted Chad upstairs. The McAlpins spent the rest of the afternoon discussing the case with Tony Mancini in an interrogation room. He pointed out ways that Logan's investigation could be discredited and jotted down a lot of notes. After some talking, Jonas MacPharlan agreed to let Chad come back. He dreaded going back to school. What was he going to say to his friends when they saw him?

He soon found out when his father pulled into the dorm parking lot about eight o'clock that night. A bedraggled Chad got out and followed them into the building. He saw somebody walking down the sidewalk and was glad it was dark. Now, if only he could make it to his bedroom without anyone else spotting him, he would be in the clear for the moment, at least.

But that was not the case. The dorm bustled with life that evening. Students wandered up and down the halls, loudly going about their business.

## LOVE'S A CRIME

He hoped they wouldn't notice, but they did. Underclassmen gave him funny looks as they walked by.

He unlocked his bedroom door and followed his parents inside. He was about to close the door when Rudy and Andy rushed out to the hall.

"Are you okay, man?" they asked in unison.

He looked away and said, "I'll be okay."

"We were worried," Rudy said.

"I'll talk to you in the morning." He closed the door and sat on his bed. The McAlpins had a lot to discuss.

The next morning, Logan pulled up the long, dusty road leading to the Dawsons' farmhouse. Two black labs barked the moment he got out. He walked quickly to the front porch and rang the bell. The door opened a crack. A middle-aged woman with curly red hair stuck her head out and glared at him. He held up his badge and introduced himself.

"I need to ask your son some questions, Mrs. Dawson."

"He's not here. And I don't know where he is."

"May I ask you some questions?"

"Suit yourself."

Connie unlatched the door and led him into the kitchen. He accepted her offer of coffee, and she poured it into a mug. She went into the living room for a moment and came back with her husband, Jack. He was wearing bib-overalls that were caked with dirt.

He shook Logan's hand and said, "What do you want?"

"I need to talk to Terry. It's urgent."

"If it's about Phillip Bishop's accident, you can forget it," he said.

"I need to talk to him."

"You think Terry had something to do with it, don't you?"

"I'm just trying to get at the facts, sir. I have proof that Phillip was killed before he got to his car."

"So you think he put him in the car? I know how it starts. The same thing happened when the cops came by before. They all ganged up on him, just because of something Phillip might or might not have overheard in the locker room. I think he overheard part of a conversation and misunderstood.

JOSEPH REDDEN

They never gave him a break, and now my son's life is ruined because of Phillip Bishop."

"That's why I need to talk to him, sir," Logan said.

"I wouldn't tell you even if I did know where he was. He heard about Phil's 'accident' and hightailed it out of here. I don't blame him."

"We haven't heard from him since," Connie added. "It's guilt by association, that's what it is."

"He has a perfectly good motive for wanting to kill Phillip," Logan said. "Do you know where your son was the night Phillip died?"

"I wish I could say he was here," she said. "But he wasn't. And I don't know where he was. But he certainly wasn't in the woods. He would never do such a horrible thing! He's a good kid. He just made some bad choices."

Jack Dawson grunted and said, "Terry learned his lesson the hard way in that juvenile detention center. He's not a minor anymore, and I'll be damned if I let you put him in prison for something he didn't do!"

"If you ask me, it's all that teachers' fault," she said. "He's the one that got Terry hooked on drugs. He's the one that got him to distribute the stuff to the students."

"They should've locked up that son of a bitch!" Jack Dawson said. "But he's a respected teacher. He only has to spend time in rehab. He's a lousy excuse for a human being!"

"Your son could have told him he didn't want to have any part in the operation," Logan said. "I've heard some stories about Terry. People say he isn't the sugar and spice you paint him out to be."

"You've got no right coming here telling us all this!" she shouted.

"Even if it's true?" he shot back.

"Get out of here!" Jack Dawson demanded. "How dare you come in here and make these horrible accusations against Terry. Get out of here!"

"I think you know where he is," Logan said.

"If I did, I wouldn't tell you!"

"Several people saw him threaten Phillip Bishop after a basketball game the week before he died. They said he tried to hit Phil and had to be pulled away. What do you say about that?"

"Students hated him. You all did everything you could to poison them against him, and it worked. You make me sick. People should be able to trust the police."

## LOVE'S A CRIME

"I'm sorry you feel that way, sir. I always try to do the right thing. That's why I joined the force. So I don't need to hear you say these things." He took one last sip of coffee and said, "I'll give you one last chance. Where is he?"

"For the thousandth time, we don't know!" Dawson snapped.

"All right, if you don't tell me, I'll find out. I'll find somebody who has a grudge against him. Maybe I'll get lucky, and that person will tell me where he is. Thanks for the coffee."

The screen door slammed on his way out. The dogs howled as he walked to the car.

Connie Dawson went over to the telephone by the counter and called Terry. "Hi, it's me. A Detective Frank Logan was just here asking about you."

"What did you tell him?"

"I said I didn't know where you were."

"Good."

"You better leave town before he finds out where you are. Do you hear me?"

"All right, I'll let you know where I am when I get there."

"Where will you go?"

"I don't know, but I'll be okay. Don't worry."

"How can I not worry? How the hell did you get in this kind of mess anyway?"

"I don't know, but it'll be okay, I promise."

He clicked off and she hung up. Jack gently rubbed her hand and shook his head.

Logan went to the courthouse's prothonotary office and sifted through a three-inch-thick file on Terry Dawson. He read the initial police reports, then the judge's instructions. He wrote down the name and number of his drug rehabilitation councilor and whipped out his cell phone. He dialed Peter Tyler's office and introduced himself.

"I'm trying to locate Terry Dawson," Logan said.

"What's he done this time?"

"The kid that nailed him about the drug operation was killed in a suspicious-looking car accident a few days ago."

"And you want to know where Dawson was at the time?"

"Yes, maybe you can help me."

"I wish I could. He skipped town, and I've been trying to locate him myself. It's the fourth time he's missed a counseling session. They never listen. When I find him, maybe I could scare him and say he can now be tried as an adult. And if he ends up in the can, I won't have to put up with him for a few years."

"Do you know where he might have gone?"

"If I knew where he was, we wouldn't be having this conversation."

"I talked to his folks, and they clammed up. They either really don't know where he is or they're covering for him."

"They always do," Tyler grumbled. "If I find him, I'd love to slap him alongside the head. But if I do find him, I'll let you know."

"I'd appreciate it, thanks."


Logan grabbed a quick bite to eat and carefully examined a map to find the New Horizons Clinic. He jotted down the route numbers to take, refolded the map, and finished eating. Then he headed out to talk to Graham Humphries. The clinic was set back in a wooded area, about a half an hour north of town.

He smiled at the receptionist and asked for directions to Humphries's room. He proceeded down an extremely narrow hallway with a rickety wooden floor. The path turned and twisted across the building. He arrived at the east wing and saw a sign that read, Drug Rehabilitation Unit. It was at the other end of the hall.

He turned the knob, but the door was locked. Then he rang a buzzer, and an orderly let him in. He flashed a badge, but a male nurse with hands of steel insisted on frisking him before he signed in at the desk. Once there, a female nurse asked to see his identification.

"I'm here to talk to Graham Humphries," he said.

"Is he expecting you?"

"No."

She motioned for the male nurse to escort him to the day room.

"This way, sir," he said.

Logan followed him into a lounge. Patients were huddled around a television. Some were reading the newspaper. Others were playing cards and smoking. The nurse pointed to a dumpy-looking man sitting in front of the window, who had on a gray sweatshirt and pants.

"Mr. Humphries, you have a visitor."

Logan went over to him and introduced himself. The orderly sat across the room and watched. Humphries had patches of red hair on an otherwise bald scalp. His face was pale and unshaven. His eyes were dark and bug-eyed. They appeared dull and lifeless. He was forty-five but looked ten years older. His teeth were yellow and so were his fingernails.

Logan took a whiff of the man's body odor and pulled his chair away.

Humphries stared blankly at him and asked, "What can I do for you, Detective?"

"I'm trying to locate Terry Dawson. I thought you might be able to help me."

He took a deep drag from his cigarette and said, "Terry Dawson. He's the last person I'd want to see."

"I take it you don't like him much."

He gave Logan a sideways glance and said, "You could say that."

"Are you afraid of him?"

"Yes, he's an angry young man. Disturbed actually. Especially after being in jail."

"Are you afraid he'll try to come after you now that he's out?"

Graham grimaced and said, "He's out?"

"Is something wrong?"

"No, I'm fine." He held the cigarette close to his mouth and inhaled deeply. Then he blew smoke toward the ceiling.

"You looked upset when I told you he was released. Do you think he would try to come after you?"

"He hasn't tried to come after me while I've been in here . . . that's why I'm reluctant to get out. I think he's capable of murder, and I think he'll try to get me."

"Why?"

"He's angry with the world. I think he blames me for the whole mess."

"Phillip Bishop's car went off Snake Turn Road."

"I heard about it. It's too bad the goody-two-shoes ended up that way. I'm not upset with him. I'm grateful he spilled the beans. I would've self-destructed if it hadn't been for him. My students owed him a lot too.

It was terrible what happened . . . it was like a nightmare. I feel bad that I got them into it. Drug abuse is a horrible thing. It destroys lives."

"I think someone killed him and put him in the car to make it look like an accident."

"You think somebody pushed the car off the road?"

Logan nodded.

"Do you think Terry Dawson did it?" Humphries asked.

"I think he was in on it. I suspect that more than one person put him in the car. Do you think he killed him?"

Graham nodded and grunted. "He was angry with him. Yeah, I'd say he had enough reason. If the circumstances had been right, I think he would've killed Phillip."

"Do you know where he could have gone?"

Graham blew smoke out his nose and said, "I don't know."

Logan handed him a business card and said, "If you hear from him, give me a call."

"The doctor says I'm doing well, and I might be discharged soon."

"Well, good for you. Thanks."

He grinned and said, "I hope I was of some help to you, Detective Logan. I really have mended my ways."

Logan waved for the attendant to take him back to the monitor desk. He signed out and walked hurriedly down the corridor.

Bill Quinn hoisted his arms up and down, then reached for a towel to wipe sweat off his face. Derek Webb was at a workout station to his right. He pushed his legs out, then toward him. They looked up to see a detective waving a badge at them. They got to their feet and went over to him. Logan felt dwarfed in their presence. They had hulking chests and gigantic arms and legs.

"I didn't do anything."

"Relax," Logan said. "I'm looking for a Bill Quinn."

"I'm Bill. What can I do for you, Detective?"

"I was told that you and Terry Dawson were on the football team. I've been trying to get in touch with him and thought you might know where he is. Have you heard from him?"

"I haven't seen him in months. And I don't really give a crap where he is."

"He's a lying piece of scum," Webb added.

"What's he done this time? You think he had something to do with Phillip's accident?"

"I just need to get the facts together. Thanks anyway." He started to go out, paused, and went back over to them. "Does he have a girlfriend?"

Quinn shrugged his shoulders and said, "He was going out with a girl named Denise Evans a few months ago."

"They split," Webb corrected.

"Do you know if he's seeing anybody now?"

Derek thought about it a moment and said, "The last I heard, he's been seeing a girl named Brenda Holmes. I don't know anything else about her though. And I don't care."

"Thanks you guys," Logan said on his way out.

Andy and Rudy listened from across the room, and watched Logan go out then they went back to lifting weights.

"That's a relief," Andy said.

"What?"

"If Logan thinks Terry had something to do with it, then maybe he'll leave us alone."

"I hope so."

## Chapter 8

Logan checked his wristwatch and yawned. Would the girl ever come out of the grocery store? He sat in his car chomping on potato chips, waiting. About thirty minutes later, he saw her exit the store carrying a lot of bags. She walked past him and got in her car. Then she headed north on Main Street. She turned left and sped down a back road that led out of town. He sped to catch up.

She looked in her rearview mirror again. That car was still following her. There was no place to turn off for another five miles and no shoulders to pull onto. She didn't want to go much faster for fear of flipping the car around one of those nasty curves. She accelerated down a hill. At the bottom, she saw a farmhouse on the right. With little time to think, she drove down the dusty road and parked behind a barn.

By the time Logan reached the top of the hill, he didn't see where she went and kept on going.

Realizing that he had lost her trail, he pulled into the next gas station he saw and waited. Ten minutes later, he saw her green Saturn zip by. He followed her to a cheap motel eight miles away and parked at the other end of the lot so she wouldn't see him. She got out of the car and looked to her left and right, then she lugged the bags to the second floor and slipped into room 207.

Brenda wrapped her arms around Terry Dawson and ran her fingers on his massive chest.

"What took you so long?" he asked. "Did you have any trouble?"

"I was being followed."

"Are you all right?"

"I think I ditched him."

He looked at the bags she brought in with her and asked, "Did you get everything?"

"Yeah, I think so."

"Good. I can't take a chance going to the store with that detective looking for me."

Logan watched the curtains close and got out to jot down her license plate number. He got back in his car and waited. About an hour later, he saw her coming out of room 207. She looked around the parking lot and walked hurriedly to her car. She got in and pulled out the motel exit.

The tires squealed as she sped down the road.

It was now his turn to pay Terry Dawson a visit. He knocked on the door, and Terry opened it a crack.

"Did you forget something, babe?"

He saw the detective waving his badge and tried to lock the door. Logan rammed against it and forced his way in. Terry towered over him and pushed him back with his large powerful hands. Logan sized up his gigantic opponent and lifted his hand up as if to call a truce. Dawson did not look like the typical drug dealer he had dealt with in the city. He was clean-cut with chiseled features and a blond crew cut. No one would have ever suspected he had been involved with drugs. He had probably gotten a lot of kids hooked on drugs with his boy-next-door looks.

"You don't know how glad I am to finally meet you."

"How did you know I was here? Did she tell you?"

"I asked some of your former football buddies the name of the girl you've been dating and the rest was easy. I figured you two couldn't stay apart for long, so I followed her. And she led me right to you."

"What do you want?"

"I think you know what I want. Where were you the night Phillip Bishop was murdered?"

"I was with my rehab counselor."

"Oh really? I just spoke to him. He says he hasn't seen you in several days. Now where were you?"

"I was with Brenda."

"She would probably lie to protect you."

"If you don't believe me, ask her yourself."

"I think I might just do that."

"Fine, see if I care."

"I'll talk to her, but if I find out you're lying, I won't be a happy camper."

Logan went back outside and Dawson shouted, "Damn!"

He sat at the edge of the bed, thinking of a plan. He called Brenda's cell phone number and said, "Hello, Brenda?"

"What's wrong?"

"A detective was just here."

"He must've been the guy that was following me. I was sure I lost him. What did he want?"

"Don't be surprised if he comes knocking on your door. If you talk to him, say you were with me when Phillip died, got that?"

"All right, but what if he finds out we weren't—?"

"Don't worry, it will be okay. There's no way he could find out."

"I hope you're right."

"You'll be okay. I'll talk to you soon. Bye."

He hung up and lay on the bed. He turned on the TV and watched the middle of a movie.


Brenda was setting the table when the doorbell rang. Her mother got up to see who it was. When Brenda heard a man introduce himself as Detective Logan, she tore down the basement steps.

"Brenda! Brenda! A Detective Logan is here to talk to you."

She heard footsteps overhead and figured she must be moving toward the family room just off the kitchen. Then she heard the basement door squeak. Her voice was more audible now: "Brenda, are you down there?"

She led him down the wooden steps and went into the laundry room. They saw Brenda sitting on a chair next to the ironing board.

Logan held up his badge and said, "I need to ask you some questions, Brenda."

They went back to the living room, and she stared blankly into his eyes.

"Where were you the night Phillip Bishop died?"

"I was with my boyfriend. We went to a party at a friend's house."

He jotted down the location and apologized for taking up their time. She scrambled to her room and dialed her friend's number.

"It's Brenda. I need you to do me a favor."


Logan paid Terry Dawson another visit at the motel.

"You'll never guess what Brenda told me. She said you both went to a party at a friend's house the night Phillip died."

"It's true," Dawson said.

"I checked with your friends. They're really loyal and probably would have lied to protect you, if I hadn't twisted the truth out of them. One of them said you weren't there. If that's the case, where were you? And don't lie to me this time."

"I was at Jonas MacPharlan's house."

Logan glared at him and said, "Don't jerk me around again."

"I'm telling you the truth."

"You'd better be telling me the truth this time, Dawson," Logan said on his way out the door. Terry peered out the window and watched him drive away. He plopped on the bed and turned on the TV.

He laughed and said, "You guys made my life a living hell, I'll make your life hell."


Logan pulled next to Hullien Hall and went into the headmaster's waiting room. He smiled at the receptionist and said, "I'm here to see Jonas MacPharlan."

"He's out for the day, sir."

"Then I guess I'll have to go over to his house."

"I'm afraid you can't do that, Detective. He and his wife are attending a luncheon in Philadelphia."

"Then I'll just have to come back tomorrow morning."

"He has meetings all—"

He left before she could give him another excuse why he would not be able to talk to him. On his way out, he muttered, "What do you have to do with all of this old man?"

\* \* \*

Logan grabbed a quick dinner before going back to police headquarters. Lieutenant Winters went over to him and said, "Working late again, Frank?"

He grunted and said, "Yeah, this boarding school case is driving me crazy. It's unbelievable. People either lie to avoid getting caught doing something they shouldn't have been doing, or they lie to protect somebody who shouldn't have been doing something."

Harry grinned and said, "You gotta love it."

"Well, I finally tracked down Terry Dawson. It turns out he's hiding out in a motel about a half an hour away. I paid him a surprise visit."

"He manages to keep himself pretty busy, doesn't he?"

"That's for sure. And he still had time to come back to campus and harass Phillip Bishop before his murder. He said he was with his rehab counselor when it happened. I knew that didn't seem right and called him right then and there. When I confronted him about his little lie, he said he was with Jonas MacPharlan. And several people said they saw him talking to him at the basketball game a week before Bishop died."

"What a coincidence."

"I'd love to know how MacPharlan fits into the picture."

"Me too."


If there was one thing Logan dreaded most, it was dealing with liars first thing in the morning. Sometimes it was necessary if he wanted to get answers. He arrived at Hullien Hall at nine o'clock and watched Jonas MacPharlan's secretary go down the hall. He slipped into the waiting room and went over to the headmaster's door. It was unlocked and he went in. Jonas wasn't there, so he sat on a wing chair next to his desk.

The door opened, and Jonas flinched when he saw him sitting there. "You startled me. What are you doing here so early, Detective Logan?"

"I have some unfinished business."

Jonas sat at his desk and looked quizzically at the detective.

"Terry Dawson told me he was at a friend's house near campus on the night Phillip was killed," Logan said. "Would you like to know who his friend is?"

"No. I think it has gotten to the point where you are grasping at straws, Detective."

"Terry claims that he was at your house that night."

"He's lying!" Jonas snapped. "You would believe the word of a felon over the word of a respected scholar?"

"He said there were witnesses who can vouch—"

"How dare you imply—"

"What's wrong, have I ruffled feathers? Why are you so upset? If you're such an upstanding citizen, you have nothing to worry about, right?"

Jonas shook his index finger at him and said, "Look here, Detective, you have been creating a disturbance on the campus. You are interfering with the learning process."

"I'm sorry, but I'm just doing my job. I have to ask these questions."

Jonas still insisted that it was a car accident, but Logan said he had enough evidence to prove otherwise.

The headmaster grimaced. "I'm afraid all your poking around is going to make things worse. Please just leave us alone."

"I can't do that, sir. Don't you want to know what really happened to Phillip? I sure do."

"I think you're making more out of it than there really is."

"I think you're hiding something. If you want me out of here, then you'll have to cooperate. Give me some answers."

Jonas leaned forward and said, "I can assure you, Terry Dawson was not at my house that night."

"Can you prove it?"

"Ask my wife. I was with her all night. Now, if you'll excuse me, I have work to do."

"All right, thank you, Mr. MacPharlan, you've been very helpful."

Logan started to close the door when he saw MacPharlan reach for the telephone. The secretary had not come back yet, so he left it ajar and eavesdropped.

"Detective Logan isn't going away," Jonas said. "He's persistent. I told you I don't want to be involved! If he finds out? You know he will. He has been snooping around. It's only a matter of time before—"

There was a long silence.

"My reputation is not ruined! I ought to—yes, but you promised."

Jonas was quiet again. A couple minute's later he said, "How do you expect me to avoid a scandal? There already is one. I don't know how I can—"

Logan heard footsteps and looked up to see the secretary coming toward him.

"What are you doing?" She pushed him down the hall and said, "Get out of here! Scoot!"

Jonas looked at the door and continued his conversation. "I'm sorry about that. It was a confusion of sorts. My receptionist was yelling at a student. Don't worry, I'll find a way."

He hung up and muttered, "Oh Lord, what have I gotten myself into?"

At two o'clock, Logan pulled into the gym parking lot and made a left turn up the long driveway that led to the headmaster's house. It was a large Georgian style home that was probably built in the 1700s. He figured that a wealthy farmer lived in it, long before it was a part of the boarding school.

He went up the cobblestone walkway leading to the house. On either side, there were well-maintained boxwood bushes. He rang the bell and rubbed his hands as he looked across the soccer field. The door creaked, and he turned around to see a petite middle-aged woman with frosted hair that was pulled back and held with a barrette.

He held out his badge and introduced himself. "I need to speak to Mrs. MacPharlan."

She smiled and said, "I'm Mrs. MacPharlan. What can I do for you?"

"I just need to ask a couple of questions, ma'am, and then I'll get out of your hair."

"Don't be ridiculous. You have a job to do, and we all need to help you. I don't know how much help I'll be though."

"Your husband thinks I'm in the way."

"He doesn't want the kids to get distracted."

She invited him in and led him across the foyer. His eyes were drawn to a magnificently handcrafted staircase. A tall grandfather clock stood prominently to the left as they approached the living room. He stared in awe at it a moment and followed her toward the entryway.

She beamed with pride and said, "It was built by an eighteenth-century clock maker from Philadelphia."

"Hmm, you don't say."

She led him into the living room and gave a brief history of the house. It was built in 1775. Most of the furnishings were reproductions. The stairs and woodwork were constructed by the finest craftsmen at that time. Charles S. Wingate was the first headmaster to live there.

Her eyes were gleaming. "Isn't it beautiful?"

Logan looked around the room and nodded his agreement. The reproductions were probably important, but he had no idea why. He sat on a chair that he thought was probably the most comfortable one in the room. It was far from that, but it was probably an antique and had to be uncomfortable. He accepted her offer of coffee, and she went into the kitchen to get it for him. He went over to warm up by the fireplace and looked at framed photos on the mantle. His eyes trained on one of the MacPharlans standing in front of a bed-and-breakfast inn. They were wearing snow skiing outfits.

She came back carrying two mugs and said, "That was taken at a quaint B and B in the Poconos. We just love it there."

"It looks nice."

"We usually spend a lot of time up there skiing, but the weather has fluctuated so much this winter that we haven't felt like going up there as much."

She handed him a mug and sat on the love seat. She offered him sugar, and he poured it into his drink. He stirred it in and took a careful sip.

She stirred her drink and said, "It was so sad what happened to Phillip. His death has had such an impact on the students."

"I bet it did."

"We had a counselor come talk to them. Some kids hold everything in, and you think they're okay and they explode later, if you know what I mean. Others let it all out. I would prefer the latter, of course. It's best not to bottle up your emotions. I prefer screaming and crying, then you can get back to normal."

Logan nodded his agreement.

She took a sip and said, "But that isn't what you came to talk to me about. My goodness, I'm sure you are quite busy."

He smiled and said, "That's okay, ma'am. I just needed to know some things about Terry Dawson. Was he here the night Phillip died?"

Her eyebrows shot up. "Why on earth would you think he would come here of all places. He's riffraff."

"Witnesses saw him talking to your husband a week before Phillip died."

She wiped her lips with a cloth napkin and said, "He was just trying to cause trouble. There was nothing to it, really."

Logan referred to his notes and said, "I just want to double-check on something, ma'am. Was your husband here that night?"

"We were here all night."

"Thanks for your help, ma'am. And thanks for the coffee."


A half hour later, he paid Terry Dawson another visit. He heard the TV blaring and knocked on the door. The noise suddenly stopped. There was no answer.

"Come on, Dawson, I don't have all day!"

Terry opened the door and grumbled. "Oh, all right."

He sat back on the bed and continued watching a stupid talk show about transvestite love triangles.

Logan turned it off and Dawson moaned, "Come on, man. I'm watching that!"

"If you don't cooperate, I'll put you in jail. Then you can actually see transvestites fighting. Now start talking. Mrs. MacPharlan told me Jonas was with her that night. Where were you? And don't lie to me this time."

"I was at home watching a movie with Brenda."

"Guess again. Her mother said she was working that night. And it's true. I checked. Were you with your family that night?"

Terry shook his head.

"So you have no alibi."

"I guess it looks that way. Are you going to arrest me?"

"If you don't watch your step, I just might. I'm watching you, Dawson. One false move and you'll end up back in jail. You got that?"

Terry waved his hands and said, "Yeah, yeah."

Logan slammed the door on his way out.

Terry leaned against his pillows and grinned.

## Chapter 9

The next morning, Chad arrived at the cafeteria before it opened. He wanted to make sure he got there early to avoid the crowd. He got his food and sat near the exit door. He saw students enter the room from the main entrance and went outside. He did not want to talk to anyone, especially Andy, Rudy, and the girls. He couldn't deal with the looks he was getting. Everyone was staring at him. He couldn't deal with answering their nonstop questions about the case. He wished they would leave him alone.

Jonas MacPharlan went over to him and said, "I would like to have a word with you."

"Yes, sir."

He followed him up the steps and glanced to his left and right to make sure no one saw them. Fortunately, the hall was empty. Jonas told him to meet him in his office and stopped to talk to Steven Simons, the dean of students.

Chad pushed through the swinging doors and saw Eddie Hastings and Scott Robbins at the end of the hall. They brushed against him as they went by.

Scott lunged at him and said, "They should've let you rot in jail."

"Shut up, Robbins!" Chad snapped.

"Get the hell away from me, freak!"

Eddie stood in between them and said, "Come on, Scott, he isn't worth it."

Chad rushed him and shouted, "You no good bastard!"

Students gathered in the hall and shouted, "Cream him, Scott! Come on, get him!"

The dean came running out of his office, followed by Jonas MacPharlan.

"What's going on here?" MacPharlan demanded.

"Nothing, sir," Eddie said. "It's under control."

"Good, I don't want to have to put you all on detention. I don't want trouble, do you understand?"

"Yes, sir," they chimed.

"Now go to breakfast and leave Chad alone."

Scott sneered at Chad as he followed the others downstairs.

Jonas glared at Chad and asked, "What's the meaning of this?"

"I didn't do anything. He started it."

He took Chad by the collar, pushed him into his office, and told him to wait there. Then he went out to the hall to talk to the dean.

Chad heard Dean Simon's voice loud and clear from the next room: "Jonas, this won't work. Students don't want him here."

"I am aware of that, Steven. I was just about to talk to him. We will discuss this later."

Jonas went back to his office and closed the door. He sat at his desk and looked sharply at Chad.

"What am I going to do with you, Mr. McAlpin? I can't have you here, stirring up trouble."

"But I didn't do anything. Scott started it."

"I'm afraid it will only get worse. You don't know how much it pains me to discipline you, Chad. You're one of the brightest students in your class. But if you stay, you'll only make things worse for yourself and for others."

Chad gulped and said, "Does this mean I'm out?"

Jonas tapped his desk and nodded. "If you weren't in such excellent academic standing, I would recommend you attend another school to avoid harassment from your peers."

Chad's eyes widened. "Then what are you saying, sir?"

"You are suspended indefinitely. I'm sorry."

"You can't do that! I'm about to graduate. Indefinitely? What does that mean?"

"I'll let you know when you can return."

"When will that be? A week? A month? When?"

"It would be better this way, with all that's happening. I've spoken to your teachers, and they understand the situation. They have given me a list

## LOVE'S A CRIME

of all your assignments. You can do your work at home and e-mail it all to me. I'm sorry, Chad, but it's the only logical thing to do."

"I can't believe this!" He stormed out and ran back to his dorm to pack. There was a knock at the door, and he went to see who it was. Andy and Rudy were there, anxious to find out what was happening.

Rudy looked at the open suitcase on his bed and asked, "Where are you going?"

"I'm on suspension till further notice," he said flatly.

"They can't do that!" Rudy cried.

"Yes, they can. And they did. You'll take care of things while I'm gone, won't you?"

"Yeah, man," Andy said.

"What will we do?" Rudy asked.

Chad lowered his voice and said, "Nothing. With the police on me, that will take some heat off you guys. Whatever happens, remember you had your chance to get out of it." He closed the suitcase and said, "Be cool. I'll be back. Tell Susy I'll call her tonight."

He slipped them a note and said, "Just a little reminder, huh? See ya!"

He went out the door, and they watched him carry the suitcase down the hall.

Rudy gulped and looked at the note. It read, "You guys are swell, but I'll get you if you tell."

They went back to their room and sat on their beds, mulling over their situation. Andy went over to the desk and rummaged through a drawer. He found a lighter hidden under a pile of junk. He lit it and held the note over the flame. They stood there, silently watching it burn.

"He's thorough," Andy said.

"He means it."

"Blackmail 101—and he's quite good at it."

"It's only a matter of time before—I say we fend for ourselves. What do we have to lose? What kind of friend is he anyway? He wants us all to go down, just to protect him. I say it's every man for himself."

"Rudy, we were friends to you when nobody else was. We set you up with Wendy. If it hadn't been for us, you'd still be a little nerd—all alone. You owe us!"

He waved his hands and shouted, "I don't owe you a thing. This is different and you know it! I don't care. I've worked too hard to lose it all now."

"So have I!"

"If you go down, I'm taking you with me." He stomped over to the door.

"Where are you going?"

"I don't know!"

"Don't rat us out!"

Rudy slammed the door and darted down the hall.

Susan and Michelle were on their beds, studying. Susan couldn't get Chad off her mind. She blamed herself. Maybe it would have been better for everyone if she had not gone back to Broad Meadow. She wished she could do things over again. She wished the boys had not gotten so worked up over her. She wished they had left her alone. She wished they had not gone to the woods that night. She wished she had not asked Phillip and Chad to talk. Maybe they weren't ready to patch things up. It was too late now. Phillip was gone. If they hadn't gone to the woods, he would still be alive and Chad would not be in trouble.

Michelle underlined a passage with a pink highlight pen and read the next page. She looked over at Susan and asked, "Are you okay?"

"Nothing's sinking in. I keep thinking about Chad."

"Same here. I don't think he killed Phillip."

"He was mad, but I know he didn't do it. Why did it have to get to this point? I can't take much more. All this fighting and hatred and everybody looking down on me. It isn't fair."

Michelle sat at the edge of her bed and said, "Talk to me."

"If it weren't for me, Phillip would be with us now. Why did they have to keep fighting over me? They were always competing for me for some dumb reason. Now he's dead. All because of me."

"You'll get through this somehow," Michelle said softly. "I'm here for you."

"I shouldn't have come back."

"You needed to be around us. You'll get through this. We'll get through it together."

"Will things ever be better?"

"They can't get any worse. Things always have a way of working out."

"I hope so."

Susan sniffled and wiped away tears. Michelle held her in her arms.


Jonas MacPharlan looked up to see Rudy standing in the doorway. "Rudy? What's wrong? You look upset."

"I have to talk to you, sir."

Jonas waved and said, "Come in."

"I did something bad—it was a mistake. I didn't know what to do."

"What happened?"

"It's this way, sir. I didn't want to do it. We panicked."

"We?"

"Chad and me. Phillip was lying there dead. We didn't know what to do. Chad and I went back to the dorm, and I drove his car back to the woods. I didn't want Chad to get into trouble, so I helped him carry Phillip to his car, and we pushed it off the road. I'm sorry I didn't say anything before. I was so worried he'd get mad at me, I didn't know what to do."

Jonas studied the wild look in Rudy's eyes. He was shaking his legs the way he did when he was really nervous.

"I'm glad you came to talk to me. Did he hurt you?"

"No."

"Did he threaten you?"

"No, I told him I'd protect him, but now I'm scared."

Jonas leaned forward and asked, "Did you actually see what happened?"

"No, but I knew it was a mistake. They just got into a fight, and Phillip hit his head on a rock. There was blood everywhere. It was all over his head, and it got all over our clothes. We could feel it—it was sticky and messy. It was on our fingers and hands."

"Why didn't you get help?"

"He was dead!" his voice squeaked. "We didn't know what else to do. Chad knew people had seen them fighting. He thought everybody would think he did it. So that's why—that's why we had to make it look like an accident. I drove his car onto Snake Turn Road, and we carried Phillip to his car and pushed it off. We took clean clothes with us and put them on. Then we drove back in Chad's car."

"Was Andy with you?"

"He went back to the dance."

Jonas removed his glasses and wiped them with a handkerchief. He put them back on and said, "That's odd, no one saw him there then."

"He said he was there. But as I was saying. Phillip was insistent. He had to talk to Chad alone to set things straight. That's when all hell broke loose. A few minutes later, Chad tore through the woods all bloody. It was bad. If you're going to expel me, get it over with. I can't stand the waiting."

MacPharlan rubbed his hands and said, "Settle down. I want you to talk to Detective Logan."

He picked up the telephone and dialed. "You won't believe who I have in my office."

Rudy jumped up and ran out of the room.

"Hey, wait a minute!"

It was too late. Rudy was gone.

"Sorry about that," he continued. "A confusion of sorts . . . yeah, Rudy. I know he's a good candidate. It was only a matter of time. What do you want me to do?"

## Chapter 10

Rudy tapped his left foot to see if the ice would crack under his weight. It was all right, so he proceeded across the pond. He slid slowly forward and heard a crack. His right foot was covered with water, and his sock was soaked. He pulled it out of the hole and headed back to the bench by the old oak tree. He stared across the pond, thinking troubling thoughts.

"I didn't mean to do it, Phil," he muttered. "I'm sorry. It happened so fast that we weren't thinking clearly. Chad made us do it. No he didn't. He gave us a chance to back out and I didn't do it. Like that would have made a difference anyway. I knew what he did. He was in trouble, and I wanted to help him. A lot of good that did me. He only cares about himself."

He picked up a rock and tossed it into the pond. It made a scraping sound as it slid across the ice.

"It's all over. I never should have told MacPharlan! He'll tell Detective Logan, and then Chad will know I told on him. Then he'll tell them everything."

He got up and went over to the stone footbridge. He looked down at the pond and wished it had not frozen over.

"God, I've always tried to do good, and you know it. But I don't know what I'm going to do now."

He wiped away tears and sniffled. A few minutes later, he wound up on the pond again.

He reached for a stick and scratched his name on the ice.

"It's the only way," he mumbled. "It's the only way."

\* \* \*

At noon, Susan and Michelle followed students toward Hullien Hall. Susan looked over at the pond and saw someone walking around in circles.

"Who's that?"

Michelle strained her eyes to see. "It looks like Rudy."

"What's he doing?"

"I don't know."

"With Rudy it could be anything."

By the time they reached the front steps of Hullien Hall, he had started to make his way toward them.

Susan looked over at him and waved. "Are you okay, Rudy?"

He apparently didn't hear her. He was walking toward the Hullien Hall guest parking lot.

"Where is he going?" Susan wondered.

"It looks like he's going back to his dorm. Who knows? Come on, it's too cold to stand out here."

They went into the building and followed the crowd downstairs. It was so jammed at this point that a line formed at the foot of the steps. They had to lean against the wall to avoid being bumped into by students coming out of the kitchen.

Rudy lay on his bed and muttered, "There's no other way."

He went over to his desk drawer and pulled out a sheet of notepaper. He sat down and wrote, "Dear Mom and Dad."

He stared at the blank sheet and continued writing.

Andy arrived at the kitchen late. By now, there was not much left to choose from. He reached for a roast beef platter and went into the cafeteria to look for a vacant seat. He went over to Susan and Michelle and asked, "Is this seat taken?"

Susan laid books on the table and said, "Go ahead."

He sat down and ate quickly.

**LOVE'S A CRIME**

Susan sighed and said, "I guess it's over. Poor Chad."

Michelle scowled and said, "Poor Chad? You can say that after the way he treated you?"

"It was just a misunderstanding."

"Your sugar-and-spice attitude won't get you anywhere."

"You don't think he actually did it, do you?" Andy asked.

"He might have a temper, but he would never do such a horrible thing," Susan said.

"But he does have a temper," Michelle said. "And we all know what he's capable of."

"I don't believe you, Michelle," Susan said. "Yesterday you said you didn't think he did it."

"He did get into some nasty fights with Phillip."

"But that doesn't prove anything," Andy was quick to point out. "It just shows you that somebody could've framed him."

Michelle nodded her agreement. "You're right. Do you think he did it?"

He met her gaze and said, "He's my friend. There's no way he could've done it. He wasn't gone long enough to—"

"Ah-ha!" Michelle cut in. "I knew you were all acting strange the day they found his body. You should know more than we do."

Andy gave her a sideways glance. "What's that supposed to mean?"

"You were all in the woods after we left."

Andy stirred his soup to distract them for a moment. He looked up at them and asked, "How could that detective arrest him anyway? It was just an accident, wasn't it?"

Michelle folded her arms and said, "I'm sure. The police aren't telling us things. And I think you know more than you're letting on."

"You're full of it, Michelle. When did you become a detective anyway?"

"Come on you guys," Susan said. "This isn't accomplishing anything."

"How long have we known each other, Andy?" Michelle asked.

He groaned and said, "Four years too long."

"And in that time, we've gotten to know each other pretty well, haven't we?"

113

He groaned and said, "Unfortunately."

"I'm a good judge of character. I know when things don't add up."

He eyed her suspiciously. "What do you mean?"

"Remember what Chad told Mr. Wriggley?"

"I try to block out his class," he said.

"Chad said Phillip was in bed, the day after the dance. Then he said Phillip wasn't there when he came back from jogging. We all know that's not true! There's no way Phillip was in bed when Chad went jogging Saturday morning. Detective Logan just proved it. Chad's blood was on Phillip's shirt. And his fingerprints were on the trunk of his car."

Andy stirred his soup and hoped she couldn't read his mind at the moment. Their prints were all over the car. What if the police had evidence to tie him to the "fake" car accident and were waiting for him to slip up?

He looked up at her and said, "Maybe it was there before."

"Come off it, Andy!" Michelle cried. "What are you guys hiding?"

"I don't know what you're talking about."

"You can level with me. I won't tell Detective Logan."

"There's nothing to tell!" he snapped.

"Come on you guys," Susan interrupted. "This isn't getting us anywhere. Chad didn't do anything."

Michelle wiped her mouth and said, "You're right, Susan. He didn't kill Phillip. But he faked the car accident. And I think you had something to do with it."

"You're really full of it, Michelle! I didn't come here to get the third degree!"

"Shut up!" students shouted.

Coach Reynolds went over to them and said, "Be quiet, Winchester. We're trying to eat here. Do you have a problem?"

"No."

"Good. Just keep it down."

Susan looked from Michelle to Andy and said, "Now see what you did? Chad needs us. We're not going to help him by yelling at each other."

Michelle changed her tone. It sounded friendlier now. "I'm sorry, Andy. I didn't mean to accuse you of anything."

"I'm sorry too."

"That's better," Susan said.

They were quiet a moment. He was eating more quickly now. Their next class was in ten minutes. Every so often, he looked around the room, searching the crowd for his roommate.

"Have you seen Rudy?"

"I saw him coming out of Mr. MacPharlan's office after breakfast," Michelle said.

Andy's voice rose. "Oh really? He cut some classes. It isn't like him to do that."

"I think this whole investigation has gotten us all frazzled," Michelle said. "Maybe he just couldn't handle sitting in classes. I can't really blame him."

He finished off his tomato soup and said, "I think he's mad at me. We got into a big fight this morning, and he walked out in a huff."

"That explains it," Michelle said.

He gave her a puzzled look. "What do you mean?"

"Susy and I saw him coming from the pond a few minutes ago. We said hello, but he didn't say anything."

"That's Rudy for you," he said.

They changed the subject. Andy listened to them talk while he finished eating lunch. He wondered what Rudy wanted to talk to MacPharlan about. He hoped he wasn't ratting him out.

The bell rang and they hurried to their next class.

The final bell rang, and Andy pushed his way through the crowded hallway. He went to look for Rudy in their room, but he was not there. He went into the lounge, but Rudy wasn't there either.

Willy Brown was so engrossed in a calculus problem, he blocked out all distractions in the room.

Andy went over to him and asked, "Have you seen Rudy?"

"I haven't seen him all day," he said without looking up from his notes. "What's wrong?"

"We had a disagreement."

"Was it a lover's spat?"

"Ha-ha, very funny."

"It's about Chad, isn't it?"

"Is it any of your business?"

"No, but I know some things you don't want people to know."

Andy looked at him skeptically. "Oh really?"

Willy adjusted his glasses and said, "Phillip never came back to get his car."

Andy shoved his index finger against Willy's chest. "Go back to studying!" He stormed out and went to his room. He hastily put on his basketball uniform and headed for practice. On the way to the gym, he ruminated about what Michelle said at lunch. She had a lot of nerve accusing him of wrongdoing. Then he thought about what Willy said. He was always a little on the melodramatic side. He should be an actor, not a mathematician. Andy sometimes found it hard to believe anything Willy "the Brain" said.

Willy, the little geek! He spent most of his time studying. Andy never saw him when he didn't have a pencil wedged between his fingers, his face in a book. He even spent his free time studying. Students talked about him behind his back and said nasty things.

Willy gave Andy the creeps. He always knew about everything that was going on even when it didn't look like he did. Andy often wondered what went on inside Willy's own little world.

"What do you really know, Willy?" he muttered.

# Chapter 11

Logan knew Chad wasn't telling the truth during the interrogation at the police station. The only evidence he had that linked him to the crime was the blood he got on Phillip's shirt during their altercation. After getting a warrant to look at his shoes, Logan found a pair that matched the plaster casts made of the footprints found on the trail leading to the road. Prints lifted from Chad, Andy, and Rudy's lockers matched the ones found on the trunk of Phillip's car. Andy's prints were also on the rearview mirror. When he adjusted the seat position, he left prints on the lever too. All he had to do was wait for the right time to arrest Andy and Rudy.

Logan knew that was only enough evidence to link Chad and the boy's to "faking" the car accident. There were no fingerprints on the rock that was used to kill Phillip. Tony Mancini could convince jurors that somebody else did it. Chad could get off on a technicality if he didn't find more substantial evidence linking him to the murder.

He also knew Chad lied about taking Phillip back to the dorm that night. He couldn't possibly have received a phone call from Terry Dawson when he was lying dead in the woods. But Terry had threatened him. And he had motive.

About two thirty, Logan went to Stewart Hall to ask Andy and Rudy if Phillip received any calls from Terry after their altercation at the gym. He knocked on their bedroom door, but there was no answer.

A boy walked by and asked, "Are you looking for Andy?"

"Both of them, actually."

"You just missed them. They should be at the gym now."

He thanked him and whistled as he strolled down the hall. Willy Brown cradled a stack of books against his chest as he climbed the steps. The door opened, and Logan collided with him. The books scattered, and he knelt down to help pick them up.

"Sorry about that."

Willy gathered a pile into a stack and evened them up. "It happens all the time. The athletes do it to get a laugh. They think it's funny. They have an IQ of a pea."

Logan handed him a stack. Willy jammed papers in his folder and wrapped his arms around the stack. He slowly got to his feet and started down the hall.

Logan walked alongside him and said, "People used to do that to me."

Willy's eyes lit up. "Really?"

He laughed and said, "I got back at them though."

"What did you do?"

"They always asked me if they could take a look at my homework. I didn't have much of a choice. They just took it right out of my hands and copied it."

"They do the same thing to me and I hate it."

"They kept getting away with it till I smartened up. I rewrote my homework with all the wrong answers."

"That's a great idea! I wish I had thought of it. I can't imagine you were ever that unpopular."

"It was hell," Logan admitted. "But I would never have gotten through the police academy if I hadn't toughened up. Hang in there. It's not so bad."

Willy flashed a bashful smile and said, "They think I'm odd. They don't think I know what they say about me. But I do. I've overheard some conversations. They say awful things."

"What do they say?"

"They think I'm a geek, caught up in my own world."

"What do they know?"

"Exactly. Phillip wasn't like that. He was a really nice guy."

"Well, somebody didn't think so."

"Did Chad really kill him?"

"I can't say right now."

"It's just awful what happened."

"I know. But don't worry, we'll get to the bottom of it." He started to go when Willy hurried after him. "Detective Logan!"

He turned around and said, "Yes?"

"You asked me if I remembered anything, to tell you."

"What is it?"

"I was studying the night of the dance and heard footsteps. I thought I was alone. I got up and just saw a shadow go out the exit door."

"Did you get a good enough look?"

"Not really. But I did hear a car engine starting. I looked out the window and saw Phillip's car pulling away."

"Do you remember what time it was?"

"About ten thirty."

Logan fixed his gaze on Willy's. "Do you remember anything else?"

"The thing that sticks in my mind is this. Phillip was real tall. It couldn't have been his shadow I saw. It was a shorter figure."

Logan's eyes gleamed. "You don't say!"

"Did I say something important?"

"Maybe." He thanked him and hurried downstairs.

Logan climbed the bleacher steps and sat on the top row. He watched the girls' basketball team file into the room and take their side of the gym. Coach Reynolds closed the partition door and blew his whistle. Ian searched for faces in the crowd and went into the locker room. He came back a couple minutes later and asked if anyone had seen Rudy. No one had.

"That's just great!" Reynolds shouted. "Where the hell is he? We've got the state finals coming up, and our team is dwindling. It's a real tragedy what happened to Phillip. Now Chad's gone and Rudy's missing. How the hell can we win without a whole team?"

Andy bravely stepped forward and said, "Coach, I'm sure there has to be a good reason why he's not here."

"You're his roommate. When was the last time you saw him?"

"This morning. Michelle and Susy saw him around lunchtime. He left his cell phone off, and I can't get a hold of him."

"As of this moment, he's off the team! I can't have this crap here!"

"But you can't do that. Rudy's always here. We need him."

"Rudy's weak. And we can't have weak players if we're going to win. It's cut-and-dried. This year we're going to have a winning team!"

Andy rolled his eyes and said, "How do you expect—?"

"I don't want to hear your lip, Andy! Just do as I say!"

Andy threw his arms in the air and shouted, "We're nothing without Phillip and Chad. We won't make it without them."

His teammates voiced their agreement.

Reynolds looked across at them and said, "I know we've lost good players. And morale is extremely low at this point, but we'll make it if you guys work harder. You just need to work at being the best. I believe in you all. And I know you won't let me down. Okay, let's get moving. Winchester, front and center!"

Logan watched Andy go over to him. The coach put his hand on his shoulder and whispered something in his ear. Andy looked irritated.

When the private conversation was over, Reynolds slapped Andy's shoulder and said, "I'm depending on you, Andy. You're the fastest runner we've got. Keep up the good work."

"But Coach, what about Rudy?"

"As I said before, he can't cut it. I'm counting on your ability to get us a winning season."

He blew his whistle, and they did warm-up exercises.

Logan wished he knew what the coach said to Andy.

About six o'clock, Andy entered the cafeteria and looked around for Rudy. He was not there, and he was starting to get worried. He went over to Susan and Michelle's table and sat down. They were also scared. It was not like Rudy to disappear like that. They wondered where he went. His cell phone had been off all day. And he wasn't returning their e-mails or text messages. As nightfall approached, faculty members were also wondering where he had gone.

Meanwhile, Logan was eating a sub at his desk. While he was away, he had received three nasty messages from Chad McAlpin's lawyer. He put off returning the calls and stared at a pile of paperwork he had put off until now. He typed a report and ate while reviewing his notes. About an hour later, he clocked out and headed for the parking lot. He could not wait to get rid of the tie that had been driving him crazy all day. He wondered if it would cut off circulation to his brain.

He sank down on his car seat, untied the knot, and pulled it off. He turned on the headlights and glanced at the rearview mirror. His neck was sore.

"Ah geez!"

He pulled onto the road and arrived at his apartment building about twenty minutes later. He chatted with Mrs. Ferguson as they went upstairs. She had just come back from the store to get her husband flu medicine.

"Are you working on any interesting cases, Frank?" she asked.

"Yeah, it's keeping me pretty busy." He chose to remain tight-lipped about the details.

She grinned and said, "I bet it is. How are you going to meet the woman of your dreams if you work at night so much?"

"I know what you mean, Mrs. Fergusson, but if I don't do it, the bad guy gets away with it."

"My niece is coming to town next week. She's about your age. Maybe you two could have dinner together."

"That sounds great. Hopefully, I can wrap up the case by then and—"

"A date would be a great distraction, Frank. It'll take your mind off it and then you can think fresh, if you know what I mean?"

He grinned and said, "I think so. That would be nice. Just knock on my door and we can set something up."

They parted on the third floor, and he went into his apartment. It wasn't Buckingham Palace. He didn't spend that much time there, so it didn't matter how small it was. As long as he had a roof over his head and a comfortable bed, that was all he needed.

When he left Philadelphia, he wanted to make the move as simple as possible. He took the six things he couldn't live without: his mattress, TV, VCR, stereo, laptop, and microwave oven. He got most of his furniture from area thrift shops. He hung his police academy diploma on the living room wall next to the one his father earned several years earlier. Next to them, he proudly hung awards and medals they had received. The last

**JOSEPH REDDEN**

picture of him with his parents hung on the opposite wall. Next to it, there was a portrait of his father in uniform with the American flag behind him. Below it, there was his mother in a bikini at the beach that must have been taken before she got married. Then there was the one he cherished the most. The one where he was in his mother's arms taken when he was about six months old.

He went into the bedroom, tossed his tie on his queen-sized bed, and unbuttoned his shirt. He laid his pants neatly on the bed and went into the bathroom.

---

Andy was reading his physics notes at his desk when his cell phone rang. He reached across the desk and pulled it open.

"Hello?"

"It's Jonas MacPharlan. Have you seen Rudy?"

"I haven't seen him all day."

"I was afraid something like this would happen," Jonas said.

"What do you mean?"

"He came to see me after breakfast and was really upset about Chad's suspension. I tried to calm him down, but it didn't seem to do any good. Where did you see him last?"

"He was acting strange at breakfast. But you know Rudy. We were heading to class, and he ran off toward the pond."

"Was he more upset than usual about what's been going on around here lately?"

"Yeah. He said something about making everything okay. I asked him what he meant, but he wouldn't say."

Jonas thanked him and hung up. It wasn't long before he gathered faculty members together to look for him. Students helped them look, but their efforts failed. After two hours, they still couldn't find him.

---

Logan took a long, hot shower, dried off, and put on a T-shirt and sweatpants. He glanced at the photo in the gold frame on the dresser and smiled. It was his favorite childhood snapshot taken on a fishing trip with his grandfather. They were wearing fishing outfits and holding their rods.

## LOVE'S A CRIME

Next to it, there was a picture of his ex-girlfriend Penny. It was the one where she was wearing a Santa Claus hat. They had just started dating then. He didn't blame her for breaking up with him. It wasn't his fault that his work consumed him.

He went to the kitchen, got a beer out of the refrigerator, and went into the living room. He turned on the television and went over to the telephone on the end table by the sofa.

Five messages blinked on the answering machine. He pressed Play and deleted three crank calls. The other two were not that important, so he decided to call back in a little while. He sat on the sofa and channel surfed until he decided to watch *Law & Order*.

The police dispatcher called about eight o'clock. "Detective Logan, I just got a call from Jonas MacPharlan. A student is missing, and he's really worried."

"It wouldn't happen to be Rudolph Preston by any chance?"

"Yeah."

"I thought so. I figured he was somewhere on campus. It's a big place."

"They looked for him for two hours and couldn't find him. His car is still there. You better get over there."

"All right, thanks."

He hung up and hurriedly changed clothes.

"A detective's job is never done," he muttered on his way to the car.

Jonas MacPharlan met Logan at the front door of Stewart Hall and told him that Rudy came to his office early that morning and admitted helping Chad push Phillip's car off the road.

"Why did he do it?" Logan asked.

"He didn't want Chad to get in trouble."

"Sometimes I just can't believe what goes on in people's minds."

Jonas sighed and said, "The poor kid."

"I need to search his room."

"Do whatever you have to. Just find him, Detective."

He led him to Rudy's room, and Andy let them in. Logan went over to Rudy's desk and did not have to do any searching. He saw something white sticking out of a textbook and picked it up. He opened it and saw an envelope with Rudy's parents' names scrawled on it. He opened it and read the note:

> Dear Mom and Dad,
>
> I'm sorry to have to write this. I'm sorry that I let you down. But I can't live with myself anymore, knowing what I've done. Now they'll all know I did it. I didn't mean for it to happen.
>
> But I had to do it. There was no other way. It's better this way. In time, maybe you'll understand and forgive me.
>
> Love Rudy.

"Damn!" Logan raced out of the room.

"What?" Andy yelled after him. He saw the note on Rudy's desk and fought back tears as he read it.

Shortly before ten, screaming emanated from the utility room. Logan ran out of the room shouting, "He's in here!"

Students crowded him and he held up his hand. "Stay back. Don't go in there!"

MacPharlan and Price entered the room and winced. Rudy was hanging from a rafter.

## Chapter 12

The Prestons were sitting next to their son, who was heavily sedated. They were both tall like he was. His father wore glasses that hung over a long nose. His hair was graying at the temples. She had a round face with abundant curly black hair and large dark eyes. She was holding his hand, in tears. She repeatedly asked what happened. Why did he do it?

Logan stood in the hall viewing Rudy's bed through the open door. He went into the room and introduced himself. "I'm really sorry about your son."

Judy Preston wiped her tears and said, "He never hurt anyone. He's always been such a good kid. Why did he do it?"

Logan looked grimly at her and said, "I don't know."

"Will he be all right?" Fred Preston asked the nurse.

"He's lucky you found him when you did, Detective Logan," she said. "The doctor said he would have been dead if it had been another few minutes."

"How long was he that way?" Fred asked.

"The doctor thinks it wasn't very long."

"Then where was he all that time?" Logan wondered.

"You'll have to ask him yourself."

"He must have been thinking about it for quite a long time," Logan said. "It's too bad he decided to go through with it."

They sat quietly by his bedside. Logan's eyes were drawn to the rope burns on Rudy's neck.

A little while later, he began stirring. His eyes rolled around, and he looked in Logan's direction.

He made guttural sounds and begged to talk to him alone. He sounded groggy. When his parents left the room, he sat up and said, "I lied, it's all my fault—it's all my fault. I had to help him. He'd tell—"

Logan leaned forward and asked, "Who? What would he tell?"

"About the papers—the exam finals—the questions. Chad said I stole them. I had to. Now my mom and dad will be mad at me. I'll be kicked out of school."

"Did he say anything else?"

"He said . . . if we agreed to stick by him that we would protect each other. After I lied, I had to tell Mr. MacPharlan. I felt so bad that I betrayed everybody that—you know."

"So Chad was holding it over your head."

"Yeah."

"And he didn't give you much choice."

"He gave me a chance to back out, but I was already into it. Please don't tell him I told you. He'll get me."

"He won't get you. He's in no position to do that."

"It's all my fault."

"Don't blame yourself."

"I didn't know what else to do." He fell back on the pillow and closed his eyes.

"Rudy, where did you go after you talked to Mr. MacPharlan?"

"I wandered around campus. There was no other way. I had to do it. I hung out in my room till lunch and left before Andy came back after school."

"Then where did you go?"

"I went into the utility room."

"Were you there the rest of the afternoon?"

"Yeah, I fell asleep in there."

"And the custodian didn't see you?"

"I was sitting behind the heater."

"When did you decide to do it?"

He choked back tears and said, "I don't know. I was working up the nerve—deciding if I should do it or not."

"You scared the hell out of everybody."

Rudy sniffled and said, "I know. Now they'll all hate me!"

Logan patted Rudy's shoulder and said, "No they won't. They really care about you."

"They won't now."

"Yes they will, you'll see."

"What's gonna happen to me?"

"Don't worry about that now. Just get better. Thanks, Rudy, you've been a big help. I'll be back to look in on you."

He opened the door, and the Prestons went back in. On his way out, he heard Rudy say, "I'm sorry about stealing the exam questions. It was a big mistake."

"It doesn't matter now," his mother said. "You're all that's important."

Before closing the door, Logan saw Mrs. Preston run her hand through Rudy's curly hair.

Her husband was sitting across from her, not saying a word.

Logan turned away slowly and said, "Poor kid, he never had a chance, with somebody like Chad."

He walked toward the elevator and punched the down button. He was about to step inside when his cell phone rang. He pulled open the lid and said, "Hello, this is Detective Logan. May I help you?"

"I have a hot tip about the Phillip Bishop case." It was a woman's voice.

"Yeah, who is this?"

"There was more to the case than drugs."

The telephone went dead.

"Hey, tell me what it is!" He shut the lid and yelled, "Damn!"


Andy checked the time. "Michelle said she was coming right back. That was a half an hour ago. Where is she?"

"Maybe she couldn't decide what to get him," Susan said.

"How hard could it be?"

"Maybe she got lost. This place is huge. There are a lot of different wings."

He tossed an old *Sport's Illustrated* on the table and replaced it with *Men's Health and Fitness*. He leaned back in the chair and read. He looked in awe at the muscle men in the full color spreads, with their enormous biceps. He glanced at his chest and abs, then at his arms and legs. He looked like a pip-squeak compared to those guys. He was going to have to spend a lot more time in the gym if he wanted to look that good.

He gasped and said, "God, look at the size of that guy's arms!"

"He looks grotesque. His veins are sticking out."

"I look like a shrimp compared to him."

Susan smiled and said, "I think you look just fine."

Michelle rushed over to them, all smiles. She waved a cluster of balloons that were tied together in Andy's face and said, "This will cheer him up."

"They're really nice," Susan said. "I like the one with the smile face."

"They're okay," Andy grumbled. "What took you so long?"

"It took longer than I thought it would."

"What's wrong?" Andy asked. "You look like a nervous wreck."

"I got off thinking about Rudy and wasn't paying attention to where I was going. I guess it's the shock of it all. I got off on the wrong wing. It's so confusing in this place."

Andy nodded and said, "Tell me about it."

Susan drew a deep breath and said, "It's just terrible what's been happening lately."

"I know," Andy agreed. "Phillip, Chad, and Rudy. What else can happen?"

"I wish this whole mess would be over with."

Michelle patted her shoulder and said, "It will be over with sooner or later."

They went to Rudy's room and chatted with his parents. He was sitting up and was more talkative now.

Michelle handed him the balloons and said, "I thought these might cheer you up."

He smiled limply and laid them by the end table. "Thanks."

Susan smiled brightly and asked, "How are you feeling?"

"Okay," he said without looking at her.

Andy looked at Rudy's neck. He was wearing a turtleneck sweater so the rope marks wouldn't be noticeable. He couldn't believe that his best friend was capable of hurting himself. He wanted to ask him why he didn't talk to him but didn't. "We all miss you," he said instead. His tone sounded flat. "Rudy stole final exam questions, and apparently Chad used that to blackmail him into helping him."

Rudy smiled, then frowned. He seemed different. He wasn't the happy-go-lucky Rudy they all knew and loved. He was subdued and mellow. His eyes were dull and lifeless. Andy snickered and said, "We played a prank on Shorty at practice this afternoon. Bruce put shaving cream in his socks when he was taking a shower after practice. And when he put them on he got it all over his feet. It was really funny!"

Everybody laughed except Rudy. He smiled and nodded. There was a long silence, and they grasped at things to say. They didn't know how to make him happy.

"How is that Preston kid making out?" Lieutenant Winters asked Logan.

"He's got a tough row to hoe, Harry."

"Did he tell you anything?"

"Oh yeah, Chad had something on him, all right. Rudy stole final exam questions, and apparently Chad used that to blackmail him into helping him."

Harry scratched his mustache and said, "Preston must have thought he'd be expelled."

"Apparently, the theft was never discovered."

"And Preston would do anything for Chad—just so his secret wasn't discovered."

"One little lapse in judgment and smack," Logan said, hitting his fist against his other hand.

"I wonder what Andy Winchester did."

"I don't know, but I intend to find out. His prints were on the trunk and in the car. Rudy lied to protect him when he spilled the beans to the headmaster."

Logan thought about the phone call he received earlier that night and tried to recall the condition of the line. There was a lot of static. It must have been a bad connection. It was definitely in a public place. He heard noise in the background. It must have been a student. Maybe an alumnus.

"What's wrong?" Harry asked.

"I got an anonymous tip when I was at the hospital."

"Anything you can use?"

"No, she said there's more to the case and hung up."

"It could have been a crank."

"I don't think so."

"Maybe she'll call back."

"I hope so."

About ten thirty that night, Chad was lying on the sofa watching TV when his cell phone rang. He reached across the end table and popped it open. "Hello?"

"Hi Chad, it's Michelle."

"Michelle? It's good to hear from you. How are you doing?"

"I could be better."

"What's wrong?"

"It's Rudy. This whole thing with Phillip has really gotten to him."

"What happened?"

"He tried to hang himself the other day. I just thought you should know."

"Oh my god! Is he—is he dead?"

"It's a good thing they found him when they did. The doctors said he would have died if it had been any later."

"Where is he? Can I see him?"

"They just took him out of intensive care and put him in a regular room. Andy, Susy, and I just got back from seeing him."

He ran his hand through his hair and said, "Oh my god! It's all my fault! This is all my fault!"

"It is your fault. You know how he acts."

"I can't believe it. Why did he do it?"

"That's what we're all wondering. Well anyway, we can't change what happened. I'm sorry, I didn't mean to come down on you so hard, it's just that we're all upset and under a lot of stress right now."

"But it's true. He was upset because of what I did."

"Don't blame yourself, there's nothing you could have done. You don't know what was going on inside his head. He must have been upset about some other things too. He was acting strange all day. We didn't see him all day, I should say. Susy and I saw him coming from the pond . . . he didn't say anything . . . it's as much our fault for not talking to him . . . he was acting strange, more so than usual. We should have known something wasn't right."

"I wish I had been there for you guys. I should go see him."

"But you can't come back. You'll get in trouble."

"I don't care. I'll be there as soon as I can. Tell Susy, I'm thinking about her."

"I will. Take care of yourself."

Andy tossed and turned in bed for what seemed like hours. He reached across the bedside table and fumbled for the light switch in the dark. He turned it on and went over to his desk to study. He could not get Rudy off his mind. He assumed Rudy slipped up and told the police everything and then tried to do himself in.

He loved Rudy like a brother. Rudy had always been there for him. It was Rudy who sat up all those nights listening when he needed to talk about personal problems. Rudy was the best friend anyone could dream of having, and how did he repay that friendship, that loyalty?

He felt bad about how things turned out. Friends shouldn't hurt each other the way he hurt Rudy. He decided it was time to do something about it. After breakfast, he drove to the police station and went over to Logan's desk and told him he needed to talk to him.

Logan smiled and said, "What can I do for you, Andy?"

"This whole thing with Rudy has gone on long enough," he said. "It's this way, sir. We forced him into it."

Logan fixed his gaze on Andy. "What?"

"Chad and I told him to cover up what we did."

Logan leaned forward and asked, "What did you do?"

"We pushed the car off the road."

"Really? Rudy never told Jonas MacPharlan you were involved. You just incriminated yourself. Start talking."

Andy felt moisture on the back of his shirt. It was cold and clammy. He rubbed his forehead. It felt hot. He gazed at the edge of the desk so he did not have to look at him.

He always tried to maintain control of his actions. If he got into a sticky situation, he usually knew what to say and how to act. By the time he finished talking, however, he contradicted himself so many times that he had no idea what he was saying.

He repeated what he told Logan a few days ago. The girls went back to campus about nine thirty, then Chad and Phillip went for their talk. He and Rudy waited for a few minutes and went to look for them. It was too dark to see anything, and they got separated. He went back to the car and waited for Rudy, who was five or ten minutes behind him. It was about ten o'clock at that point. Chad met them about fifteen minutes later.

"So what you're saying is that Chad was in the woods for about forty-five minutes," Logan said. "Let's assume the fight took five minutes, but it probably seemed like fifteen. You and Rudy went to look for them and got separated. Maybe you found Phillip lying unconscious and hit him on the head with the rock."

"Are you saying I killed him?"

"I'm only trying to examine all possibilities."

"I loved Phillip like a brother. Why would I want to kill him?"

"Why don't you tell me? I found out that Phillip told authorities about the drug operation. What did he know about you?"

"Nothing."

"You had a spotless academic record. Maybe he knew something bad about you that you might not have wanted others to know."

"I don't know what you're talking about!"

"Come on, there has to be more to it than that."

"I didn't do anything!"

"What happened when Chad came back to meet you?"

"He told us Phillip was dead."

"What did you do?"

"I went to check on him."

"Were you alone?"

Andy rolled his eyes and huffed. "Yes."

"How long were you gone?"

"About ten minutes."

"So you had the means and opportunity to hit Phillip on the head."

Andy lurched forward and shouted, "I didn't do it! He was already dead when I got there. I swear it!"

"Are you sure he was dead? Did you check his pulse? You were all panicking. Maybe you thought he was dead when he was just unconscious."

"He was dead, I swear it!"

"Are you sure? Maybe you did it wrong."

"I've had lifesaving classes! He was dead!"

"Why didn't you use CPR?"

"I tried, but he was gone."

"Were you jealous of Phillip's athletic abilities?"

"I was envious, but that's no reason to kill him. I mean—I didn't do it."

Logan sneered and said, "Well, it's just a thought. I'll find out if you're hiding something. I talked to Rudy at the hospital. He told me Chad threatened to tell Jonas MacPharlan that he stole final exam questions last year, if he told anyone about pushing the car off the road. What did he have on you?"

"Nothing. I didn't do anything, I swear!"

"Come off it, Andy. You and I both know Chad threatened to reveal your secret. What did you do that was so bad you would help fake a car accident to prevent him from revealing your secret? Come on, you can talk to me."

"I didn't do anything!"

Logan's coworkers looked over to see what was happening, then went back to work.

"All right, don't tell me. But I'll find out. You can bet on it. And by the way, you're under arrest."

## Chapter 13

Ian Reynolds was in the middle of eating dinner when he got the call. He arrived at the police station about seven thirty. Andy had just turned eighteen, and a parent didn't have to be present. It was a good thing Ian was not allowed to see him, because he felt like reaching in the cell, and shoving his fist down Andy's throat.

"Thank God you're here," Andy said when they were in the courtroom. "I'm so sorry I had to call you like this. I couldn't call my folks. They would've been pissed. You're the only one I could think of."

"Let's just get you out of here. We'll discuss it later."

"Please don't say anything to Mr. MacPharlan, he'll kick me out!"

"That's asking an awful lot, kid," Ian growled. "If I do that, I could get my ass canned too."

"Please don't say anything. I'll perform twice as hard. I'll triple that. Please just don't say anything."

"Okay, I won't say anything. But we'll have to work out a deal. I'll think about what that will be later."

"Thank you."

Coach Reynolds got up to get coffee while a public defender talked to Andy about legal matters. Time dragged as they waited for his case number to be called. His legs felt like rubber as he approached the bench. He stammered "guilty" to the charge of criminal mischief and conspiracy and the judge set the trial date and bail amount.

Then he waited in holding like Chad had done before him. He was released into the coach's custody two hours later.

## LOVE'S A CRIME

They didn't say a word, the whole way back to campus. When Ian pulled onto Broad Meadow Road, he said, "I'm ashamed of you, Andy. What's wrong with you anyway? Moving a corpse? Faking a car accident?"

"We panicked and—and it seemed like a good idea at the time. I'm sorry."

Ian glared at him. "Tell that to Phillip's parents."

A couple minute's later, he pulled into the Stewart Hall parking lot and slowed down to let Andy out.

"You don't know how lucky you are that the court is in session on Wednesday nights," Ian said. "I won't say anything to Jonas. But I'm not letting you completely off the hook though."

"What do you . . . what do you mean?"

"First thing tomorrow morning, you're going to go to his office and tell him everything."

"He'll kick me out."

"I'll have a little talk with him. You've had a clean record up until now. Everybody makes mistakes. And besides, at least you didn't kill Phillip, right?"

Andy gulped and said, "He was already dead when we got to him."

"If Chad can finish up at home, maybe MacPharlan can work out some kind of similar arrangement for you, if the situation comes up."

"I knew you'd see it my way."

"I'll see you at practice. Try to get a good night's sleep. The state championship is riding on it."

"Thanks. And I'll pay you back for the bail money too. Good night." Andy pulled the door handle and got out.

The next morning, Andy delivered on his promise. He went to Jonas MacPharlan's office and told him everything he said to Logan. It was the hardest thing he ever had to do, but confessing really did ease his guilt. During his free period, he went back to his room and lay on his bed. He thought about how hellish the past twenty-four hours had been. He worried what his parents would think when they found out that he had been arrested.

They wouldn't understand. Then his thoughts flashed on Rudy. He couldn't believe what Rudy had done for him.

"Rudy, you caught yourself," he muttered to himself. "You protected me, and you tried to kill yourself because of me. Why did you do it?"

Finally, he couldn't take it anymore. He got on his hands and knees and pulled out the paperback book he hid under the bed. He removed the joint he had stashed in it and stuffed it in his pant's pocket. Then he went outside and walked hurriedly toward the pond.

When Tony Mancini found out that Andy and Rudy confessed, he wanted to meet with Logan. Once again, they sat face-to-face in the interrogation room. Logan was in no mood for an argument.

"Your buddies just sold you down the river without a paddle," Logan said.

Chad shook his head and groaned. "I can't believe it. I covered for them, and this is the thanks I get?"

"Why don't you start over again? Tell me what really happened that night in the woods."

Chad looked at his father and said, "I'm sorry."

William shook his head and looked at his son in disbelief as he relayed the whole ugly chain of events as they happened. When he was finished, William and Tony exchanged uneasy looks.

"So you left your friend in the woods to die and stuffed him in his car to make it look like he was killed in a car accident," Logan said.

"I didn't mean to. I just panicked. And then . . . and then I got them to help me fake the accident. I swear I don't know anything about the rock that was hidden under the bush."

At that point, Mancini asked to speak to Chad alone. Logan got up and went out of the room.

"What's going to happen to me?" Chad asked Mancini.

"It doesn't look good, Chad."

William took a deep breath and looked sadly at his son.

"But it isn't all bad," Mancini continued. "Up until now, you have maintained a clean record. The evidence suggests that Phillip died in the woods. And no fingerprints were found on the bloody rock, so you can't be linked to that part of the crime."

"That's a relief," William said.

"Not necessarily," Mancini said. "If you did use that rock to hit Phillip on the head, the police could find additional evidence to link you to the crime."

"But I didn't do it."

"I believe you," Mancini said. "But you still have to pay for faking the accident."

Then he went over new legal strategies and discussed Chad's options.

William looked at him and asked, "What do you think his chances are?"

"Now that Chad has changed his story, the ball is in a different court. Jurors might take pity on him. Maybe they'll realize the horror he must have felt and go lenient on him. If the case is tried without jurors, a judge might not be as sympathetic."

"So you think a jury trial would be better?" William asked.

"It could be. Either way, you'll have jail time to worry about."

Chad drew a deep breath and said, "How long . . . how long do you think I'd have to be in prison?"

Mancini frowned and said, "I don't know."

They sat in silence for quite a while. Chad decided to take his chances and change his original statement and confess to faking the car accident. When Logan returned, he sat across from them and asked, "So have you made a decision?"

Mancini did all the talking. Chad signed a written confession and underwent the same grueling legal headache in front of another judge. He could still stay in his parents' custody as long as he agreed to make court appointments. When the McAlpins left the police station, Tony started working on Chad's defense.

Andy was shivering. Michelle turned her attention from something Mr. Fletcher was saying to look at him. It was warm in the classroom, but Andy was cold.

"Are you okay?" she whispered.

"I'm fine," he said.

He was half listening. Mr. Fletcher was saying something about a Grecian Urn. The poet apparently coughed out his lungs from TB when he was in his early twenties. It wasn't a pleasant way to go. Andy's interest piqued when he heard him mention something about *Frankenstein*. It was only a momentary interest because Mr. Fletcher launched into a discussion of the romance poets.

Andy couldn't stop thinking about his current legal ordeal. He didn't know why things had gotten so out of hand. When the bell rang, he barely managed to get through his other classes. He changed into his basketball uniform and went to the gym. It seemed like it took forever to get there. His legs felt rubbery. His walking was labored. By the time he reached the gym, he was really tired. He dribbled the ball down the court before practice started. His heart was racing, and he felt clammy.

The coach blew his whistle and had them run up and down the court to warm up. Andy couldn't keep up and lagged behind them. They gave him funny looks as they turned to go by him. He started to turn but only made it a few feet. He clutched his chest and collapsed on the floor.

Coach Reynolds blew his whistle and rushed over to him. The boys stopped in their tracks and shouted, "Andy!"

## Chapter 14

Andy was starting to come around. He opened his eyes and took a moment to focus. He stared at the monitors he was hooked up to, then at the IV that was attached to his arm. He looked at the clock on the wall. It was about five o'clock. He didn't know how he got there.

A nurse smiled at him and said, "I see you're in the land of the living now. I'll get the doctor."

Dr. Thomas Cooper entered the room and asked, "How are you feeling, Mr. Winchester?"

"Like I was run over by a truck."

"You're really lucky your coach could drive you here. You have an irregular heartbeat. And your blood pressure was through the roof. We're monitoring it with IV hydralazine."

Andy pointed to the IV on his arm and said, "What's this all about?"

"That's to hydrate you. It will give you fluids."

He squirmed and said, "It's uncomfortable!"

"I know, but it will make you feel better in no time. Now I just need to ask you some questions. Are you under any stress?"

"Yeah, I guess so. I'm trying to finish up at Broad Meadow and get into the state championships."

"Well, let's not worry about basketball right now. Does your family have a history of heart disease, Mr. Winchester?"

"I think so."

"Are you on any prescription drugs?"

"No."

"Did you take any drugs before basketball practice?"

Andy eyed him suspiciously and said, "No. What does that have to do with anything?"

"I'm just trying to rule out possible causes. We can't mess around here. You came really close to having a heart attack."

His eyebrows shot up. "Really? Oh my god!"

"If you don't level with me, you could go into cardiac arrest. Do you have a heart condition?"

"No."

"Then why would somebody that is in as good shape as you are almost drop over from heart failure? We'll need to do a stress test to see if there's something wrong with your ticker. Have you ever had an EKG?"

"No."

"We'll make it as quick and painless as we can. For starters, we'll need to take a blood sample."

"You will?"

"Are you afraid of needles?" the nurse asked.

"I just don't like getting poked with them!"

"It's for your own good," Dr. Cooper said. "We need to do a complete blood work up to see what could be causing the problem."

Andy cringed when the nurse shoved the needle in his arm.

"There you go," she said. "That didn't hurt now, did it?"

Andy kept his mouth shut. She collected the blood sample and went out of the room.

The doctor handed him a cup and said, "You'll also need to pee into this."

"Why do you need to do that?"

"You're in good shape. We just need to find out why you collapsed."

Andy handed it back to him and said, "I don't think that will be necessary."

"What aren't you telling me? Come on, it's your life we're talking about here."

"It's purely confidential, right?"

"Anything you tell me stays between the two of us," the doctor assured him.

"I smoked pot before basketball practice . . ."

* * *

Ian Reynolds was asleep in the waiting room with a magazine on his lap. A nurse tapped his shoulder to wake him up. "You can see the patient now."

He followed her into the room and saw Andy lying on an examination table. He was hooked up to a monitor. He had lost the color in his cheeks. His face looked ashen. He looked at the coach and smiled.

"Are you all right now, Andy?" he asked.

"I could be better. I'm sorry for all the trouble I'm causing."

"Don't worry about it." He pulled a chair next to him and said, "Do they know why you fell down?"

"The doctor thinks it's from stress," he lied. "I guess everything that's been happening lately is a lot worse than I thought."

The nurse came back to check on him.

"When can I leave?" Andy asked.

"We're waiting for your blood pressure to go down," she said.

"How long will that take?"

"It will take a while. Why don't you try to take a nap?"

"I don't see how anybody could sleep with all these things attached to you," Andy groused.

She winked at Ian and smiled. "It's a way of preventing the patient from escaping, I guess."

"See how you'd like lying here with all these wires hooked up to you."

"I wouldn't like it much, but it's important. The doctor will be in to check on you in a few minutes."

"Thanks, ma'am," Ian said.

"This really sucks, Coach."

"I know. Take it easy."

"It's easy for you to say."

"You're feisty, so you must be feeling better. Just lie back and try to sleep."

Ian waited until he fell asleep and got up to get coffee. When he came back, the doctor was checking Andy's blood pressure again. Ian pulled up a seat by Andy and observed.

"I thought you'd faint when I mentioned having to get a blood sample from you," Dr. Cooper said.

"What do you expect? I hate needles."

Ian burst out laughing. "Now I've heard everything. As big and strong as you are, Andy, to recoil in fear over the mere mention of getting a shot is the funniest thing I've ever heard."

"I'd like to see you try it."

"I'm not the one with the problem."

"I should hope not," Dr. Cooper interjected. "It looks like your blood pressure has stabilized, Andy."

"Does that mean I can go back to Broad Meadow now?"

"I think it would be best to keep you here a little while longer to check on it. We still have a few more tests to run. We need to do a Syrum Toxicology screening. And we have to check your kidney functions and potassium levels. And we have to do a comprehensive cortisol level profile to check your liver."

"You have to do all that? I'll be here all night."

"I know, but it's really important that we do these tests," Dr. Cooper said. "Just lie back and watch some TV. I'll be back in a few minutes to see how you're doing."

"I can't believe this," Andy said when they were alone. "Why does it have to take so long?"

"They just need to make sure everything is okay."

"I've taken up so much of your time the past couple of days. You must hate me right now."

Ian shook his head and grunted. "I don't hate you, Andy. I'm disappointed in some of the decisions you made that night in the woods. You know you can talk to me about anything, right?"

"Yeah."

"What's up? Why did you fall down like that?"

"I'll tell you later."

"We aren't going anywhere."

"I can't talk about it now."

"All right. You know where I am. Just remember. You'll owe me one."

Andy nodded and grinned. They watched the middle of a basketball game on the TV overhead. About two hours later, Dr. Cooper told Ian he could take Andy back to Broad Meadow.

**LOVE'S A CRIME**

Ian pulled into a parking spot and helped Andy out of the car. When they went inside, boys stared at them as they walked by. The coach helped him into his room and left a Do Not Disturb note on his door.

The next day, people didn't know quite what to say. After a while, they asked him if he was okay. After what happened to Phillip, Chad, and Rudy, the girls hovered around him like a hawk. "Are you sure you're all right?" Michelle asked.

"I'm fine," he said. "It's just stress. I'll be okay. But thanks for caring." He held out his arms and pulled her into a tight hug.

"We're just worried, is all," she said. "So many horrible things have happened the past few weeks. I just don't want anything to happen to you."

"I know you don't."

Susan hugged him and said, "If there's anything you need."

"Thanks for being there for me, you guys," he said.

With all that was happening lately, Jonas MacPharlan did not need to hear a lecture from Chad's father. He listened to him rant, trying to get a word in.

"I'm sorry, Bill. Students are distracted as it is, I can't let him come back."

"I donate a lot of money to Broad Meadow, Jonas."

"And we really appreciate it."

"I don't have to do it. If you don't let Chad finish up there, I'll talk to my attorney. Maybe board members should start looking for a new headmaster."

"No, you don't have to do that. He can come back. I don't think he would jeopardize his academic career by fleeing."

"Good, I thought you would see it my way."

Jonas hung up and told his receptionist to take messages. He couldn't handle another phone call at the moment. This mess with Andy was the last straw. He hoped nothing else would happen. If it did, he was worried that he would lose his job.

## Chapter 15

Chad drove through the school's archway and waved at girls who were walking toward the Victorian house across the road from the student center. They pretended not to see him and went inside. When he got to his dorm, he received the same cold treatment from guys who he thought were friends. They yelled, "Go home, killer!"

"Leave me alone, I'm not a killer!"

He went to his room and turned on his stereo. Andy knocked on the door, and he refused to let him in.

"Come on, Chad, let me in!"

"Leave me alone, you little traitor!"

Andy forced his way in and said, "I can't believe MacPharlan let you come back here again."

"I guess he likes jailbirds."

"I wouldn't have wound up in jail if it hadn't been for you. Just don't tell anybody."

"I didn't force you to confess. You brought it on yourself."

"I would've kept quiet, but this whole thing with Rudy got to me. I had to talk to Logan. He confessed and tried to kill himself."

"I know." He was quiet for a moment. "Can we see him?"

"Yes, but I'm sure he won't want to see you, since you're the one that caused him to do it."

"You had a part in it."

"He kept me out of it. He told Logan I was here the whole time. He said he helped you push the car off the road."

"I warned him."

## LOVE'S A CRIME

"Give it up. You were already in deep trouble. You forced him to act. He had no choice."

"That's bullshit and you know it. I told you guys that you didn't have to help me."

"You didn't give us much choice once we got into it. We thought friends helped each other. You used us. You knew we would help you and then you turned on us. Now, Rudy is lying in a hospital bed. When he gets better, Logan will probably arrest him too. This is all your fault. We wouldn't have had to fake the car accident if you hadn't killed him!"

Chad waved his hands and shouted, "You know that isn't true! Somebody else did it."

"You actually believe your own lies."

Chad brushed up against him and shouted, "Shut up!"

"Did you ever think that maybe you deserved this?"

"That's it!"

Chad hit him on the chest, and Andy pushed him onto the floor. Chad grabbed his legs and forced him down with him. They rolled around hitting each other. The door flew open and dorm supervisor, Mike Anderson, stood over them.

"Break it up, you two!" he shouted. "You don't need this right now, Andy."

"But he started it!"

"I don't give a rat's ass who started it. Come with me."

He grabbed them by their collars and led them to Jonas MacPharlan's office. He told him what happened, and the headmaster asked to speak to them alone.

Jonas glared at Chad and said, "Just because your father persuaded me to give you another chance, don't press your luck, Mr. McAlpin. I will be watching your every move. If you make another mistake, you are out of here permanently. Am I making myself clear?"

"Crystal."

"I also don't want you two to be in the same dorm together. So Chad, you are moving to Hullien Hall."

"But Mr. MacPharlan," he whined.

"I want you out of there by the end of the day. Now get moving."

"Damn," Chad said under his breath.

He got up and walked hurriedly out of the room.

Jonas looked at Andy and said, "I understand you fell down at basketball practice the other day. How are you feeling now?"

"A lot better," he said. "I guess it was just from stress."

"Well, try to take it easy. I don't want anything bad to happen to you."

"Thank you, sir." He started to get up to leave when MacPharlan said, "I am not finished with you, Mr. Winchester."

Andy sat back down and stared blankly at him.

"I'm sorry about your medical emergency, but that doesn't give you an excuse to act the way you do. I'm tired of straightening out scuffles between you boys."

"It won't happen again, sir."

"You're right, it won't happen again. I won't allow it. From now on, I'll be watching you as well. Do you understand?"

He gulped and said, "Yes, sir."

Jonas lifted his index finger and said, "Now get out of here!"

"Whatever you say, Mr. MacPharlan."

He closed the door, and Jonas heard his footsteps creak along the corridor.

Chad had to wear an electronic tracking device whenever he left campus.

On Sunday afternoon, he went to visit Rudy at the hospital. Rudy's eyes lit up when he saw him enter the room. He pulled up a chair and sat by Rudy's bedside.

"Michelle told me you were here. I'm sorry it's taken so long for me to get in to see you. How are you feeling?"

"I'm okay. How about you?"

"I could be better. This whole thing with Phillip is nerve-wracking."

"I know."

"I'm sorry I got you into this mess."

"It wasn't your fault. I'm the one that tried to . . . do it."

"If it hadn't been for me, you wouldn't have done it."

"Let's not talk about it. MacPharlan let you come back?"

"Yeah, my dad talked to him."

"What's happening at school now?"

"Andy fell down at basketball practice the other day."

"Really? Is he okay?"

"It was just nerves, I guess. I'm not really sure. It happened before I came back. It was really weird though. Everybody was asking him if he was okay. I feel bad because I didn't know anything about it. We got into this nasty fight when I got back, and MacPharlan told me to move into Hullien Hall."

"That's too bad."

"The coach has been treating him with kid gloves. He hasn't been at practice."

"Andy must really be sickly if the coach would do that with the state championship riding on it."

"I know."

"Did he let you back on the team?"

"Yeah. At least that's one good thing that's happening for me now."

"What did the guys say when you went to practice?"

"There was a lot of friction, if you know what I mean. But the coach screamed bloody murder at them."

"Is Andy up to playing?"

"He is now. He has to be. We have one more game. And then the semifinals." He crossed his fingers and said, "And then, hopefully onto the state championships."

"I'm rooting for you guys."

"Thanks."

They chatted about nothing in particular, then Chad asked, "What did you tell Logan?"

"That we pushed the car off the road."

"And you left Andy out of it?"

"Yeah."

"He thought you implicated him and told Logan he helped us."

"Really? Why did he do it? I was trying to keep him out of it."

"He felt bad that you wound up here. Logan arrested him on the spot."

"Oh my God! Andy did that because of me!"

"Yeah."

"I guess he must've gotten out on bail. MacPharlan let him come back too?"

"I don't think anybody knows about it yet."

"How did you find out?"

"My lawyer told me. I had to change my original statement, and now I'm in an even bigger mess. It was perfectly simple. I told them that we all went back to campus and Phillip drove his own car back to Snake Turn Road. You had to chicken out and spill the beans to MacPharlan."

"I panicked, I'm sorry. I didn't know what you were telling him at the police station. I thought . . . I thought you were gonna tell him about Mrs. Bradshaw. What did you expect me to do? You were holding it over my head."

"I kept my end of the bargain. I didn't say anything about it. And then you cracked and implicated me. What did I ever do to deserve it?"

"I thought you were going to tell. I couldn't take that chance. If MacPharlan found out what I did, he would have kicked me out. Does he know?"

Chad shook his head and said, "I don't think so."

"If Logan arrested Andy, he'll probably come after me next."

"I'm sure he will."

"He's probably just waiting for me to get out of the hospital."

"Calm down, Rudy. I didn't come here to get you upset."

"Well, then you shouldn't have started in on me about talking to MacPharlan."

"Can we just drop it? Let's talk about something else."

"I don't know what else there is to talk about beside this legal mess you've gotten us into."

"I don't need this right now. I'm sorry you're here, and I hope you get better soon." Chad got up and stomped out the door.

Logan saw Chad leave Rudy's hospital room and went over to him. "Hello, Chad. A little birdy told me you were here. Are you finding out what Rudy blabbed?"

"I told you what happened, Detective Logan, so why don't you leave me alone?" He quickened his pace, and Logan rushed to catch up.

"I'm trying to help you, Chad. You might have pushed the car off the road, but I don't think you actually killed him."

Chad stopped and stared at him. "At least somebody believes me."

"Tell me what really happened. Somebody had it in for both of you. Don't you want to know who it was? You've got your whole life ahead of you. If you don't cooperate, you'll go to prison as an adult when you turn 18. Come on, talk to me."

They went to the closest lounge and sat down. Chad leaned over and stared at the carpet design.

"Can you remember anything else that happened that night? Come on, think hard."

"I don't remember."

"It's been a while, and you've had time to forget. Something must have slipped your mind. Just think carefully. It's important that you remember everything."

He relayed the unfortunate set of circumstances that happened in the woods that night. This time, however, his time line was skewed slightly. It took Andy a lot longer to come back to report that Phillip was dead than it did in his previous account. He did not feel the least bit guilty about implicating Andy. He felt Andy had it coming.

"So you're saying that there was a chunk of time that Andy was alone in the woods?"

Chad looked him square in the eye and nodded. "It looks that way."

"When you guys went back to the site where Phillip fell, did you see blood on his forehead?"

"Yeah, it wasn't like that when I left him there."

"Okay, so Phillip fell and you ran back to the car. You weren't gone long before Andy went to check on him."

"What does that prove?"

"That Phillip was lying there for a few minutes with nobody around. When you went to tell Andy and Rudy what happened, it wouldn't have taken long for somebody to hit him on the head."

"Will that prove that I didn't do it?"

"I don't know. It's circumstantial evidence right now. Unless we find something we overlooked, we have no proof. Can you remember anything else?"

"I'm telling you exactly what happened."

"I get the feeling you aren't telling me something."

"I told you everything that happened, I swear. They were just as responsible for pushing the car off the road as I was, and they didn't stop me from doing it."

Logan rolled his eyes and said, "You didn't give them much choice. Rudy told me he stole last year's final exam questions. And he said you threatened to tell Jonas MacPharlan. Then he tried to take his life."

"I never intended for that to happen, I swear! You have to believe me."

"What is Andy's secret?"

"I don't know what you're talking about."

"You know damn well what I'm talking about. You had something on Andy. It was something so bad that he agreed to help you fake the car accident. I bet you threatened to tell Jonas MacPharlan everything if he confessed. It's the same thing you did to Rudy."

"You're wrong! They're my best friends. I would never—"

"If you had just talked to me in the first place, things would've gone a lot better for you."

"I was scared. Everybody knew we had been fighting and would think I did it."

"What do you have on Andy?" Logan persisted.

"I told you I don't know what you're talking about."

"Maybe you might change your mind with a longer stay in jail. You'll be in worse shape if you aren't honest with me." He handed him his business card and said, "Call me if you remember anything else."

Logan popped his head in Rudy's door and waved.

"Hi Rudy, mind if I come in?"

He smiled and said, "Go ahead."

"You look a lot better than the last time I saw you."

"Thanks."

"How are you doing?"

"I'm okay, how about you?"

"Oh, I can't complain."

"Everybody's been in to see me today. You just missed Chad."

"I saw him. We had a little chat just now. That's sort of why I stopped by. I need you to clear up something he said."

"Okay."

"When you first saw Phillip lying in the woods, was his forehead bloody?"

"Yeah."

"According to Chad, there was no blood on his forehead when he left to meet you guys."

"Somebody must have hit Phillip on the head after he left then."

"How long did it take you guys to look for Chad and Phillip?"

"I'm not sure. About ten minutes."

"That's funny, he just told me it took you guys a lot longer than that."

"Really? Why would he say that?"

"Maybe to make it look like you guys did it."

Rudy shook his head and waved his hands. "I don't believe he would do a thing like that. He's just out to protect himself. And he doesn't care if he incriminates us."

Logan flipped through his notes and said, "When you guys went looking for them, you got separated, right?"

"I wasn't that far behind Andy. I wouldn't have had time to do in Phillip and get back to the car. I can't believe he would even suggest that I did it. Phillip was like a brother to me."

"I don't think you would have had time to do it either. I didn't mean to upset you, Rudy."

"I thought we were friends! Chad is only out to help himself!"

"I'm sorry." He asked him about the basketball team to change the subject.

"Andy collapsed during basketball practice a few days ago."

Logan's eyes widened. "Really? Is he all right?"

"It was probably just from stress. The tournament is coming up soon. I wish I could be a part of it."

"You have more important things to worry about right now. Just do what the doctors say and you'll be out of here in no time, okay."

"Okay."

A few minutes later, Logan glanced at the wall clock and said, "I have to get going. Behave yourself."

Rudy grinned. "I'll try not to. Thanks for stopping by."

Logan turned and waved at him on his way out the door.

\* \* \*

Early Monday morning, Logan caught Andy before he went to his first period class. They sat on a bench in front of Hullien Hall, and Logan asked him if he was all right after his fall at basketball practice.

"I'm fine," he insisted. "Who told you?"

"Rudy."

"How's he doing?"

"A lot better, I think."

"Good. I've been meaning to go see him. But so much has been happening lately, I haven't had time to do it. But that's not what you wanted to talk to me about. What do you want? Class is about to start."

"This won't take long." He asked him once again about the events that unfolded in the woods that night.

"I already told you what happened!" he protested.

"I know, but I need to clear up some things," Logan said. "There were two times when you were alone and could have conked Phillip on the head with the rock. Chad just told me you were alone in the woods for quite a while."

Andy balked at the suggestion that he killed Phillip.

"When they didn't come back from their little chat, you went to look for them."

"Rudy went with me," Andy corrected.

"That's true. But you two got separated, remember?"

"He couldn't have gotten that far behind me. I wouldn't have had time to hit Phillip on the head and hide the rock We had flashlights. Rudy would've seen me do it. He got back to the car right after I did."

Logan looked sharply at him, considering it a moment. "Okay, perhaps you're right." He glanced at his notes and said, "When Chad told you Phillip fell down during the fight, you went to check on him. When you came back, you told the guys that he was dead, and they went back there so you could show them."

"I still wouldn't have had time to do it."

"That may be, but Chad said Phillip's forehead was bloody, and that it wasn't like that when he left to find you two."

## LOVE'S A CRIME

Andy shook his head and grunted. "It figures. When I saw him lying there, I held the flashlight beam on his face. There was blood all over the place. If he's trying to suggest I did it, he's a liar! I can't believe that scumbag. I thought we were friends!"

Logan closed the notepad and said, "I guess you don't really know people. I didn't mean to upset you."

He started toward the parking lot and heard Andy shout, "Damn him!"

---

Chad breathed heavily as he worked out after basketball practice. Andy entered the room and stood in front of him. They were the only people in the weight room at that hour.

"Logan stopped by to talk to me this morning," Andy reported.

Chad hoisted his arms up and down and said, "He asks too many questions."

"And you talk too much."

Chad stopped what he was doing and looked at him icily. "He just asked a lot of follow-up questions. Nothing to worry about."

"It's funny how your version of what happened doesn't jibe with what Rudy and I told him."

"What do you mean?"

"You know full well what I mean! You made it look like I was by myself in the woods a lot longer than I was!"

"I don't know what time things happened."

"The hell you don't! You were just trying to shift the blame off yourself and onto me."

Chad got up and wiped his face with his towel. "Phillip's head wasn't bashed in when I left him there. And you were in the woods alone for quite a while."

Andy got in Chad's face and shouted, "That's bullshit and you know it! There was blood all over the place when I went to check on him. You hit him and are trying to make it look like I did it!"

Chad pushed Andy back and said, "I didn't do it. You're living in fantasyland."

153

Andy was about to slug him when Ian Reynolds stomped into the room and shouted, "What's wrong with you guys! I'm sick and tired of all the fighting!"

"Andy started it," Chad cried.

"I don't care who started it!" His screams echoed across the room. "I've had enough of all the bickering! We'll never get anywhere with all the fighting!" He turned to face Andy and said, "You don't need all the stress right now."

"I'm fine, Coach."

"You're not fine. You collapsed during practice."

"But Coach, that was days ago. I'm fine now."

Ian ran his fingers through his buzz cut and said, "All right. Just keep away from each other for a few hours. Blow off steam. Then tomorrow afternoon I want you two to bury the hatchet. I don't want you guys to blow it for us."

"Sorry, Coach," they chimed.

Ian looked at Chad with disdain. "This is your fault, McAlpin. You shouldn't have come back. You're causing too much trouble."

"You need me!" he shot back.

"I don't need you that badly! If we don't get into the tournament, I'll hold you personally responsible."

Chad waved his hands and shouted, "All right, fine! I don't need to take this anymore!"

He glowered at Andy and marched out of the room.

Ian looked back at Andy and said, "Try to save your strength."

"I'm fine," he insisted.

"Just ignore him. Try not to think about the investigation and we'll get through this, okay?"

"All right, Coach." He watched Ian go out and started his workout.

He moved his arms up and down till he worked up a sweat. He thought about what Chad said earlier, his anger reaching the boiling point. He lifted the weights with such an intensity that sweat pored down his face like tears.

"Damn it!"

## Chapter 16

Ian Reynolds shielded Chad from the onslaught of protesters as they approached the gymnasium.

"Go away! Let us through."

A woman held up a placard that read, "Go Home Murderer!"

"I didn't do it!" Chad insisted.

"You have no right being here!" she yelled.

"Go to hell!" he shot back.

The crowd surrounded them. They had to elbow their way across the parking lot.

"They should have kicked you out!"

"They shouldn't have let you back on the team!"

"I hope you rot in jail!"

Andy jabbed one of them in the gut and pushed through the throng. The mob was unrelenting.

He looked at them like he was going to eat them alive, and they backed away. "Get the hell away!" he screeched.

They made it across the parking lot and had to contend with reporters and a TV news crew who were camped out at the front door. They shoved microphones in their faces and asked Chad the same questions: "Did you really kill Phillip Bishop?"

Chad waved his hands and shouted, "I didn't do it! Get the hell out of here or I'll smash your camera into smithereens!"

They clamored behind them as they entered the building.

"Did your father pull strings to let you play today?"

"I said get the hell away from us!"

They got in Andy's face and blocked him so he couldn't move. A woman stuck the microphone in his face and asked, "Do you feel up to playing after your panic attack?"

He pushed it toward her with a violent thrust. "It wasn't a panic attack. I'm fine now."

Security guards swarmed around them.

"Get them the hell away from us!" Ian commanded.

They led the press out the front door and said, "Let them get through!"

When they stepped foot on the basketball court, they had to contend with angry fans waving similar signs from the bleachers.

Chad shook his head and groaned. "I don't believe it."

Ian took him aside and said, "Just ignore it. Concentrate on the game. You've worked hard, and you don't need to blow it now. That goes for the rest of you guys."

It wasn't long before the players walked single file onto the basketball court when their names were called. They received the same harsh treatment from the Tilton Wildcats as they brushed past them. Chad snarled at them from the sideline.

It wasn't the way to start a game, especially when their nerves were shattered as they were with all the horrible things that had been happening lately. Tigers teammates could feel the unmistakable tension between Andy and Chad. These obstacles did not add up to a pleasant mixture.

Chad and Andy could have chilled the room with the icy looks they gave each other at the start of the game. Andy tossed Chad the ball with such force, it was a wonder it didn't bore a hole through his hands. He leapt into the air and slammed the ball into the hoop. Chad gave him a congratulatory thump against his chest, which nearly sent him flying backward.

Ian blew his whistle and called for a time-out. Then he pulled them aside and shouted, "What the hell's wrong with you guys? Just put aside your differences. We've worked too hard to blow it just because you're mad at each other!"

"Sorry, Coach," they replied in unison.

"Now get back out there and work together!"

## LOVE'S A CRIME

\* \* \*

A TV camera crew panned the players running up and down the court.

Patients gathered around the lounge and watched the game on a locally televised TV channel.

Rudy wished he could have been there to cheer on the team in person. He screamed with excitement when Andy slammed the ball into the net. He practically vibrated when Chad did the same thing a few minutes later. The Tigers and Wildcats were tied at the end of the second quarter.

He glanced over at the girls and said, "I'm sorry that I'm ignoring you."

"It's okay," Susan said. "If you were in the game, we wouldn't be able to talk to you anyway."

"The coach really laid into Andy and Chad."

"He's out of control," Michelle said. "He needs to calm down."

"I can understand that Chad and Andy would be in each other's faces," he said. "Especially when so much is riding on it."

"I avoid them at the end of every sport season," Michelle said.

"It can get crazy," Susan agreed.

Rudy reached for the bowl of pop corn on Susan's lap and chomped like mad. When the game came back on, he slapped his forehead when Andy didn't score. The ball bounced off the board and slammed onto the floor instead.

Rudy waved his hands in the air and shouted. In the process, he practically knocked over the bowl.

Susan gently tapped his shoulder and said, "Be careful."

"Sorry." His attention was back on the game.

Right now, the Tigers had slipped behind. Fans suffered a stressful afternoon as the Wildcats continued their winning streak.

Logan was watching the game at his grandfather's apartment in Jenkintown. At one time, Charles had the energy to play basketball with Frank. He had to take things slowly now.

"Andy Winchester is a powerhouse," the announcer said. "It wasn't long ago that he collapsed at basketball practice. Now he's a force to be reckoned with."

At that moment, Andy tore into an opponent that was much larger and taller than he was. A shouting match ensued, and spit flew out of their mouths. It wasn't long before their coaches had to break them up.

"Winchester is known for his hot temper," the commentator continued. "Now it's on display for everybody to see."

Logan shook his head and grunted. Ian Reynolds was shaking his fist at Andy. Andy waved his hands in the air and marched over to the bleachers. His substitute ran out to take his place.

Charles groaned from his seat in front of the TV. "That kind of behavior is unprofessional."

Frank nodded in agreement. "Tell me about it, Gramps."

"He's a hothead, but he runs like a rocket."

"I know."

When there was a commercial break, Charles pulled himself up with effort and pushed his walker over to the kitchen table. He got another beer and walked laboriously back to his seat.

Frank stood to help him sit, but he defiantly did it on his own.

"Are you all right?"

Charles grumbled and said, "I'm fine. Why wouldn't I be?"

"I just feel bad that I'm not around to help you as much as I should be."

"You're busy. I wouldn't expect you to change one thing in your life to help me."

"But you were always there for me when—"

"Don't be ridiculous. I've always been independent. I don't need anybody's help."

"I'm sorry."

"What are you sorry for?"

"I don't know."

"I take it back."

"What do you mean?"

"There is one thing you could do differently. You could take more time to relax."

"I would love to do that, but this case I'm working on is keeping me really busy."

## LOVE'S A CRIME

"You say the same thing every time I talk to you. What's so special about this one?"

When the game came back on, Andy and Chad were at it again. Once again, the coach yelled at them. Frank pointed to the screen and said, "They're mad because I pitted them against each other."

Charles's forehead creased. "You don't say?"

Frank went over the details as briefly as he could and said, "They're really mad at each other."

Charles took a handful of potato chips and said, "I would be too if my best friend did that to me. But I suppose it had to be done."

Chad scored again, and the fans went wild.

"So how is the case going?"

Frank grimaced and said, "Not well. I've got loads of evidence to prove that the boys faked the car accident but nothing to link any of them to the actual murder."

He fixed his gaze on his grandson and asked, "So what are you going to do about it?"

"I'm not sure."

"What do you think you're overlooking?"

"If I knew that, I could have cracked the case by now."

"It'll come to you."

"I hope so."

"Get away from it for a little while. You'd be surprised what the subconscious can do. Have you heard from Penny lately?"

Frank frowned but didn't look at him. "The last I heard she was seeing somebody."

"I think you should give her a call."

"I've thought about it, but I don't get around to it."

"That's just procrastination. You risked getting shot at on a daily basis when you were in Philadelphia, but you wimp out when it comes to making a simple phone call."

"I know what you mean. And I know exactly what you're trying to do."

"You work too hard. You need to relax. Maybe you'll be able to crack the case if you take some time off to unwind a bit."

"Maybe you're right."

Charles grinned and said, "I'm always right."

\* \* \*

On Sunday afternoon, Andy went to see Rudy at the psychiatric unit at the other end of the hospital. They sat in the lounge and watched a basketball game with some other patients. Some people were reading while others played cards or backgammon.

At halftime, Rudy led him to his room so they could talk privately.

"I'm sorry I haven't been in to see you lately," Andy said.

Rudy grinned and said, "Don't worry about it. You've been really busy."

They went into the room, and Rudy plopped on his bed. Andy looked around at the modest accommodations and pulled up a chair next to him.

"So what's happening at school?"

Andy told him about the latest couple that broke up. Then Rudy asked, "Are you okay now?"

"Everybody keeps asking me that. I'm fine. But thanks for asking."

"Chad came to see me last weekend."

Andy rolled his eyes and grunted. "I bet he did. Was he trying to find out what you told Logan?"

Rudy nodded and said, "Logan stopped by right after that and started pumping me full of questions about that night in the woods."

"I know, he came to talk to me the next day."

They compared notes for a moment. When it came to Chad, they both weren't happy.

"He's trying to make it look like we were in the woods a lot longer than we were," Andy said. "Can you believe Chad tried to make it look like I did it?"

"But you were gone for a few minutes when you went to check on Phillip, remember?"

"And his head looked like it had been bashed in. There was blood all over the place, right?"

"Right."

"I couldn't possibly have had time to do all that, right?"

"I don't see how."

Andy was quiet a moment. Rudy studied his expression and said, "What's wrong?"

"It just occurred to me. It's really my word against yours. I was by myself. You just saw the body when we all went to look at it. A lawyer could point that out. Who would jurors believe? Him or me? He insists that Phillip's head wasn't all bloody when he left him there. And we both are in agreement that his head was bloody when we found him there. They'll probably try to turn us against each other."

"Well, if they are, they're doing a fine job of it. That's what Logan did. Isn't that the reason you guys were fighting during the game?"

"It showed?"

"I thought you were gonna rip each other's heads off. It's a miracle you guys won."

Andy pushed a strand of hair out of his eyes and said, "I had a few time-outs though."

"Maybe it's a good thing you were pissed off. You took out all your anger and rage on the game and won."

"Not by much." He held his fingers close together and said, "Just by a smidgen."

"It was tense, that's for sure. I was practically chewing my nails! I wish I could have been a part of it."

"There's always baseball season. Your job is to get better, okay? I'm sorry that I got mad at you just before you—"

"It's okay."

"No, I feel bad about the things I said to you. And to think that you left me out of your confession. I feel like a rat."

"It's okay."

"I got so upset that I went to Logan and confessed."

"You didn't have to do that."

"I had to. And I left you out of it. He arrested me on the spot."

"I know. Chad told me."

"He probably would have arrested you, but you wound up here. So I would try to stay here as long as you can, if you know what I mean."

"It's been on the back of my mind the whole time I've been here. He'll probably be waiting to pounce on me when he finds out I'm being discharged."

"Any word when you'll be getting out?"

"I still have some issues to work on," he said flatly. "I wish I could be back at school with you guys."

"Oh, I wish you could be too, buddy. We miss you."

They spent the rest of the afternoon playing cards on Rudy's bed. When it was time for dinner, Rudy thanked him for coming and walked to the front door with him. They waved good-bye to each other, and Rudy watched him go out the large, thick door.

The next day, there was a one-page newspaper spread about the game. There was a large picture of Andy Winchester holding the ball in midair above the fold. To the right, there was a side bar article about him. The headline read: BOY WONDER FALLS AND RISES. It went on to talk about his mysterious collapse at basketball practice several days earlier and how he managed to get back in the game to help the Tigers get into the state championship. The reporter painted him as a hero.

Below his picture, there was a much smaller one of Chad shielding his face with his hands as he entered the gymnasium. The reporter wrote a slanted article about the murder investigation. Logan grumbled as he read a distorted paragraph about him. When he was finished reading, he tossed the paper to Harry Winters.

"Look on the bright side," Winters said. "At least the guy spelled your name right."

"Can you believe my name would be in a basketball write-up?"

"I'm amazed that they let McAlpin play. He caused a big ruckus."

"That's an understatement." He pointed to the side bar story and said, "It's interesting about Winchester's fall, isn't it?"

"I know."

"Kids in as good shape as Winchester shouldn't just drop over like that."

"So what do you think?"

"I have some theories. And stress isn't one of them. If you know what I mean."

Harry nodded and said, "It is really a mystery, isn't it?"

\* \* \*

Logan tossed and turned in bed. Fleeting thoughts about the case flashed through his head. He got up to read for a little while. Anything was better than not being able to sleep.

Maybe he was just trying to avoid it. When he got stumped, his subconscious always went back to that moment . . .

His eyes grew heavy, and he drifted into a fitful sleep.

He approaches the door, as if in slow motion. It is the same door he has seen so many times before. He is always in a hurry but never gets there in time.

He has his hand on the knob, ready to pull it open. His hands feel limp, and he can't turn it.

He hears the screams.

He pulls out his weapon, ready to fire. But it's a toy gun.

He tries to speak, but words fail him.

Then he hears the gunshot . . .

Logan awoke with a start. His heart was racing. He flicked on the light on his bedside table and reached for the mystery novel he was reading.

# Chapter 17

"After a roller-coaster ride of a season, the Broad Meadow Tigers have managed to get into the state championships," droned the announcer. "They face an uphill battle today as the Tilton Wildcats battle it out. They won't give up without a fight."

Fans crammed onto the bleachers like sardines, in eager anticipation. Soon after the game started, they sat practically at the edge of their seats in what was shaping up to be a nerve-wracking afternoon.

Ian Reynolds slapped his forehead and yelled at his team, as usual. They had to play well today. There was no room for errors. The stakes were too high. Andy and Chad had apparently worked out their differences and scored the most points.

They were now tied at twelve points each. Rudy chewed his fingers as he watched. He leaned forward and wove his legs in and out. He let out a high-pitched shriek when Andy missed a shot. The next few minutes were nerve-racking as the Wildcats jumped ahead. They now led the Tigers by eighteen points.

As the afternoon wore on, he could tell the game was taking its toll on his friends. He wished he could be there to give them a much-needed burst of energy.

Rudy sprang to his feet after he witnessed a couple more blunders on his teammate's part. He came back after a commercial and hoped they would get their act together.

Logan couldn't believe that Chad and Andy were allowed to play, but figured there was enough security there in case they tried to flee. He watched Tilton jump ahead a few more points. He shook his head and grunted as he watched Chad leap over the hoop. It was a slam dunk.

The camera panned on audience reactions. Broad Meadow students came dressed as Tigers. Their faces were painted with orange stripes. Children had even gotten into the act. The Tiger mascot pranced about on the sidelines. Logan practically choked on his beer when he saw Terry Dawson in the crowd. *What was he doing there?*

Ian watched nervously from the sidelines. With only four minutes on the clock, it would take a miracle to win. Andy zoomed across the court, slipping in between players that practically dwarfed him. There was no time for screwups.

He tossed the ball to Chad, who was at the right spot to make the perfect shot. He leapt into the air and smacked the ball through the hoop with a vengeance.

The fans' screams were deafening. The Tigers pulled ahead six points.

Ian blew his whistle and called for a time-out. Andy reached for a jug of water and gulped it down in nothing flat.

Ian tapped his shoulder and asked, "Are you okay?"

He drew a deep breath and said, "I'm fine."

He slapped water on his face and darted back onto the court. Two more minutes . . .

It wasn't long before two huge guys surrounded him. Chad came to the rescue, pushed them out of the way, and Andy tossed him the ball. He hurtled it into the hoop seconds before the final buzzer sounded. Broad Meadow beat Tilton 48-42.

He covered his eyes and hunched over. His teammates hoisted him over their shoulders and paraded him around the room while fans went wild. He opened his eyes and watched people rushing toward them.

Logan went to the local TV station and viewed footage of the game. Every time the camera cut to fans, he slowed it down. Then he saw what he was looking for. Terry Dawson had been there too.

"I don't believe it! There he is again."

The videographer shot him a puzzled look and asked, "Who?"

"Does the name Terry Dawson ring a bell?"

He thought about it a moment and said, "Oh yeah. He got kicked out for peddling drugs."

"And he did some jail time. Well, he likes to hang out at the games, and I'd like to know why." He thanked him and headed back to his car.

A week later, the Broad Meadow Tigers celebrated their victory at a black tie gala. It was at a banquet hall at a hotel about ten miles from campus. Rudy signed himself out for the evening so he could share in the festivities. He was standing in the lobby with his parents when his friends got off the bus.

Andy flew into his arms the moment he saw him. "It's good to see you!"

Rudy grinned and said, "I wouldn't have missed this for the world."

Chad slapped Rudy's shoulder and said, "You look great, man!"

"I only wish I could have been there with you guys."

"I'm glad you came," Andy said.

They followed Coach Reynolds into the banquet hall and sat at a long table in front. Ian was seated in between them. Friends and family were sitting at tables around the room. Michelle and Susan went over to congratulate their friends. They looked stunning in their evening gowns. Susan was wearing royal blue. Michelle's outfit was burgundy.

Chad looked at Susan and glowed. "Thanks for coming."

"I'm so happy for you," she said. "Congratulations."

"You deserve it," Michelle added.

"We'd better get our seats," Chad said. "I'll talk to you later."

Ian stood and said, "I want to thank you all for coming. We made it. I always knew we would. Isn't this the best basketball team ever?"

Guests clapped and whistled.

"We had so many obstacles this year, it's a wonder we made it this far. I just want to take a moment to remember Phillip Bishop. He was a powerhouse, whose life was cut short."

Everybody bowed their heads while he said a prayer. Then he went on to talk about how well the team worked together.

## LOVE'S A CRIME

Andy never felt comfortable wearing a suit. He constantly loosened his tie. It was choking him. He glanced over at Chad, who looked really good all dressed up. It looked like he was born wearing a tie—he was that comfortable.

Rudy yawned and looked at his parents. He didn't think the coach would ever stop talking.

Everyone laughed when Ian started joking about funny things that happened that season.

"And what can I say about Andy Winchester . . ."

Logan watched a clip of the party on the eleven o'clock news. The reporter was standing in the doorway with the banquet table behind him.

"It was a somber moment when Coach Ian Reynolds paid tribute to Phillip Bishop who was murdered earlier this year," the reporter announced.

Footage cut to Ian in the middle of talking. "You were a great guy, Phillip, and we're going to miss you."

The reporter was talking to him in person now. "How do you feel at this moment?"

"Extremely proud of the team," he said. "They did a phenomenal job this year. And I'm proud of everything they did to get us here."

"You have a reputation for being obsessed with winning. Is that true?"

"Well, if I wasn't, we wouldn't be here today. It just shows you what hard work and discipline can do. The guys might have hated me for being such a hard-ass at times, but we got into the state championship and won. Tilton gave us a run for our money."

Footage cut to Chad McAlpin. The reporter shoved the microphone in his face and said, "How do you feel right now?"

"Ecstatic. We worked our butts off and we made it."

"A few weeks ago, you were arrested in connection to the Phillip Bishop murder. Have you heard anything new about your case?"

"I can't say at the moment."

"Did you kill him?"

"I didn't do it."

"You were let out on bail and they let you play?"

"Why shouldn't I have been able to play? I deserved to be there."

"Did people treat you differently?"

"I got a lot of negative comments thrown my way, but I had to just let it all slide by and concentrate on the game."

The reporter was interviewing Andy now. He asked him about his collapse at practice, and he said the same thing he had said before. He was fine.

The reporter shoved the microphone in Rudy's face and asked about his suicide attempt.

"I was really upset about what happened to Phillip," he said. "It was the biggest mistake I've ever made, but I'm working through my personal problems."

Footage was back on the reporter. "The Broad Meadow Tigers have overcome a season of ups and downs. And now they have a trophy as their reward. This is Rory O'Connor reporting live at the Franklin Hotel . . ."

Logan grumbled and said, "You'd better enjoy all the attention now, McAlpin. You'll get yours eventually."

# Chapter 18

Logan stared at the telephone. Maybe his grandfather was right. He always lived with the fear of getting shot at but was just as scared of relationships. He dialed Penny's number from memory, and her voice message picked up.

"Hi, it's Frank. It's been a while. I just wanted to see how you're doing." He left his new phone number and hung up.

He didn't expect her to call back. He was surprised that she did.

"I'm so glad you called," he said. "I didn't like how things turned out the last time we saw each other."

"I didn't mean to get so upset. I'm sorry."

"I was just wondering if you wanted to meet for coffee."

"Aren't you busy cracking a case?" The tone of her voice was heavy with sarcasm.

"I need a little break."

"Okay." She told him the name and address of a quaint coffee shop, and he told her he'd meet her there about eight o'clock the next evening.

Frank saw the sign for Really Fine Brew on the awning and went inside. He saw her sitting in the corner, facing the door. Her face beamed when she saw him. She was now sporting a red due and looked fabulous. They hugged each other, and she kissed him on the cheek.

"It's good to see you," they said in unison.

"You look great," he said.

"So do you."

They ordered coffee and caught up. They only talked about pleasant memories. They avoided talking about why they broke up. It was a taboo subject.

"How's Gramps?"

"As feisty as ever. He's working with a physical therapist for his bum knee. He hobbles around a lot."

"Oh, that's too bad."

"He'll be okay. How's your family?"

"They're fine."

He sipped his coffee and said, "I thought you were going with somebody now."

"Are you keeping tabs on me? No—we broke up a couple months ago."

"What did he do wrong?"

"He wasn't you."

"Really? Are you saying what I think you're saying?"

"What do you mean?"

"Are you sorry we broke up?"

She leaned forward and grinned. "Well, let's just say that six months is a long time to be apart. Absence makes the heart grow fonder, you know."

"I thought about calling or e-mailing you but didn't get around to it."

"What stopped you?"

"I thought you were mad at me."

"I wasn't mad at you, Frank."

"What's your excuse?"

"I figured you wouldn't want to talk to me." She poured another cup and stirred cream in it. "And then I got really busy at work, and I started seeing Dan."

"What does he do?"

"He works at the same bank I do but at a different branch."

"Oh."

"He didn't think I was over you, and I finally realized he was right. So we broke up."

"You're starting to get a reputation in that department." He leaned forward and grinned. "So is it true? Do you still have the hots for me or what?"

"You think highly of yourself, don't you, Mr. Big Shot Police Detective. What if I told you I was madly in love with the firefighter that lives in my building?"

"Then I'd say you were moving from cops to firemen. Maybe you have a thing for hero types. I'm not sure what the psychological term for it is though."

She burst out laughing. When she calmed herself down, she asked, "Are you seeing anybody now?"

"No, I'm married to my career at the moment. I can't believe I just said that."

"So it's the same old same old?"

"I guess it looks that way. I've spent a lot of nights eating dinner at my desk."

"You can't keep doing that."

"That's what my grandfather said."

"Well, it's true. And I know why you're doing it. Are you still having the nightmare?"

"Once in a while."

"You keep busy so you don't have to think about what happened."

"Maybe."

"If you had spent more time with me and less time at work, we might have stuck it out."

"I know. I'm sorry."

"You'll never change. You're so obsessed with your work that you don't take time to be with the people that care about you."

"I really would love to be able to do that. But—"

"If I don't do it, a dirt bag will get away with murder," she mocked. "You'll never change, Frank."

"I'm sorry. It's what I have to do. Being a cop is in my blood."

She folded her arms and rolled her eyes. "How many times have I heard that before? No one will ever want to settle down with you if you keep doing what you're doing."

He held her hand and gently caressed it. "After this case, I'll go away with you to celebrate."

"When will that be?"

"Soon."

"So you're about to make a big bust or whatever?"

He shook his head and said, "No, it might be a little longer than that. I'm sort of at a dead end right now."

"Uh-huh. So what else is new? It sounds like the same excuse you kept giving me when we were dating."

He took everything she said into consideration. "You know, you're right. Maybe it would do me some good to get away for a few days to clear my head."

She regarded him skeptically a moment. "So you would actually tear yourself from the case longer than two minutes? That's incredible."

"I think you've handed out your share of sarcasm tonight, Penny. I'll prove to you that I can change."

"All right. Where do you want to go?"

"How about the Poconos?"

A week later, they spent the day skiing. Late that afternoon, they warmed up by the fire in the lounge. Then they had dinner at a cozy restaurant at the hotel.

"I haven't gone skiing in years," Penny said.

"It's been a while for me too," he admitted.

"I really didn't think you could drag yourself away from work. Congratulations."

"You were right. It really does feel good to get away for a little while to clear my head."

He was glad the Broad Meadow Tigers were celebrating their state championship victory at the Poconos. It gave him the perfect chance to go skiing while still keeping his eye on things at the same time. But Penny didn't have to know that.

They were in the middle of a deep conversation about their favorite movies when he seemed lost in thought. He saw Jonas MacPharlan holding another woman's hands. They were totally oblivious to other people in the room. His face twitched when he saw Logan. He literally looked like a deer caught in headlights.

Penny tapped his arm and said, "Earth to Frank. What's wrong?"

He pointed across the room, and she turned to look at them.

"You see that man over there? He's married, but that's not his wife."

## Chapter 19

Jonas MacPharlan pulled Logan aside and begged him not to tell his wife that he saw him with another woman at the restaurant. Logan decided to hold it against him for a little while. A little suffering was a good thing for detectives, not for a cheating spouse. It wouldn't take much to get him to spill the beans about who he was talking to on the phone. Logan put that on hold for now. He had more important things to look into.

His frustration grew as he tracked down leads that didn't pan out. He only had evidence that the boys faked the car accident and their confessions. He couldn't lift a print off the rock used to kill Phillip Bishop. There were also no tracks leading to and from the bush where it was hidden, which meant the murderer went back in daylight and swept away his or her footprints.

In early April, he went to the first night baseball game. It would give him a chance to relax and get away from the case for a little while. As he drove into the school, he thought about how beautiful the campus looked this time of year. The pond looked like a watercolor painting as splashes of purple and white reflected off trees. Sunlight dappled through the cherry blossoms up the tree-lined lane. It was a wonderful day to be outside.

When he pulled into the gymnasium driveway, the parking lot was full. He parked on the grass next to a gray SUV. He walked toward a set of wooden bleachers and found an empty seat on the top row.

It was the bottom of the fourth inning. Andy started shouting at the umpire. Tempers flared, and a referee reprimanded them. The fight was broken up and the game resumed.

Logan took note of everyone who was there. It looked like Andy had been spending a lot of time working out lately. His muscles were gigantic, and were bordering on grotesque for a boy of his height and weight. He was one damn fine athlete, that was for sure. And he ran faster than anyone on the field.

Terry Dawson was in the crowd. He seemed to be everywhere. Michelle and Susan were sitting a few feet away from him. Coach Reynolds was just as nasty when it came to baseball.

He was chewing someone out for making a careless blunder. He seemed more concerned with the girls than the run his team had just given up. The past few weeks had really put a toll on all the students, in one way or another.

Chad hit a home run. On the way back to the dugout, he smiled at Susan. She glared at him.

"You should have transferred when you had the chance," Michelle said. "He's getting to you."

"I can't do that. Chad needs me."

"You don't owe him anything. He treats you like garbage."

"I've always loved him. I never really expected—" She looked over at the field and cringed.

"He has an effect on you. It's not good living in the past. It didn't help Phillip."

"I didn't want to upset him. Maybe you're right." She got up and cautiously made her way down the bleacher steps. Michelle went after her.

Jonas MacPharlan watched them move across the bleachers. He was deeply concerned about Susan's emotional state but was not sure what he could do to help her. He knew Chad meant well. But he also knew that young men at that age often did not know how to treat young women. Maybe in a few years he would learn how to be more sensitive to a woman's feelings.

He thought about the telephone conversations. He was an intelligent man and wondered how he ever got into this predicament. Watching the game did not relieve his anxiety. Surely, there had to be a solution. But he could not think of any at the moment.

Andy was at bat again. It cracked and he sent a fly ball toward the bleachers. Logan leapt up to catch it and threw it to the catcher. The game

## LOVE'S A CRIME

was tied and went to an extra inning. Broad Meadow won 7-5. The winners paraded back to the gym with Coach Reynolds by their side.

Logan filed out with the crowd, still looking for Terry Dawson. He saw him go into the locker room and waited in the gym until the players had gone. He heard Terry's voice echo in the lonely locker room.

"Here it is. Do you have my money?"

"No man." It sounded like Andy.

"Then I guess you don't get any."

"I promised I'd come through. Don't I always?"

"You're always late and I'm tired of waiting."

The locker banged.

"Please, I know I promised I'd give it to you, but I'm having a cash flow problem. Just give me a chance."

"I always give you chances. You blew it this time."

"Please, Terry. I'm really stressed out and need it. Coach Reynolds is putting the heat on me. Just this once, then I won't bug you again. Please, I give you my word."

The locker banged again.

"Your word isn't worth crap!" Dawson shouted. "Give me the money by tomorrow night or I'll make your life a living hell."

Logan went in and peered around a row of lockers. There were no windows, and the room looked dark and dreary at night. He caught a glimpse of a prescription medicine bottle that Andy stuffed in his pocket. Dawson kicked a trash can in Andy's direction and stomped across the room. Logan ducked around the corner to avoid being spotted. Luckily, Terry did not see him.

When he was gone, Logan saw Andy sitting on a bench, rubbing his head with a towel. He flinched and looked up at the detective.

"What's in your pocket, Andy?"

"Nothing."

"Don't give me this crap! I heard everything. What's in your pocket?"

Andy reached in his pocket and pulled out the pill bottle. It was blank on the outside. Logan popped open the lid and looked inside.

He shook his head and looked scornfully at Andy. "Now I'm getting a better picture. Steroids. You don't need them. Why are you using them?"

Andy averted eye contact. "I had no choice. Coach Reynolds told me that he would cut me if I didn't run fast enough."

"So this is what Chad had on you, isn't it?"

"Yes."

"You had to help him because if people knew, you'd get kicked out, and your chances of getting the scholarship would fly out the window, right?"

"Yeah."

"It meant that much to you?"

"Yeah."

"Your parents make enough money to send you here. Why did you need a scholarship?"

He met Logan's gaze. "My dad's in financial trouble with his business. He had enough money saved for me to finish out the year. I'll graduate in a few weeks. He said I'll be on my own after that. You might think I'm a geek for wanting to go to college that badly, but it's my one chance to play at the college level. Coach Reynolds told me he thought I could make it to the pros."

"There are other ways, Andy."

"I didn't think about it that way. When we saw Phillip lying there dead, I guess we panicked. We weren't thinking clearly. I was thinking about being kicked out and did anything he wanted."

"Did Phillip know you were doing steroids?"

"Yes."

"Maybe he was a threat and you had to stop him from talking."

"No, he was my best friend! I would never—"

"Maybe he was just unconscious when you went to check on him. Maybe you hit him on the head with the rock."

Andy punched the locker and shouted, "That's not true! I didn't do it. You've got to believe me."

"How long did it take you to go look at Phillip's body before you went back to the car?"

"I don't know. Maybe about five or ten minutes."

"That gave you plenty of time to hit him on the head with the rock. Well, it's just a thought. I'll see you later."

Andy buried his face in his hands and rocked his body.

\* \* \*

Logan sat at his desk, leafing through a medical almanac. He found the section on steroids and skimmed it. The list of side effects included acne, oily skin, and hair loss. If combined with other drugs like marijuana, it could cause a rise in blood pressure or a heart attack.

He whistled and said, "It sounds just like what happened to Andy. Why didn't I figure it out before? He must've smoked pot before basketball practice. That's why he collapsed."

He continued reading and took notes. The telephone rang, jarring his concentration.

"Townsend Police Department. Detective Logan speaking. How may I help you?"

"I have more information about the Phillip Bishop case." It was that woman again.

He perked up and said, "Yeah?"

"I can't talk about it over the phone."

"Who is this?"

"A friend of Susan's."

"Michelle?"

"Yes."

"Are you okay?"

"Meet me at the football field under the bleachers in an hour."

She clicked off before he could ask another question. He grunted and said, "This case gets mysteriouser and mysteriouser."

## Chapter 20

Michelle waited for Logan under a street lamp in the gymnasium parking lot. It was too bright, so she moved closer to the baseball field so no one would see her. She almost lost her nerve. But it was something she had to tell him. She glanced at her wristwatch and said, "Please hurry, Detective Logan."

By the time Logan got to the campus, it was starting to get dark. He pulled into a parking spot, and wandered along the sidewalk that led to the gym. He heard a noise in the bushes and stopped. He slowly approached it and pointed his flashlight in the direction of the sound. He saw someone lurking behind the bush, but it was too dark to get a good look.

"Who's there? This is Detective Logan. Identify yourself."

He moved closer and got a better glimpse. The figure had broad shoulders like a man. He tore across the soccer field, Logan at his heels. He made it about halfway across when Logan tackled him. He beamed the light in his face and said, "Chad, what are you doing here?"

"I overheard Michelle arrange to meet you and hid in the bushes so she couldn't see me. I was worried about her, so I followed her."

"With all that's been going on lately, you could have really scared somebody."

"I'm sorry, I wasn't thinking. I have to run."

He watched Chad blend into the darkness as he darted across the grass. Logan went toward the football field and unlatched the gate.

\*   \*   \*

Michelle looked at the bleachers and saw someone coming toward her.

"I thought you'd never get here," she said. "It's urgent that I tell you this. It was horrible what—"

She screamed and fell on the ground.

Logan heard footsteps on the pavement. He waved his flashlight across the field and saw someone slip into the night. He raced toward the bleachers and found Michelle lying very still.

# Chapter 21

Faculty members sat jammed together around the headmaster's living room. A heated argument ensued and they were talking over each other. Jonas's face twitched as he looked at his colleagues and wondered who he could count on for support and who would betray him.

Board Member Gail Stockdale shook her head and said, "Last year's drug bust debacle was bad enough, but now we have to contend with Phillip's murder and what happened to poor Rudy. We can't afford another scandal."

"A lot of parents have been calling and e-mailing me," Dean Simons interjected. "They don't like what's going on here one bit. And I don't either."

"It's going to affect enrollment," Assistant Headmaster Price added. "It's too late to pull their kids out now, but parents are threatening to put them somewhere else in September."

"We can't afford to lose more young people," Gail said.

"Students have been under a lot of stress around here lately," Nurse Grier said. "I don't think the grief councilor was much help. I think it just made the kids feel more on edge."

Alumni Affairs Director Victor Conrad shot Jonas an accusatory look. "Fault rests solely on you, Jonas. You lack leadership skills."

"It isn't my fault."

"We don't want to hear your excuses," Victor replied angrily.

"Calm down," Coach Reynolds said. "Arguing won't solve anything."

"Ian's right," John Fletcher agreed. "We need to keep levelheaded about it."

## LOVE'S A CRIME

Victor shook his index finger at Jonas and said, "I hope this is the last time we have to sit in an emergency meeting. I warned you, Jonas."

MacPharlan looked at him with such intensity, it was as if his eyes bore through the man.

"Well, I guess you don't give me much choice," he said. "Do I get a chance to defend myself? Or is it guilty until proven innocent?"

"I say we vote on it," Victor suggested. "All in favor of firing Jonas, raise your hands."

That idea was met with much dispute. So it was decided that they would have an anonymous ballot.

Lillian MacPharlan sneered and said, "It figures you people would want to hide the dagger you're digging in my husband's stomach. You are a bunch of cowards!"

Jonas gave her a look of disdain. "Lillian, you're not helping matters."

"The very idea that you let that murderer back on campus," Mrs. Ashton snapped. "It's an outrage!"

"I understand how you feel, Eudora," Jonas said. "But Bill McAlpin insisted that we let him back in. He threatened to sue if we didn't do it."

She folded her arms and scowled. "Well, it clearly isn't working. Chad McAlpin is causing a disruption."

"I swear to God, Jonas, if there is one more incident, I'll have to shut down Broad Meadow," Victor warned.

"Your idol threats don't frighten me, Vic," Jonas said. "Besides, you don't have the authority to do that."

"Come on you guys!" Coach Reynolds cried. "We aren't getting anywhere here."

"Do you know how much money we've lost in the past two years?" Victor continued. "If tuition drops as a result of the current problems, we'll have to close the doors."

Jonas looked at him and rolled his eyes. "Give me a break, Vic! This school has withstood a lot of hard times and pulled through. In another year or two, people will forget all about the drug bust and Phillip Bishop's car accident."

"It wasn't a car accident," Victor said. "Chad McAlpin killed him and made it look like an accident."

"Oh come off it, Victor," Ian said. "It hasn't been proven that he—"

"He did so do it! Don't you dare defend him."

"I'm not," Ian said. "I'm just saying that there are a lot of other people here. Maybe Terry Dawson did it. He had a lot of motive."

Victor fell silent a moment and said, "Well, Chad looks suspicious."

"Why don't we decide when Detective Logan closes the case," John Fletcher suggested.

"That's a good idea," the librarian agreed.

"All right," Victor said. "I'm willing to wait until Detective Logan solves the case. This is a matter that we will have to address this summer."

"Oh good, I'll have time to pack," Jonas said.

"Your sarcasm isn't helping matters," Gail said.

Jonas was about to respond when they heard a siren screeching down the road.

"It sounds awfully close," Gail said.

They all got up and peered out the window.

"It's pulling into the gymnasium parking lot!" Gail shouted.

Lillian gasped and said, "Oh my god! Not again!"

Victor looked sharply at Jonas and said, "I meant what I said, Jonas."

Lillian was quick to defend her husband. "Not now, Vic. Can't you see we've got an emergency situation going on here?"

Jonas ventured outside to see what was happening.

Paramedics lifted Michelle's limp body into an ambulance and whisked her to the emergency room. She was placed in ICU with a concussion. Meanwhile, Logan and uniformed police officers searched the area where she had been standing. Ball field lights were turned on so they could get a better look at the grounds surrounding the bleachers.

Logan knelt down where she had fallen and shone light on a blood splotch. He slowly, but methodically, moved the flashlight toward the blacktop to see if the person responsible left behind a blunt object. He did not see anything in the shrubbery behind the bleachers. His colleagues could not find anything either, so they decided to call off the search until sunrise.

An officer unlatched the fence gate, and he followed them out. Jonas MacPharlan was there waiting for him. "What's going on? I saw the ambulance lights and wondered what happened."

"Michelle Martin was attacked," Logan told him. "Where were you about a half an hour ago?"

Jonas leaned on the fence and said, "You think I did it? Why would I want to hurt her?"

"It's just routine, sir. Where were you?"

"I was having a board meeting at my home."

Logan looked across the parking lot at the headmaster's house. It looked like a short walk to the bleachers from there. Several cars were in the driveway.

"Is everybody still there, sir?"

"They are still there, but we couldn't get much accomplished with all the distractions."

"I need to talk to them."

He followed MacPharlan across the parking lot, and they walked down the driveway, toward the front porch. He looked down at the headmaster's right leg. He was limping. It was the first time he had ever seen him without the cane. When they approached the house, Logan saw faculty members peering out the bay window. They went inside, and Lillian MacPharlan rushed into the foyer with a wild-eyed look.

"Good evening, ma'am," Logan said. "I'm sorry to disturb you again, but somebody attacked Michelle Martin."

She gasped and said, "Oh my god, is she all right?"

"Paramedics took her to the hospital. I called them, and they said she's in ICU right now. I need some information."

She led him into the living room, and the teachers had moved away from the window. Logan apologized for the interruption and told them what happened. They talked over each other.

"Will she be all right?" asked John Fletcher.

"She'll be out of commission for a while, but I hope she'll be okay."

John shook his head in disbelief and said, "Who would do such a horrible thing?"

"That's what I'm trying to find out, sir."

He looked around the room and asked them what time they got there. Most of them arrived about seven thirty. Others arrived late. His eyes trained on Board Director Gail Stockdale. He thought he recognized her from somewhere. Then it dawned on him. She was at the Poconos hotel restaurant with Jonas MacPharlan.

Realizing what Logan was probably thinking, Jonas hoped he would not give them away. He looked at his wife. Fortunately, her eyes were on the detective. He gazed out the window, hoping his eyes would not betray him. He wasn't very good at sneaking around. They all maintained poker faces.

"What time did you get here, ma'am?"

"At about quarter to eight," Gail said.

"Did you see or hear anything unusual when you got here, ma'am?"

"I don't think so."

"Did you see anyone wandering around the gym?"

"No, it seemed to be empty."

"Think carefully. It might be very important."

Lines creased her forehead as she pondered the moment she pulled into the headmaster's driveway.

"I saw a girl by the gym, but she was too far away for me to get a good look. I was in a hurry anyway."

"What did she look like?"

"I went by too fast to get a good enough look."

"Did you see anyone else?"

Gail shook her head and said, "I'm afraid not. I'm sorry."

"If you can remember anything else, please give me a call at the police station."

"I don't think I'll remember anything, Detective."

"Sometimes you would be surprised what seemingly unimportant event can be remembered." He looked around the room and asked, "Did you hear anything at about eight o'clock?"

"We were too busy talking to notice," Jonas said.

"I was probably making coffee about then," Lillian MacPharlan said.

"Show me," Logan said.

Lillian led him into the kitchen. It was a large room with a cutting board in the center and an antique wood stove at the opposite end. He looked out the window, but it was too dark to see anything.

"What's out there?"

"The garden."

"I bet you can see the bleachers too."

"During the day. If you look hard enough through the trees and bushes."

He followed her back to the living room and asked some more questions. Then he showed himself out and drove to the girls' dorm to give Susan the bad news. He knocked on her door, but there was no answer. He headed down the hall, checking nameplates as he went. He stopped when he saw the one for Mary Weller and Wendy Holmes. He knocked and Mary invited him in. He saw Wendy sitting at the edge of her bed with an open spiral notebook. Susan was sitting on a folding chair next to her. A textbook was lying on the bed with yellow highlighted passages on the open pages. Susan glanced at the wall clock. It was about nine thirty, and she knew something had to be wrong if he was there at such a late hour. Her eyes widened.

"What's wrong?"

"I'm afraid I have some bad news," he said. "Michelle called and asked me to meet her under the bleachers. She wanted to tell me something. But somebody tried to prevent her from talking to me."

"What do you . . . what do you mean?" Wendy asked in alarm.

"Somebody attacked her," he said.

Susan put her hands to her face and screamed, "Oh my god!"

Wendy went over and put her arms around her.

Mary shook her head in disbelief and said, "Oh no! This can't be happening!"

"Not again," Wendy said. "Is she okay? Did you catch the guy who did it?"

"I'm afraid not," he said. "She's in the ICU right now."

"What kind of monster would do such a thing?" Mary wondered.

"I don't know," he said gravely. "That's what I'm trying to find out. I just need to ask you a few questions. Where were you about eight o'clock?"

"We've been studying for a history test," Mary said. "Just ask around. Girls have been bothering us all night, wanting to borrow things. Who would do such a horrible thing? Can we see her?"

"Why don't you call the hospital tomorrow morning and see if you can go in to visit her."

He thanked them and said, "I didn't mean to upset you."

On his way out, he saw the girls wrap their arms around Susan in a tight huddle.

Susan choked through tears and said, "Why is this happening?"

Logan went to Andy's room and saw him studying with Chad. When he told them the bad news, they were just as shocked as the others.

Andy slammed his fist against his hand and shouted, "Who did it? I'll get him!"

"We don't know yet," Logan said. "But violence never solves anything. Let the police handle it."

"It's horrible!" Chad cried. "I don't believe it."

Logan concentrated his attention on Chad and said, "Where did you go after I saw you earlier tonight?"

"I came back here."

"That's funny, you were running in the opposite direction the last time I saw you. Where did you go?"

"I went to the student center to get some snacks, and then I came back here, I swear. Why would you think I had something to do with it?"

"For the first time, I'm not accusing you of anything, Chad. The attack happened right after we bumped into each other. You couldn't possibly have been in two places at the same time." Logan glanced over at Andy and asked the same questions he asked the others earlier that evening. He was also studying with a classmate at the time Michelle was attacked. He thanked them and showed himself out.

Logan arrived at the hospital about eleven o'clock and went to see Michelle. Her head was bandaged, and she had been sedated. A nurse told him to come back when she could talk. He paced the hall outside her room, talking into his tape recorder.

"This case has been one surprise after another. What was Michelle Martin trying to tell me? Whatever it was, it involves someone at the school.

Maybe she knows who killed Phillip Bishop. The question is, who knew she was going to meet me? I've got to find out for her sake. She obviously didn't do it. Rudy can also be scratched from the suspect list. He tried to hang himself out of guilt for pushing Phillip's car off the road. Graham Humphries was in rehab, so that leaves him out.

Andy and the girls were studying with friends when Michelle was hit on the head. Jonas MacPharlan was having a meeting at his home at the time. And the woman he's having an affair with was there right under his wife's nose. Coach Reynolds was also there with a room full of witnesses. It's a quick walk from the headmaster's house to the bleachers, however. Any one of those people could have slipped out for a few minutes without being noticed, to go make a phone call or to go to the bathroom.

Maybe Chad did do it. He was with me before she was attacked but disappeared in the other direction. So it seems unlikely he would have had time to reach the bleachers before the attacker got there. Unless he slipped behind the headmaster's house and cut through the garden and through the trees.

I'll have to find out where Terry Dawson was tonight. I'll also have to look around the bleachers again when I can take a better look in daylight. Maybe the suspect left behind a clue."

Logan and his colleagues were searching for clues under the bleachers at the crack of dawn. Two uniformed officers used weed whackers and worked their way through the bushes behind the bleachers. Lieutenant Winters and Logan were cutting weeds ten feet away.

"Do you have any idea who might have done it?" Winters asked him.

Logan cut a branch and said, "Jonas MacPharlan."

"The old man?"

"I've never seen him without his cane. Last night, he didn't have it. So it's got to be somewhere out here."

"Did you see it when you went to his house?"

"No, but there were a lot of people there. And I don't know where he usually keeps it anyway."

"It does seem suspicious."

"And there's something else that's interesting."

## JOSEPH REDDEN

Harry looked at him inquisitively. "What's that?"

"Mrs. MacPharlan said she was making coffee about the time of Michelle's attack. The kitchen window overlooks the back of the bleachers."

"Do you think she could have seen anything?"

Logan shook his head and said, "I don't think so. It's pretty dark, especially with all those bushes and trees. But she's the only one who could have slipped out for a few minutes unnoticed. Especially if she said she was going to make coffee."

"That's a thought."

"She doesn't really have motive."

"That's true."

"The house is pretty close to the bleachers, but she wouldn't have been able to run very fast in high-heeled shoes."

They knelt down and ran their fingers under the shrubbery. Then, Officer Daniel Lewis shouted, "I found something, sir."

Lieutenant Winters and Logan went over and knelt next to him. Officer Lewis pointed to a shiny metal object sticking out of the grass. Logan sifted through the dirt with his fingers and unearthed an eagle medallion.

"I'll be damned!" he exclaimed. "Here it is!"

He dug out the rest of the cane and studied it. There was a crack next to the emblem and what looked like a bloodstain on the eagle's head. He placed it in a large evidence bag, and took it to the station. No Prints were on it, which meant the person wore gloves.

About noon, Logan went to Flannery's Tavern about five miles from campus. He ordered a seltzer and chatted with the bartender. He was a heavy set man with a scruffy beard and a chain tattoo on his left arm.

"Did you work last night?" he asked.

The man grunted and said, "Yeah, it's the third night in a row I've pulled a double shift."

"I know how you feel. I've been working on this case that's been driving me crazy. In fact, I was up late working on it last night."

"Really." He didn't seem terribly interested in the detective's problems.

"Yeah, a Broad Meadow student was attacked last night."

"That's too bad! Is she all right?"

"She's in intensive care. I'm just trying to figure out who did it."

"Who would do such a thing?"

"That's what I'm trying to find out." He handed him a snapshot of Terry Dawson and said, "He's a regular here, isn't he?"

"I've seen him around. He's a real troublemaker."

"Was he here last night?"

He handed the photograph back to him and said, "Yeah, he was here all right. He was sitting there at that table in the middle of everything, watching the Phillies game. He was really bombed out of his mind and was arguing with a buddy about the game."

"Damn!"

"What's wrong?"

"All my suspects have alibis."

Logan grabbed a late dinner again. He didn't like it much, but it was getting to be a way of life for him lately. About ten o'clock, he went to the gymnasium. The custodian was whistling as he mopped the locker room floor. This time he made sure he didn't surprise the old man. He waited for him to turn around before he went into the room.

He looked up and saw Logan in the doorway. "You again. What do you want?"

"About eight thirty last night, a female student was attacked under the bleachers. Were you here?"

"Yeah."

"What time did you get here?"

"About a half an hour before that."

"Did you see anybody outside?"

"Nobody was hanging around out there, but I did see a girl walking toward the gym a few minutes after eight. I didn't see where she went. I went inside."

"Are you sure you didn't see somebody else?"

He shrugged his shoulders and said, "No, I didn't see anybody else. I'm sorry."

"Well, thanks anyway."

JOSEPH REDDEN

\* \* \*

Logan went back to police headquarters and reviewed his suspect list. He started with Phillip Bishop's name and reasons why someone might have murdered him. He put stars next to primary suspects and scratched off the names of people who were no longer suspects.

> Phillip Bishop: ambitious athlete and scholar who was hit on the head with a rock after fighting with Chad McAlpin in the woods. Chad was jealous because he was going out with Susan Williams. Phillip turned in Terry Dawson for drugs. He also knew Andy Winchester was using steroids. Phillip dumped Michelle for Susan. Michelle never got over it.

> Chad McAlpin: he was seen arguing with Phillip a few days before Phillip's death. Jealous of him for stealing his girlfriend, Susan Williams. He went to the woods to talk to him. They got in a fight. Bishop fell and hit his head. He went back to tell Andy and Rudy. Andy went to investigate, came back, and reported that Bishop was dead. Chad was in charge of making it look like Bishop died in a car accident. He threatened Andy and Rudy into silence with secrets they didn't want revealed. (Maybe Phillip was still alive, and he thought he was dead when he went back to Andy and Rudy). I saw him running into the night, prior to Michelle's attack. No one saw him until after the attack.

> Andy Winchester: aggressive athlete. Displays great strength in sports due to steroid use. He and Rudy went to look for Chad and Phillip and got separated. Maybe he found Phillip lying unconscious and hit him with the rock. He was so desperate to play well, he paid Terry Dawson to get him steroids. Chad knew about it and was blackmailing him to keep quiet about pushing Phillip's car off the road. Phillip Bishop knew about Andy's steroid use, which was a possible threat to Andy. Maybe he was going to tell, and Andy had to prevent him from talking. Andy would have given anything to get the scholarship because he had a chance of

being in the pros. He needed the scholarship because his parents were having financial trouble. Andy was so upset about what he did to Rudy that he confessed to faking the car accident. After I arrested him, he got out on bail and smoked pot. The steroids and marijuana didn't mix, and he collapsed at basketball practice. (Interestingly enough, Coach Reynolds handled both his arrest and the medical emergency. Maybe he knew that he was doing steroids and looked the other way. I'll have to look into it).

Chad had been in the woods for several minutes before Andy and Rudy went looking for them. It was dark, and they got separated. That gave Andy plenty of time to hit Phillip on the head with the rock and get back to the car before the others came back.

He got back to the dorm at about 10:20 p.m. to get Phillip's car. Willy Brown saw Andy (or rather his shadow) exit the dorm. Chad and Rudy drove back in Chad's car. Last night, he was studying with a friend when Michelle Martin was attacked. I'll have to talk to his friend to see if that is really true.

Rudolph "Rudy" Preston: got in over his head. He agreed to help Chad. Guilt ridden, attempted suicide. Chad blackmailed him with a threat of going forward about Rudy's theft of final exam questions. Rudy also was alone in the woods that night. He had enough time to hit Phillip Bishop on the head when he was probably lying there unconscious. Rudy was still in the hospital at the time of Michelle's attack. That can mean one of two things: (a) Rudy can be crossed off the suspect list or (b) Rudy killed Phillip and someone else hit Michelle. It could have just been an isolated incident. I need to look into it.

Jonas MacPharlan: headmaster. Uneasy about the investigation. He doesn't want me around. He wants to avoid a scandal and told the press it was a car accident. I overheard him talking to someone on the phone who seems to be calling the shots. (I saw him with Gail Stockdale at the hotel restaurant at the Poconos. Maybe somebody else caught them together and is blackmailing him. I need to look into this.) Jonas said he was with his wife the night Phillip Bishop died. His wife confirmed it. He was having a faculty meeting at his house at the time Michelle Martin was attacked. Officer Lewis found his cane between the house and the bleachers. His prints would be on it anyway. There's no way he could have left the meeting, unless he excused himself to make a phone call or something. No other prints were found on it, which means the attacker wore gloves.

Ian Reynolds: competitive coach, had apparent axe to grind with Phillip Bishop. Maybe he's jealous. He pushes his players too hard. He left the dance about nine o'clock to work out at the gym on the night Phillip died. The janitor saw him. He was at the faculty meeting at the headmaster's house when Michelle Martin was hit on the head. He bailed Andy out of jail and took him to the ER when he fell down at basketball practice. It makes a lot of sense that he knew about Andy's steroid abuse. Maybe he and Terry Dawson were in on it. If Phillip found out about it, that's plenty of motive for killing him.

Terry Dawson: star football player gone bad. He had it in for Phillip for turning him in for dealing drugs last year. Motive: revenge. He said he was with Jonas MacPharlan at the time Phillip died, but it turned out he was at home without an alibi. He was watching a baseball game at Flannery's Tavern when Michelle Martin was hit on the head.

Michelle Martin: close friend of Susan, Phillip, and Chad. She was in love with Phillip and was upset that he loved Susan more. She drove the girls back to campus at 9:30 p.m. She dropped Mary Waller and Wendy Holmes off at the dance and drove Susan back to the dorm. She gave her a sleeping pill and said she walked back to the dance at about ten. Mary and Wendy said she got there about eleven. It doesn't take that long to walk from her dorm to the student center. Where was she?

(Tanya Kestler saw a car pull out of the parking lot about the time Michelle said she left. Maybe Michelle went back to the woods and killed Phillip. Or maybe she just went back and saw who hit him. Maybe the killer saw her and had to shut her up. She definitely had information about the case and someone tried to shut her up. Or it could be an isolated incident).

Susan Williams: a year ago, she had a nervous breakdown and was under psychiatric care at the William G. Wallace Memorial Hospital near Chicago. She was in the middle of the rivalry between Chad McAlpin and Phillip Bishop. She was studying with Mary Waller and Wendy Holmes when Michelle was attacked.

Logan stared into space and looked at his notes again. He crossed Rudy's name off the suspect list and turned on the tape recorder. "Loose ends to follow up on:

How did Michelle's attacker know she was going to meet me at the gym? Was it an isolated incident?

Did someone overhear her talking to me on her cell phone?

What does she know?

Where was she for about an hour the night Phillip was murdered?

Did Michelle go back to the woods and see who killed Phillip?

Why was the coach so mad at Phillip?

Did he know about Andy's steroid abuse?

Who was Jonas MacPharlan talking to on the phone?

What is Susan hiding?"

He tapped his pen and looked back at his notes.
"The problems between Phillip Bishop and Chad McAlpin stemmed around Susan Williams. The case seems to come back to her. Why?"

## Chapter 22

Logan went into Michelle's room and sat by her bedside. Her head was wrapped in bandages. Her eyes had a vacant look about them. It looked like she was drugged up on painkillers. She managed a smile and said, "It's good to see you, Detective Logan."

"How do you feel?"

"Pretty good now. They gave me painkillers."

"Who did this to you? What were you trying to tell me?"

"Get her out of there before she's next."

"Who?"

"Susy. It's horrible what happened."

Logan held her hand and said, "Michelle, look at me. It's important. You have to tell me who hurt you."

She closed her eyes and said, "She didn't want anybody to know. The poor thing."

"What didn't she want people to know?"

"She was pregnant . . . oh, I promised her I wouldn't say anything."

"That's okay. I'll tell her I forced it out of you."

"You took advantage . . . I'm so doped up on painkillers I'd say anything . . . it's not fair . . . I can't let her be hurt . . . don't let her be hurt . . . not like the way she looked when she was bruised . . . I tried to help her, but she turned away."

"Did someone hurt her?"

"It was just awful . . . I warned her, but she wouldn't listen."

"Come on, Michelle. Tell me who did this to you. Is it the same person who hurt Susan?"

"I thought it was a safe place to talk—nobody would be around."

"Who did this horrible thing?"

Her eyes closed and she fell asleep. He got up and headed out the door. A tall dark-haired man carrying a bouquet of flowers passed him in the hall. Logan saw him go into Michelle's room. He stood in the doorway and saw him holding her hand. Then he spoke quietly. He had a New England accent. Then it dawned on him. He was one of the teachers at the headmaster's house on the night of her attack.

She opened her eyes and took a moment to focus. Her face brightened when she saw him. He leaned over and kissed her on the cheek.

"Hey, babe," he said.

"You came."

"How do you feel?"

"Like I was run over by a truck."

He gently rubbed her hand and said, "Poor baby. I'm so sorry. I wish I could have been there for you."

"There's nothing you could have done. It happened."

"I hope they catch the guy that did it and let him rot in jail."

"I hope so." She yawned and said, "I'm not much company."

"It's okay."

She closed her eyes and went back to sleep. He sat there holding her hand.

Logan went over to a lounge just down the hall and eyed the hallway while he waited for him to leave. To get on the elevator, he would have to head that way. He peered down the hall and saw a nurse go into Michelle's room.

"I just have to check on her," he heard her say.

"Oh, let me get out of your way then," the man said.

"It won't take long."

"Is there a vending machine?"

"It's in the lounge down the hall on the right."

The man entered the room and shoved coins into the slot. He pressed the button for Sprite. It popped out, and he reached down to get it. He pried open the tab and sat down. He gazed out the window, then looked at Logan.

"Oh, Detective Logan," he said. "I don't know where my brain is today. Remember me, I'm John Fletcher. I'm an English teacher at Broad Meadow."

"That's right. You were at the headmaster's house last night."

"It's horrible what happened."

"I know."

"I just thought I would stop in to see how she's doing. It's horrible. She's one of my best students."

"It's hard to believe that she's your student. If you hadn't told me you were her teacher, I would have thought you were one of her classmates. It's my mistake."

"I get that all the time."

Logan grunted and said, "So do I."

"That's what you get when you're blessed with young looks. How old are you?"

"Thirty."

"I'm twenty-three."

"You don't say. I could've sworn you were a student. It must be hard teaching kids that are so close in age with all their raging hormones."

"It is. I think a couple of the girls have a crush on me. It's flattering, but they spend way too much free time coming to see me after school."

"To check you out, no doubt."

He smiled and said, "Yeah, but . . . but I let them know I'm not interested. I try to maintain a teacher-student relationship with them."

"Well, if that's the case, why is it that I saw you kiss Michelle when I stopped by to see her a few minutes ago?"

"It wasn't . . . it wasn't what it looked like."

"Really? I would've done the same thing if my girlfriend was in the hospital. But she isn't a student. You're here to see your girlfriend, admit it."

"Now look, I could get into a lot of trouble if . . . if word got out that—"

"You'll get in trouble big time, that's for sure. The very idea that a teacher would be messing around with his student."

"It's . . . it's not like that, I swear."

"It looks that way to me."

"There's a perfectly logical explanation. You were right. I am way too young to be in this situation. I suppose . . . I suppose I got in over my head. Michelle isn't like the other young women. She's sophisticated. Worldly.

She acts a lot older. She doesn't get mixed up with guys her own age. Sure, she hangs out with Andy Winchester. But it's a platonic relationship."

"So you were getting some action with her."

"You're way off base there. She just turned eighteen."

"She's still your student. You should have gotten her to switch teachers."

"I know, but I thought I could handle it. When I . . . when I realized I had feelings for her, that it wasn't a simple crush . . . I told her she should switch classes. She was just about to turn eighteen in a few months, and we . . . and we decided to cool it down some. She switched classes, and we maintained our distance. This semester, she signed up for my class. We figured it was only a couple more months, so what the hell. When we were around each other, privately, I used self-control. It was really difficult, but that's what we did. We had to."

"I'm getting a better picture here," Logan said. "Did Phillip Bishop know about you two? He seemed to know everybody's business."

"I should hope not."

"Let's say he did know. That would give you both plenty of motive for conking him on the head with the rock. If it hadn't been for her attack, I'd think she might have done it. But that doesn't leave you out. Where were you the night Phillip died?"

"I was at the dance. You can ask around. I was there for several hours."

Logan jotted it down in his notebook and said, "Okay, I will. But that doesn't let you off the hook. Maybe she decided to tell MacPharlan about you two."

"She would never do that!"

"Maybe you two got into an argument and you hit her on the head. It's a short walk from the headmaster's house to the bleachers. All you had to do was swipe the old man's cane and wham!"

"How could you even suggest that I would want to hurt her? I love her!"

"Well, it gives you plenty of motive. Does MacPharlan know about you two?"

"No, and please don't tell him. Nobody can know. My career will be destroyed if word gets out about this."

"You should have thought about it before you got involved with a student."

"But she just turned eighteen."

"I don't think the school board will see it that way. Or the authorities. Or her parents."

Logan started to get up to go, then turned to face him. "One more thing. Do you live near the school?"

"My house is just down the road from the student center."

"Michelle told me she went back to the dance after she took Susan back to their dorm. Her friends said she didn't get there till about eleven o'clock. That means she had about an hour that's unaccounted for. Did she go to see you?"

He hung his head and said, "Yes. But nothing happened, I swear. I got a phone call, and she went back to the dance. Please don't report this, I'm begging you."

"You know I can't do that. But I'm willing to wait till I find out who's behind the attack and Phillip's murder."

"Thank you."

"The matter will be straightened out, at any rate," Logan said on his way out of the room.

Logan headed down to the psychiatric ward to look in on Rudy. Maybe he knew what happened to Susan. He rang the doorbell, and a female staffer let him in. He flashed his badge to the nurse at the monitor desk and said, "I'm here to see Rudy Preston."

"Sign in please," she said.

He scribbled his name and the time on a sheet and followed her down the hall. She knocked on the door and said, "Rudy, a Detective Logan is here to see you."

Logan went inside and saw him sitting at a small desk. He was slaving over an open book and had an intent look on his face as he wrote in a spiral notebook. Wadded papers were strewn at his feet. He was wearing gray flannel pajamas.

Logan smiled and said, "Hello, Rudy. Everybody misses you. How are you feeling?"

"I'll be okay," he said quietly.

"It looks like they keep you pretty busy here."

"I'm trying to get caught up on last week's homework. Mr. MacPharlan is letting me do everything from here."

"That's nice of him."

"I might not have graduated on time if he hadn't let me do this. How is everybody?"

"Things are a little tense after Michelle's attack."

"What . . . what happened?"

"You haven't heard? I'm sorry, I assumed they told you."

"They don't tell me a thing! They don't want to upset me. What happened?" Logan relayed the whole ugly incident and said, "They just moved her out of intensive care. She's here right now."

Rudy sprang to his feet and said, "I've got to go see her!"

"I went to see her a few minutes ago. They gave her painkillers that made her groggy. She was about to tell me something but fell asleep. It was something about Susan. Do you know what she might have been trying to tell me?"

"Not a clue."

"I think it has something to do with her breakdown last year. I'm sure I already asked you this, but do you remember if she acted differently back then?"

"I know she was really upset. But I just figured she had gotten into a fight with Chad or something."

After a five minute question-and-answer session, Logan realized it was leading nowhere. He left and headed back to the school to talk to Susan.

It was about two o'clock. Little did Logan know it, but that was the hour the cows crossed the road for their afternoon feeding. He couldn't get around them and sat behind the wheel fuming as he watched them slowly file across the road.

He shook his fist in the air and shouted, "Come on!"

He glanced at his wristwatch about ten minutes later. Then he looked in disbelief at the cows on the road. They were just standing there. A farmer was prodding them across the path, but that did not seem to do any good. They were not moving. The man nudged the ones in back, forcing the other ones to keep walking. There was a traffic pile up in both directions.

## JOSEPH REDDEN

He watched the last cow cross the path and checked the time again. He sat there for eight minutes, but it seemed a lot longer. He grumbled at the farmer and sped down the narrow road that led to the campus.

He pulled into the all-familiar guest spot at Hullien Hall and walked over to Susan's dorm. There was no answer when he knocked on her door, so he turned the knob and went inside. She was on her bed, reading an English literature text. She looked up at him and said, "I already talked to you, Detective Logan, and I can't do it again."

"I won't be long. Please, it's important."

She hesitated before making a decision. "Okay."

He pulled a swivel chair near her bed and said, "I have to ask you some very personal questions. I wouldn't ask if I didn't think it was relevant. Why did you really go to the hospital last year?"

She looked sharply at him and said, "I told you why. I was upset about things."

"I now know that isn't exactly true. Michelle told me you were pregnant."

She cringed and clasped her right hand over her face. "But she promised not to say anything."

"I got her to talk about it when she was on painkillers. I'm sorry, but it had to be done. You clammed up, so I had to do something. I think you got pregnant and went as far away as you could to get an abortion."

She burst into tears and rocked her body to and fro. "You had no right!" she screamed through tears.

"Who was the father?"

She looked away and said, "Nobody here."

"Michelle was trying to tell me something before she was attacked. She knew what happened because you told her everything. You are close friends who often confided in each other. You told her, didn't you?"

She wiped her tears and sniffled. "No, Michelle found out that someone else was involved with the drug incident. She told Phillip and he was going to tell, but somebody got to him first. Poor Michelle."

"Who was it?"

"I don't know. I tried to get her to tell me, but she wouldn't. She didn't want me to get involved."

"What did she do when you told her you were pregnant?"

"She cried with me."

"Did you tell the father?"

She shook her head and averted eye contact.

"Did you tell the school nurse?"

She shook her head.

"Was it consensual sex?"

"Yes, he . . . he told me he loved me."

"My gut instinct tells me that's not true. Why would you be acting so nervous? Michelle let it slip that she didn't want you to get hurt. She insisted that you get away from school quickly. Why do you suppose she would be so fearful for your safety?"

"I don't know. A lot of awful things have been happening around here lately. I suppose she just didn't want me to be next. She always looks out for me."

"Were you raped?"

She cringed and said, "No! Why would you think that?"

"It's just a hunch. You can tell me anything."

"Why should I trust you after taking advantage of Michelle like you did?"

"You know it was for your own good. Now come on, talk to me."

"I swear nothing happened!"

"Some people around here remembered that you had bruises about a year ago. How did you get the bruises?"

"In a skiing accident. It was on a class trip to the Poconos."

"Who got you pregnant, Susan? You can tell me, I'm your friend."

She screwed up her face and cried, "Phillip!"

A few minutes later, Logan went up to Chad's new dorm room on the third floor of Hullien Hall. He heard music blasting as he walked down the hall. He asked a boy which room was Chad's, and he pointed to one, halfway down on the right. He knocked on the door, and Chad glowered when he saw him.

"Detective Logan, what are you doing here?"

"I just have some things I need to have cleared up."

"Make it snappy. I'm in the middle of something."

He led Logan into the room, and the floor creaked under their weight. At this hour, late afternoon sunlight wafted across the slanted ceiling and shone on the desk. It was a lot nicer than the room Chad was in before.

Chad went over to the stereo and lowered the volume. Logan gazed out the window and said, "You've got a nice view."

"You can see a lot more of the grounds, that's for sure. You can even see the pond."

"It's a nicer room."

"It's a lot bigger. But it got cold at night this winter."

"I bet it did. It's an old building."

Chad looked at his desk, then back at Logan and said, "What do you want?"

Logan continued with the small talk and then asked, "Where did you go after we bumped into each other the other night when Michelle was attacked?"

"I got snacks at the student center, and walked around a little bit. I needed time to think."

"Time to think under the bleachers with Michelle?"

"Hey, wait a minute, I thought you said you believed me."

"Well, I just found out something that makes me curious about you again."

Chad shook his head and glared at him. "Give me a break! Everybody assumes that because I'm back at school again that I hurt her. It wasn't me. There's no way I could have bumped into you and gotten there in time. No way."

"It took me five minutes to get to the field by foot. You were running. Maybe you ran behind the headmaster's house and back to the bleachers that way. You could have beaten me there."

"I told you, I wasn't there!"

"Then where were you?" Logan pressed.

"I went back to my room."

"Did anybody see you?"

"Everybody's in and out."

"Well, it's just a thought."

"Is this what you do? Harass people all the time?"

"Only people that aren't telling me the truth."

"Why would I hurt Michelle? She's my friend. I resent you accusing me of doing it."

"I'm sorry, but I have to ask these questions."

"Is she up to seeing visitors yet?"

"I stopped by a little while ago, but she was too groggy to talk. When I was there, she said some things about Susan that concerned me."

"What did she say?"

"I think it has something to do with when she had the nervous breakdown last year. Can you remember how she acted before she went away? Did she say or do anything out of the ordinary?"

Chad looked out the window and watched students walk across the grounds. Logan had a knack for stirring up painful memories.

"I was really upset with her at the time," he said at length. "I could tell something was bothering her, you know, but she wouldn't open up. I begged her to talk to me and then she just acted distant."

"When was this?"

"Around Thanksgiving break. When we came back, she was really quiet. It was creepy."

"I'm going to shift gears for a moment," Logan said. "Is it true that she had a skiing accident on a class trip to the Poconos?"

Chad gave him a puzzled look and said, "She didn't go with us. She was sick that weekend."

Logan's eyes lit up. "Thanks, Chad, you've really been a big help this time."

"What did I say?"

"I'll explain later." He got up and walked hurriedly out the door.

Chad shook his head and groaned. "What was that all about?"

A few minutes later, Logan went back to the scene of Michelle's attack. He studied the line of trees and bushes separating the bleachers from the MacPharlan's backyard. Then he looked at the garden that stretched from the east side of the house over to the shrubbery.

He went to the backyard and took note of the neatly mowed lawn and noticed a row of trees had been cleared to lay a path from the backyard to the ball field. There was a fence at the end of the trail. The bleachers were five feet from the fence. He unlatched the gate and wandered over to the bleachers. He went back to the gymnasium parking lot and retraced his steps the way he did it the night Michelle was attacked. He stopped and looked in the direction he saw the attacker running. Then he went over to the gymnasium entrance and retraced his steps back to the bleachers.

"Michelle was standing facing the gym," he said. "And the person who hit her was walking toward her. He couldn't have been running toward the road. I would've seen him."

He went back to the clearing and retraced his steps to the MacPharlan's backyard. He checked his wristwatch. It took two minutes to walk from the bleachers to their kitchen door in back of the house.

He went into the gym to see if the custodian was there. Maybe he saw something that night. He saw a light on in the coach's office and turned the knob. Ian Reynolds flinched and looked at him in surprise.

"Oh, hello, Detective Logan. You startled me."

He apologized and said, "You told me if I wanted to work out to come over. I couldn't find a key to the weight room."

"Well, I was going down myself. Come on."

He followed the coach into the weight room. Reynolds had him lie on the bench and lifted the bar over his hands.

Logan took a deep breath and said, "It's too bad about Rudy and Michelle."

Ian grimaced and nodded his head. "The poor kids."

There was a long silence as the workout continued. Metal clapping on metal drowned out Logan's grunts and heavy breathing. Then Coach Reynolds put the bars back on the stand, and the detective rested a moment. He sat up and wiped his forehead with a towel.

"What time did you say you arrived at Jonas MacPharlan's house the night Michelle was attacked?"

"About quarter of eight."

"Did you walk to his house from the gym?"

He rolled his eyes and said, "Yes, what does that have to do with anything?"

"Did you see Michelle?"

"No. To tell you the truth, I wasn't really paying that much attention."

"Did you see anybody hanging around outside?"

"If students had been wandering around, I wouldn't have known it. My mind was on getting to the meeting. I walked in with Gail Stockdale."

"You're sure you didn't see anyone?"

"I'm sure. We were talking about the terrible things that have been happening around here lately. She was really upset."

Logan lay back on the rack, and Reynolds handed him the bar. Frank hoisted his arms straight up and bench pressed a set of ten.

"This case is hurting the kids," the coach said.

"And the team's performance," Logan added.

"That's right. Their minds are elsewhere."

"True," Logan wheezed. "It's too bad about Andy."

Coach Reynolds placed the barbell back on the rack and looked down at Logan. "What happened?"

"Didn't you know?"

"Know what?"

"He was expelled."

Ian looked at him suspiciously and said, "Oh?"

"He told Jonas MacPharlan that he was doing steroids."

The coach's face turned bright red.

"Is there something wrong?" Logan asked.

"No!" He stomped out of the room.

When Andy reported for baseball practice, the coach stared at him in disbelief.

"I thought you got expelled?"

"What do you mean, Coach? I've been expelled? What for?"

He glared at him and said, "You didn't say anything?"

"No, why would I?"

"Oh, I get it. Played for a fool! I fell right into his hands!"

"What are you talking about?"

"Never mind. Did you tell Detective Logan anything about your steroid use?"

"He forced it out of me. I didn't mean for it to—"

Reynolds punched his desk with his fist and shouted, "That's just great! Andy, you're cut if you screw up again! You hear?"

"But, Coach, Logan forced it out of me!"

"I don't want to hear it. Just get the hell out of here!"

Andy closed the door on his way out and heard Reynolds shout, "Damn!"

That night, Chad went to visit Michelle. When he got there, he saw Logan at her bedside. She was sitting up and looked a lot more responsive than the last time he stopped by. It looked like they were in the middle of something, so he waited in the hall. They didn't see him.

"How are you feeling?"

"Better."

"Are you trying to compete to see how many Broad Meadow students have to seek medical assistance?"

She managed a smile and said, "It seems that way, doesn't it?"

"You look a lot better. And you seem more alert."

"I was totally out of it the other day. I barely remember you were here."

"I know. It was just awful."

"That's an understatement."

"Are you up to answering a few questions?"

"I guess so."

"Did Susan tell you who got her pregnant?"

"No, but I assumed it was Chad. That would probably explain the tension between the two of them."

"Did she say when conception occurred?"

"I think she said it was about a year and a half ago. The end of November. Around Thanksgiving vacation."

Chad was so filled with rage when he heard that Susan had been pregnant that he stomped down the hall and punched the elevator button with a vengeance. He ran his fingers through his hair, cursing under his breath. Passersby gave him funny looks. People waiting to get on the elevator decided to take the next one going down.

He didn't get her pregnant. That was for sure. The only other person it could have been was Phillip. It all made sense now. The way she acted after Thanksgiving break. The way Phillip swept in and stole her from him. It was because he got her pregnant. They had been lying and sneaking around behind his back the whole time, pretending to be his friends.

"Damn him!" he shouted at the top of his lungs.

He stomped toward the parking lot, the keys shaking in his hands. He slipped onto the car seat and slammed the door with a fury. He sat there a moment, in stunned silence, holding his hands to his face. Then he sped out the exit and took his anger on the road.

He floored the accelerator on the twisty back roads. The wheels squealed as he sped around the bend. He failed to negotiate the turn and wound up in the other lane. A pickup truck was plowing toward him. The road was so narrow, there were no shoulders. He slammed on the brakes, and the car skidded violently as he righted himself. He lost control of the vehicle, and it slammed into the field.

The pickup truck driver rolled down his window and shouted, "Learn how to drive, dumb ass!" Then he sped off.

Chad was too stunned to move. He took several deep breaths, trying to calm down.

"Oh my god!" he said repeatedly.

When he calmed down, he backed down onto the road and was more careful driving back to campus.

## Chapter 23

That night, Chad tossed and turned in bed. His thoughts were on Phillip and Susan. He couldn't believe they had been sneaking around behind his back. He couldn't believe Michelle knew her secret. They all lied to him, and he demanded answers.

The next day, he tried to figure out the best time to talk to her alone. He decided to wait until after school. Students sensed a cool chill between the two of them. Chad gave her dirty looks. She avoided eye contact. They were both unusually quiet.

When the final bell rang, Susan filed out with classmates. Chad pushed his way through the crowd to catch up with her.

"Wait up, Susy!"

She looked back at him and said, "I'm really busy. I don't have time to talk to you now."

She went down the front steps and walked hurriedly down the sidewalk. He reached for her arm and pulled her toward him.

"Did Phillip get you pregnant?"

"No, leave me alone!" She pulled her arm free and ran to get away from him.

He went after her and yelled, "I won't leave you alone until you talk to me."

She stopped in her tracks and turned to face him. "Detective Logan promised he wouldn't say anything. I knew the investigation would come to this."

"He didn't tell me. I overheard him talking to Michelle at the hospital."

"Everything would have been fine, if he hadn't been so nosy. You wouldn't have had to know."

## LOVE'S A CRIME

"That's not fair!" he shouted. Students stared at them on their way by. He waited till they were alone again. "We went out with each other, damn it! I had a right to know! You could've at least told me you were seeing Phillip. I wouldn't have been happy about it, but I would've gotten over it. You all lied to me. I thought you were my friends."

"I didn't want you to know."

He put his hands on her shoulders and looked into her eyes. "Phillip was close to you because he got you pregnant. He was lying to me the whole time. Talk to me!"

She squirmed to pull free and said, "I can't talk about it!"

"Fine, I know somebody who will tell me what I want to know!"

He saw Logan coming up the walkway from Hullien Hall. He went over to him and said, "Detective Logan, I need to talk to you."

"Not now." He walked hurriedly to catch up to Susan.

Chad ran to catch up to him and shouted, "But Detective Logan!"

He followed him into Susan's dorm and saw her let Logan into her room and close the door.

He went outside and waited on a bench by the front door.

"Why did you lie to me, Susan?" Logan asked.

She pushed a strand of golden hair out of her eyes and said, "I don't know what you mean."

Logan glanced at his notes and said, "Michelle told me you got an abortion about the same time you checked into the psychiatric hospital in Chicago last year. Why didn't you tell me?"

"She had no right!"

"She's only trying to help you, Susan. Here's the way I see it. Phillip is dead and can't defend himself. That's why you named him as the father. You're protecting the real father, aren't you? Did he threaten you?"

"No!"

"So Phillip wasn't the father. Talk to me. I can help you."

"I can't."

"Because you're in danger?"

"No."

"Is the father on campus now?"

"No!" She ran out of the room.

He ran after her but didn't see where she went. He decided to try her later. Maybe she would talk about it then. When he went outside, Chad was waiting for him.

"I didn't mean to cut you off like that, Chad. You wanted to talk to me?"

"I need to talk to you in private."

"Okay."

He led him up to his dorm room and closed the door. Chad sat at the foot of his bed and said, "I overheard you talking to Michelle at the hospital yesterday. Why didn't you tell me Susy was pregnant?"

"I promised her I wouldn't. It's up to her to tell you."

"But she won't. She lied to me!"

"I'm sure she had her reasons. She won't tell me who got her pregnant. Maybe you can help me figure it out. Did you have sex with her?"

"No, she wasn't ready and I didn't want to pressure her."

"If you didn't make love to her, then maybe Phillip did. Maybe he got her pregnant."

Chad clenched his fist and said, "I just can't believe that Phillip got her pregnant. The little—"

"I think you found out about it and killed him out of revenge. Everybody knows you were angry with him."

"It wasn't like that!"

"So you did kill him?"

"No, you're twisting my words!"

"Someone who is as calm and collected as you are can certainly lose his cool."

"I swear I didn't do it! I just found out about this yesterday. Why won't you believe me?"

"Because you had motive. And you were at the scene of the crime. And you admitted pushing him off the road."

"That's all I did, I swear!"

Logan referred to his notes and said, "You told me Susan wasn't acting like herself around Thanksgiving break, a year and a half ago. She told Michelle that's about the time she got pregnant."

Chad scratched his head and said, "Wait a minute. Susy went home early for Thanksgiving break last year. Phillip and I were at his folks' house. It couldn't have been him. He was with me the whole weekend. I remember, because he teased me the whole time about missing her, and we talked to her for hours on the phone."

"Maybe she was mistaken about the date of conception. It could have been off a week or so. Can you think of anything else?"

"Not really."

"How did Susan act before she left for Thanksgiving vacation?"

"I don't remember. She left before I got to say good-bye. She had afternoon classes free and I had a class. I was pretty upset with her. We talked on the phone and she apologized. There was something she wanted to talk to her parents about. They told me she didn't get there till a day later. That is pretty strange. It's not like her."

"How about when she came back from vacation?"

"I'm not sure."

"Was she happy, sad, angry?"

"She was mad at me. We got into a fight, and now that I think of it, she was irrational. She wouldn't let me touch her. It seems to me she was hanging around Michelle a lot after that. Then things were back to normal for us. I wonder if Phillip could have gotten her pregnant before vacation. If that's so, the dirty bastard was sneaking around behind my back the whole time. How could I have been so stupid? They were doing it right before my eyes, and I wasn't paying attention."

"Relax, I think she's protecting someone."

"Who?"

"That's what I'm trying to find out. I think she told Michelle what happened."

"And she was going to tell you, only somebody tried to kill her."

Logan nodded and said, "Exactly."

"Did anybody else hang around with her?"

"Not really."

"Well, if you remember anything else, give me a call." He thanked him and went out the door.

\* \* \*

"Susan wasn't herself that weekend," Mr. Williams told Logan. "When Chad called, she perked up a bit. Then she was droopy. We thought she was just missing Chad. I hope we have been of some assistance, Detective Logan."

"You have. Thank you, sir. I'll tell her you said hello." He hung up and decided to get some lunch. He went to the diner down the street from the police station and got a meatball sandwich. While he waited, he sipped a soda and thought about the case. Who got Susan pregnant? And what was Michelle trying to tell him? Was she trying to name the father?

Chad leaned over Michelle's hospital bed and whispered her name. She opened her eyes and said, "Oh, hello, Chad."

"I've got to know something. Who got Susy pregnant?"

"How did you know?"

"I overheard you talking to Logan yesterday. Now come on, it's important. Who was the father?"

"Phillip."

"I heard you say she got pregnant just before Thanksgiving vacation. I was with him that weekend. It couldn't have been him."

"The doctor could have been off by a week or so."

"I don't think so. She told you, and you were going to tell Logan, and the guy hit you on the head. Who did this to you?"

She yawned and said, "I don't know. I didn't get a good enough look."

He leaned closer and said, "Come on, you do know. It's the same person that got Susan pregnant and killed Phillip because she also told him, didn't she? That's why he was killed, wasn't it? He was going to tell the police. Who got her pregnant?"

Michelle closed her eyes and said, "Ask Susan."

He gently nudged her to wake up again and said, "She won't tell me. Come on, I'm not leaving until you tell me."

"I promised her I wouldn't say anything."

"Who did it?"

She was about to respond when a nurse entered the room and told him she needed to check on Michelle. When he came back a few minutes later, her parents were sitting by her bedside. He went to his car and headed back to campus.

Logan ducked around a row of lockers and listened to Coach Reynolds's pep talk before a baseball game. He wished them good luck, and everyone ran outside with the exception of the coach and Andy. Logan saw Ian slip something to him.

He slapped Andy's shoulder and said, "Go to it Tiger! You can do it, with the little incentive I gave you."

Logan stepped out from around the locker and saw Andy race out the door.

Ian smiled and said, "Good afternoon, Detective Logan. I don't have time to talk now. The game is about to start."

"I guess you forgot you told me you despised people who cheat."

"I do."

Reynolds walked hurriedly down the hall, and Logan ran to catch up.

"I'm finally getting the picture. You're supplying steroids to your players with Terry Dawson's help."

Ian froze in his tracks and looked back at him. "You're way off base, Detective Logan."

"Don't lie to me, Reynolds. It's all over. I saw Terry Dawson slip the steroids to Andy. And then I did some digging. He has a friend who is a security guard at a pharmaceutical company outside of Philadelphia. He has a key to the medical supplies and can get any drugs he wants, for a price, of course. He owed Dawson a favor. Are you working with him?"

"It isn't what it seems."

"Why don't you fill me in then? How long have you been supplying these little incentives to your players?"

Reynolds waved his hands and said, "What can you do? Once everybody does steroids, you can't have an even game. It's a matter of survival. Now if you'll excuse me, I have a game to win." He went outside, jogged across the field, and got in line with his players.

Logan watched him bow his head during the national anthem and said, "What a lying piece of scum." He went back to his car and pulled out of the parking lot.

Susan found a typewritten note pinned to her bedroom door that read, "Susy, please reconsider. Love, Chad."

She ripped it off and locked herself in the room. She turned her radio up as loud as it would go and refused to come out.

She opened her spiral notebook to a blank page and started to write a letter. Then she ripped it up and tossed it in the trash can. At two thirty, she packed a bag and slipped down the hall, leaving her radio on. She pulled out of the parking lot and drove off campus . . .

It wasn't until about six o'clock that the girls realized Susan was missing. Jonas MacPharlan made all the appropriate calls, knowing full well that his job was on the line after this incident. At the meetings, he would continue to insist that it wasn't his fault. He just hoped his colleagues would support him. She wasn't at her parents' house. And she wasn't at her favorite hangouts.

It wasn't long before Logan was looking for yet another missing person at Broad Meadow.

When he arrived on campus, a frantic Jonas MacPharlan greeted him at the entrance to the girls' dorm. "I'm so glad you're here," he said, practically out of breath. "One of the girls saw her go into her room after school. Her radio was blaring for hours. About six o'clock, somebody finally went in to get her to turn off the blasted thing, but she wasn't there."

"Did she say where she was going?" Logan asked.

"She didn't say a word to anyone. We checked all her favorite hangouts, and she wasn't at any of them. Do you see the harm you've caused with this investigation? Susan is fragile. I'm afraid this has driven her over the edge. You have to find her."

"I'll need to take a look in her room."

"Do whatever you have to. Just find her."

## LOVE'S A CRIME

Logan went to her room and looked around. Nothing seemed out of the ordinary. Her bed was made, and her books were neatly stacked on a shelf. He searched desk drawers and leafed through spiral notebooks. Maybe she wrote something to indicate where she went. He flipped to the last page. It had yesterday's date, April 12. She jotted three pages of history notes and half of a fourth page. There seemed to be no indication of where she might have gone.

He went over to the trash bin next to the desk and saw torn pieces of paper sticking out of it. He leaned down and picked them up. There were two handwritten notes, written by separate people. He pieced together one that read, "Susy, please reconsider, Love, Chad." Then he put together the one she wrote. He sifted through the trash can but couldn't find the rest of it.

He stuffed it in his jacket pocket and went back to police headquarters. By late afternoon, he had checked every motel in the area. He ran a credit card check and found out she was in a motel about thirty minutes away.

He knocked but there was no answer. He opened the door and cautiously entered the room, followed by a female officer. They saw Susan lying sprawled on the bed with pills strewn on the quilt next to her. The TV was blaring in the background.

They rushed over to her and Logan shouted, "Oh my god! What did you do?"

He checked her pulse. It felt weak. She opened her eyes and stared blankly at him. His voice was soft and gentle. "Thank God you're all right. You scared a lot of people. You're going to be okay, just hang in there."

She started sobbing uncontrollably. She trembled so much that the mattress shook.

"It's all my fault," she said repeatedly.

"No, it's not."

"Phillip was murdered because of me. If I had kept it to myself—"

"Don't say that. Just lie back. You're going to be okay. We're going to help you."

He called 911 and said, "This is Detective Frank Logan of the Townsend Police. I'm at the Rain Tree Motel in Jasper. There's a young woman here who swallowed a bottle full of aspirins. It's room 105. Please hurry."

She was taken by ambulance to the same hospital where Michelle and Rudy were staying. Twenty-four hours later, Logan went to check in on her. He hoped this was the last time he would ever have to visit a Broad Meadow student at the hospital. He handed her flowers and sat by her bedside.

"Why did you do it?" he asked softly.

"I was scared. I didn't want everybody to know how dirty I am."

"You need to talk to me now, and you can't run away this time, huh?"

"I want this all to be over with, but I'm scared."

"We're all scared from time to time, Susan. The more you hold it in, the more it will keep haunting you."

She was in tears. He gently rubbed her hands and said, "I've been scared a lot too. You've got to trust me, please."

"I can't."

"I think I know who hurt you. But I need you to confirm it. Please talk to me."

She sat up slowly and reached for a glass of water and said, "It's a long story . . ."

## Chapter 24

Chad browsed through the selection of Get Well cards on the shelf. He wanted to find the perfect one to give to Susan. He found one he liked and bought a half dozen pink roses to go with it. Before going up to her room, he sat in the waiting room and wrote,

Dear Susy,

I know we've had our differences in the past. It's easier telling you things in writing. I feel bad about what I did to you. I should have been more understanding. What I'm trying to say is that I'm nothing without you. You had to end up here for me to realize how much you mean to me. Let's start over. I'll never act so pigheaded again. It can be good again.

Love,<br>Chad

He sealed the envelope and dashed into the elevator before the doors closed. He pressed the flowers against his chest so they would not get crushed in the crowd. His heart raced as he watched the floor numbers rise. When the bell rang for the third floor, he filed out with other passengers.

He checked the room number and went inside. Rudy was sitting up in bed, grinning at him. Chad gave him a puzzled look and said, "Rudy, what are you doing here?"

"It's good to see you, man. Are you looking for Susy?"

"Yeah, where is she?"

"We switched rooms."

Before he could explain, Chad bolted out of the room. When he reached Rudy's old room, he saw Susan lying in bed.

"Chad, you can't be here now," she said.

A nurse went over to him and said, "You can't be in here now."

"But I have to talk to her!"

"You'll be in the way."

"In the way of what?" He looked up in time to see a doctor in surgical greens going toward Rudy's new room. A cap covered his head. Logan appeared from around the corner and started following him.

"Detective Logan!" Chad boomed. "They won't let me—"

Logan pulled him down the hallway to the right and motioned for him to be quiet. The doctor turned to see who was yelling but didn't see them and kept on going. Logan peered around the corner and saw him walking toward Rudy's new room.

"What are you doing?" Chad asked Logan.

"I don't have time to explain. Just stay put."

He hurried to catch up to the doctor. Chad was on his tail.

Rudy's head was covered with blankets. The doctor yanked a pillow off the bed and pressed it on his face. Rudy managed to pull his hands free to get away from the man's grip. The doctor leaned on him and pressed harder. During the struggle, Rudy grappled blindly for his mask and pulled it off.

Rudy lifted his head from the blankets and shouted, "Coach Reynolds!"

"Rudy? You son of a bitch!"

He started to head out when Logan and Chad appeared in the doorway. Susan slipped in behind them and said, "Are you looking for me, Coach Reynolds?"

"I guess you didn't know about the room changes, huh, Coach?" Rudy said.

Reynolds tried to make a quick exit, but Logan blocked his escape. He hit the coach in the gut, pushed him into the room, and slammed the door. Ian lay on the floor clutching a chair leg. Chad stood with his mouth agape as he looked at everyone in the room.

"It was only a matter of time, Reynolds," Logan said. "Everybody knew Susan was here. I made that information clear to Jonas MacPharlan. I figured you would come to stop her from talking. But you were too late. She told me everything. I bet you didn't figure we'd switch rooms."

"I don't know what you're talking about," Ian said.

Logan grunted and said, "Uh-huh, and I suppose you were just fluffing Rudy's pillow too."

"I was just horsing around, wasn't I, Rudy?"

"You tried to kill me!" Rudy squeaked.

"Just like you tried to kill me," Michelle said from the doorway.

"That's right," Logan said. "She was trying to tell me something, and you tried to kill her. It all had to do with Susan. She had a deep dark secret that she was ashamed of. Phillip Bishop knew about it too and was going to talk to the police. You couldn't let that happen and had to kill him."

Ian waved his hands and shouted, "You're crazy!"

"You raped her a year and a half ago and threatened to make her life a living hell."

Chad lunged at Ian and socked him in the face. "You bastard! You son of a bitch! I trusted you! I thought you were my friend. And what did you do? You killed my friend and hurt Susan? And you tried to kill Michelle? And you tried to make it look like I killed Phillip! What kind of monster are you?"

Reynolds pushed him down and punched him repeatedly on the chest. Logan raced over, pulled him off, and continued talking after everyone had calmed down. Ian sat on the chair, glaring at the detective.

"She told me she got into a skiing accident on a class trip to the Poconos. She didn't think I'd ask her classmates. She was sick that weekend and couldn't go. She was really dealing with the trauma of being assaulted by someone she trusted. She was sexually assaulted.

"She found out she was pregnant and had an abortion. She had an emotional breakdown and was admitted into a psychiatric hospital in Chicago. She just wanted to get as far away as she could. She used the breakup with Chad as an excuse. She didn't want anyone to ever know what you did to her.

"She was discharged a couple months later. She didn't want to go back to Broad Meadow, but her parents wouldn't listen. They felt it was best for her to be around her friends. She went back to the same school with the coach that raped her. You threatened to kill her loved ones if she called the police, didn't you? She was afraid you would kill her. She had to keep it bottled up inside."

"You have no proof!" Reynolds shouted. "It's my word against hers! Who will the court believe? The word of a revered athletic director or a snot-nosed rich kid who had relationships with two boys. They went into the woods the night Phillip died. He was probably screwing her!"

Chad started to go after him again, but Logan pulled him back.

"You son of a bitch!" Chad screeched. "Let me at him!"

Logan tightened his grip on Chad and slowly dragged him over to a chair. He pushed him down and said, "Don't move."

Susan sat next to Chad and patted his arm.

Ian continued, unfazed. "You know what will happen, Logan? They'll make her out to be loose."

Ignoring the coach's comment, Logan continued, "Susan was terrified when she went back to Broad Meadow. She was afraid to go near you, Ian. She finally confided in Michelle. She told her the coach asked her to help him in the office after a game one night, and he attacked her. Some time later, she confessed to her that she had been pregnant and had gotten an abortion."

"Any one of the guys could have gotten her pregnant!" Reynolds protested. "You can't prove any of this."

"Yes, he can," Susan wailed.

"It was a terrible thing that happened, but no one would have to know," Logan went on. "You threatened to kill Susan's friends and family if she told them what happened. By now, her relationship with Chad was strained. Phillip was deeply concerned about her welfare, and they spent a lot of time together. She told him what the coach had done. He gave her moral support, and they started dating. Michelle and Phillip respected her wishes and kept the secret but had a hard time keeping quiet about it.

"Somehow you found out that Phillip knew what you did, Ian. He must have threatened to tell the police, and you had to do something about it. He turned in Terry Dawson, so you figured he would do the same to you.

## LOVE'S A CRIME

By now, Chad was jealous of him, and everybody had seen them fight in public. Chad could easily be framed. You followed them to the woods and parked up the road so they wouldn't see you. You know the area that's popular with the kids and found a place to hide. You heard Chad and Phillip arguing and watched their fistfight. Phillip hit his head on a rock, and Chad panicked. He ran through the woods, and you had the perfect opportunity. You went over to Phillip, grabbed a rock, and hit him on the head. Then you hid the rock under a bush and went back to the campus. The next day, you must've gone back to get rid of your footprints.

"Everything that happened after that fell into place for you, Ian. You couldn't have planned it better yourself. The boys tried to make it look like Phillip drove his car down the embankment. To make their plan work, they had to get his car. Chad drove back to campus with Andy and Rudy. Andy went to the dorm to get Phillip's car and clean clothes. When he got in, he had to push the seat forward so he could drive. They lifted Phillip's body into the car and left it in neutral when they pushed it down the hill. Then they changed into the clean clothes and went back to campus.

"Chad had enough information about his pals to blackmail them. Rudy stole final exam questions last year and got so upset, he ended up here. Andy was doing steroids and didn't want anybody to know. He slipped and told me his version of what happened. They all told me different stories. Which one was I to believe? They told me the same basic story but told it differently to protect themselves. Andy was so upset about what happened to Rudy, he went to the police station and confessed. He didn't know that Rudy had kept him out of it when he talked to me earlier. In his version, he left Rudy out of it.

"I arrested Andy on the spot. He didn't want his parents to know that he had been arrested, so he called you to bail him out, Ian. He knew you and Terry Dawson were supplying him with the steroids and that you would keep your mouth shut. When he got out, he smoked some pot, which didn't react well with the steroids. When he collapsed during basketball practice, you took him to the emergency room, Ian. Once again, he knew you wouldn't blab it to MacPharlan. It was your dirty little secret.

"Michelle called me, and we arranged to meet under the bleachers. She was going to name Susan's rapist but didn't get to tell me because you attacked her, Ian. You lived up to your threat to kill Susan's friends if she

221

told them what you did to her. If I hadn't been at the gym last week, you would have killed Michelle too."

"You bastard!" she cried.

"How could I have hit her?" Reynolds asked. "I was at Jonas MacPharlan's house the whole time."

"It is true, you were at the headmaster's house that night," Logan said. "But before that, you must have overheard Michelle talking to me on her cell phone. You knew she knew and had to be stopped. So you went to the meeting and must have excused yourself to make a phone call or something.

"You went into the foyer, grabbed MacPharlan's cane, and went out the back door. It's a short walk to the bleachers from their house. You hit her on the head, hid the cane in the shrubbery, and went back through the kitchen door. You couldn't come back with the cane because there was some blood on it. My colleagues and I searched the area around their house three times. The last time we looked, a police officer found a couple of blood spots on the eagle emblem.

"Susan was so upset by now that she told me Phillip got her pregnant. She figured that dead people can't defend themselves. She wanted to throw suspicion from the coach."

"I had no choice," she said.

"Ian, I delved into your background and discovered you had a history of abuse," Logan said. "I checked records of all female students who attended Broad Meadow in the past ten years. Five had similar marks on their bodies. When I found out about Susan, it dawned on me. I remembered looking at the yearbooks. A couple of those cheerleaders I read about didn't finish up here. The librarian said one of them had a nervous breakdown. Now I know why. They told me interesting stories about a certain coach who forced himself on them. Unlike Susan, those girls did not return the following year. They all said they were so ashamed they were afraid to talk about it. They said the coach threatened to kill their family members if they told. They are willing to testify—"

Reynolds shook his head and said, "What proof do they have? A good lawyer will throw that theory out the window. You can't prove I did anything to Susan. She was probably sleeping with him."

"I'll say you tried to kill me," Rudy cut in. "And it's true! Everybody saw it!"

"I was just standing over your bed when they came in. I was holding your pillow."

"You're full of shit!"

"Give it up, Ian," Logan said. "It's over! Right after Michelle was attacked, Jonas MacPharlan 'misplaced' his cane. I got suspicious and paid him a visit. He couldn't explain how the blood spots got on the brass eagle head. He also couldn't explain how the blood got on the shrubbery. Then I played hardball. When you all went to the Poconos after you got into the state championship, I went up there to go skiing with my girlfriend. Guess who I saw at a hotel about ten minutes down the road?"

Ian snarled and said, "I don't have time for guessing games, Logan. Get to the point."

"Okay, you asked for it," Logan said. "Jonas MacPharlan was having a romantic rendezvous with Gail Stockton."

There was a collective gasp around the room.

"Gail and old man MacPharlan!" Chad cried in alarm. "I don't believe it."

"He was more than willing to talk to me when push came to shove. He caved in. He told me everything I wanted to know. He's not that good at sneaking around. It turns out that you caught him in a compromising position, Ian. You blackmailed him into silence. He suspected you were pumping your athletes with steroids but looked the other way. One day, when I went to talk to him in his office, I overheard him talking to somebody on the phone. It sounded like the other person was calling the shots. And now I know why. He was talking to you, Ian. You were making good on your blackmail threat. You were both nervous that I would find out that you were giving your athletes steriods. At least, that's what you wanted Jonas to think. He was already in hot water about the drug bust, he didn't need another scandal. He didn't have to know what happened in the woods.

"He told me how you provided each other with alibis for the night Phillip Bishop died. Lillian MacPharlan originally told me she was with her husband that night. But when she learned about Jonas's extramarital activities, she was more than willing to tell me everything. She was lying to protect him. It turns out she wasn't watching videos with her husband that night. She was shopping with friends. After the stores closed, they had coffee and talked. She arrived home a short time after Phillip Bishop was killed.

"You had just overheard Michelle plan to meet me at the bleachers. You slipped out of the meeting and put on a glove you probably had in your jacket pocket. After you hit her, you tossed the cane in the shrubbery, and went back inside."

Coach Reynolds was quiet now. It was the first time he had nothing to say.

"How did you find out that Phillip knew about Susan's secret?" Logan asked.

"I overheard a conversation on our way home from a game one night," Reynolds said. "It sounded like Phillip knew something, so I confronted him. That's when I found out he knew. We argued, and he threatened to tell the police. I knew I had to do something. I had to make sure he wouldn't tell. I heard Rudy say something about going to the woods, and I decided to follow them like you said. But I couldn't be too obvious, so I left the dance a few minutes after they did. I know that area like the back of my hand. And it's true, I knew where they'd be."

"So you drove to the gym and talked to the janitor to provide yourself with an alibi," Logan said.

"How did you know?"

"It took me a while, but I figured it out. You went to the weight room, which is in the basement, and way down on the other end of the building. You went out the back door and drove off campus. You knew you would be gone a while and wouldn't be missed. The janitor was mopping the locker room floors, and you knew that would take a while. There are no windows in the locker room, so he would not be able to see or hear you drive away. He also had the radio on real loud, so he wouldn't have been able to hear anything."

"That's right. I drove to the woods and parked way down the road so they wouldn't see me, just like you said."

"But how did you know where Phillip would be?" Logan wondered.

Ian got up and slowly backed his way to the door and said, "He used to talk about his favorite spot by the leaning oak tree. I started walking toward it and heard them arguing. Then I heard one of them fall. I couldn't make out who it was. I headed in the direction of the fighting and saw Phillip lying on the ground. Chad tore through the woods. Then I reached for the nearest rock and you know the rest. I went back to the gym and went in through the weight room back door. I had to take a shower. I had to get the blood off me. I had extra clothes in my locker and got dressed. Then I made sure the janitor saw me come back upstairs."

"How did you find out Michelle knew her secret?" Logan asked.

"I wasn't sure if Michelle knew, so I decided to keep an eye on her. After dinner, I was in the cafeteria and overheard her say she would meet you there. I couldn't take a chance, so I followed her. And I did everything you said I did. I took the cane and went out the kitchen door. I saw her there, right where she said she would be and went over and hit her with it."

"You bastard!" Michelle shouted.

Ian backed toward the door and said, "I had no choice."

"You know, it's all very ironic," Logan said.

Reynolds glared at him and said, "What do you mean?"

"You didn't have to do anything. In all likelihood, the case would have been dismissed. Susan washed away the evidence that you raped her. It would have been your word against hers. And as you keep reminding us, you're a respected coach. No one would have believed her anyway."

The coach reached in his pants pocket and pulled out a penknife. He hoisted Susan up and stood there with his left arm around her chest. He held the blade against her throat and said, "If you come near me, I'll kill her."

Logan reached for his gun and said, "Put the knife down, Ian."

Reynolds ran out, dragging Susan with him. Logan and Chad were at his heels.

"Stop or I'll shoot! Police! Everybody get out of my way!"

An orderly was pushing a gurney toward them. Reynolds pushed Susan on the floor and raced down the hall. Logan knocked it over and kept moving. Chad helped Susan up, and she collapsed in his arms. Reynolds scrambled down the stairs, Logan right behind him. When Ian reached the lobby, he darted out the entrance door. Andy was coming from the parking lot and waved at him.

"Hi, Coach."

Reynolds could care less at this point. He zipped right by him. Andy smiled and waved at Logan. He wasn't in the mood to be chatty either.

"What's going on?" He stood with his mouth agape and watched Logan chase after Coach Reynolds.

Logan tackled him, and they landed in the shrubbery. He punched Ian in the ribs and forced his hands behind his back. He cuffed him and said, "Ian Reynolds, you are under arrest for the murder of Phillip Bishop. You have the right to remain silent—"

"What are you doing?" Andy asked in alarm.

"Not now, Andy." He shoved Ian into the backseat of his car and sped out the exit.

Andy shook his head as the car disappeared from view.

"I can't believe it," he muttered.

# Chapter 25

Andy stared at his friends in disbelief as they told him what just happened. They were so excited, they were speaking on top of each other. Rudy was talking so fast, Andy couldn't understand a word he was saying.

"You should've been here, man!" he said repeatedly.

Andy shook his head and groaned. "The coach actually tried to choke you?"

"Yeah, man!" Rudy exclaimed. He was practically vibrating.

"I don't believe it!"

"It happened."

"I can't believe we were talking to a murderer on a daily basis," Michelle said. "It's creepy."

Andy nodded and said, "I know. He should win an acting award."

"I can't believe all the horrible things that happened this year," Chad said.

"I can't believe anyone would want to go to Broad Meadow in the first place," Rudy said. "You either wind up in jail or hospitalized or murdered."

"I was just in jail," Chad said. "I didn't end up in the hospital."

"Well, at least we didn't end up in jail," Michelle and Susan said in unison.

Rudy chuckled and said, "Andy should win the prize. He was in the ER, and he was in jail."

"Then I'd say it's going to be a tie, Rudy. When you get out of here, Logan will probably arrest you for helping us to move Phillip's body."

"I know."

"I guess I can forget about my athletic scholarship now."

"And our shot at college," Chad put in.

"Just think about finishing up and worry about that later," Susan suggested.

"Let's talk about something more pleasant," Michelle said.

Rudy's face brightened. "The school should have new bumper stickers made up that read, "My Broad Meadow son/daughter is a jail bird, not a murderer."

Michelle scowled at him. "It doesn't sound catchy."

"It's not a very good endorsement for the school," Susan added.

"Maybe this is better. 'My Broad Meadow son/daughter was not jailed or hospitalized.' We could leave the 'not' part blank. They can take their choice whether their kids were or weren't jailed or hospitalized."

The girls cringed and shook their heads. The boys were laughing hysterically.

"Come on you guys!" Michelle cried. "It's not funny."

"It's in bad taste," Susan agreed.

Rudy leaned back in his seat and burst out laughing. "Can you believe parents putting something like that on their cars?"

Michelle looked at him and rolled her eyes. "You're nuts, Rudy!"

"The stickers could be collector's items. I need all the money I can get for my defense fund."

Michelle folded her arms and shook her head. "You're not that famous. Who would want to buy a sticker from you?"

"You never know. People are weird about things like that."

The girls looked at each other and said, "Rudy!"

He waved his hands and said, "What? People are weird."

"I can't wait till graduation," Michelle said. It was a welcome change of subject.

About an hour later, Logan entered the room carrying a bouquet of flowers. Susan's face brightened when she saw them.

"They look beautiful," she said.

"I thought they would cheer you up." He set them on the windowsill next to Get Well balloons and pulled a chair next to them. "You look a lot better, Susan."

"Thank you."

"How are you feeling?"

"Better. It's hard though."

"I know. You just need to take your time. You've had a lot to deal with lately."

"I'm supposed to talk to a rape counselor tomorrow morning."

"That's good. You really need to talk about what happened. Let it out."

"It's a horrible thing to deal with. I can't stop thinking that somehow it was my fault."

"Don't think that way. He violated you and left you with an emotional scar for the rest of your life. You should never feel like you were wrong. He was wrong and will pay for it."

Andy shook his head in disbelief. "I can't believe he did all those horrible things."

Logan nodded and grunted. "It's true."

"And to think that I looked up to him," Rudy said.

Michelle grimaced. "He's not my kind of role model. How could somebody be that horrible?"

Logan turned to face her. "Sometimes the least likely people commit the most brutal crimes."

"Doesn't he have a wife and kids?" she wondered.

"Yeah, she's a nice lady," Chad replied. "They have three boys—one is a baby."

"At least he won't hurt other girls," Susan said. "It's a horrible thing to deal with."

"I can't believe you kept it to yourself for so long, Susy," Chad said. "To think that you had to be around him all the time, knowing the horrible thing he did to you. It's unbelievable. You're so brave."

"I did what I had to do."

"I would've beaten the crap out of him if I had known."

Michelle shook her head. "That would have only made things worse."

Chad looked at her and said, "I don't know how you kept the secret, Michelle."

"It was really hard. But it had to be done."

Chad focused his attention on Susan again and said, "And all along I thought Phillip stole you from me. He knew about what the coach did and was just trying to protect you. I just wish you had talked to me."

"I should have told you, but I couldn't."

"I just wish you had confided in me in the first place, Susan," Logan said.

"I'm sorry. I was just scared."

"I know. You had good reason to keep quiet."

"That's for sure!" Michelle cried. "I wasn't very nice to you when we first met."

"You were like a pit bull is more like it," Logan corrected her. "And now I know why. You were just trying to protect her."

"I should have called you sooner, but I didn't know if I could trust you or not."

"Sometimes it takes a while to gain a person's trust."

"I didn't make it easy for you. I'm sorry."

"You shouldn't be sorry, Michelle. The coach threatened to kill Susan's friends and family if word got out. You didn't want anything bad to happen to her."

Susan looked at Michelle and said, "Speaking of keeping secrets, why didn't you tell me you were going out with John Fletcher? You don't have to hide things from me."

"I know. I would have told you eventually."

"Will he get in trouble?" Michelle asked the detective.

"That is a matter left up to the school board. But if you switched out of his class before you turned eighteen, I'm sure he'll be all right. You weren't dating before then, were you?"

"We avoided each other like the plague."

Susan snickered. "It's true. She spent a lot of her free time studying."

"I guess that's why you gave me the brush-off," Andy said.

"I'm sorry."

He grinned and said, "At least I know that my competition has a name. So I still have a shot, right?"

Michelle giggled and said, "No comment."

"Well, it was worth a shot. If things don't work out with him, you know where I'll be."

"I'll keep that in consideration."

"What's going to happen to us?" Rudy asked Logan.

"Moving a corpse and faking a car accident are serious offenses. You'll probably be charged with criminal mischief and conspiracy." He looked over at Andy and Rudy and said, "You could both be charged as accessories. If you're lucky, the judge will give you a suspended sentence with community service or something. We'll just have to wait and see."

"I'm sorry I was so difficult, Detective Logan," Chad said.

"I've worked with people a lot harder to deal with than you, Chad. And I must say, you're one of the best liars I've ever been around. But I don't think that's something to be proud of."

"How can I ever thank you?"

"A check in the mail will be fine."

Everybody laughed.

The next day, Ian Reynolds's mug shot was on the front page of the newspaper. The headline read: HIGH SCHOOL COACH ARRESTED FOR MURDER.

By Kim Weston

TOWNSEND—State Championship winning basketball Coach Ian Reynolds of Broad Meadow was arrested at Union Hospital Tuesday for the alleged murder of student, Phillip Bishop last January. Townsend Police Detective Frank Logan apprehended Reynolds when he apparently tried to strangle student Rudolph "Rudy" Preston who was a patient there. According to Logan, Preston was not the intended victim. In something you might see in a movie, Logan used Preston as bait to lure the coach into the room. Logan said Reynolds was really trying to kill student Susan Williams whom he raped more than a year ago.

"He threatened to kill her loved ones if she told them what he did," Logan said. "When he found out she told Bishop, he hit him on the head with a rock in the woods. The blow killed him."

On the night Bishop died, he went to the woods with his friends. He got into an argument with teammate Chad McAlpin. Bishop fell and hit his head, and McAlpin went to get help.

"Reynolds witnessed the altercation," Logan said. "When McAlpin left, he hit him on the head with a rock. It was that blow that killed him."

According to Logan, McAlpin got his friends to help move Bishop's body. Andy Winchester and Rudy Preston helped put him in his car and pushed it off Snake Turn Road.

In April, Logan said he got a tip from Michelle Martin, a friend of the rape victim. She also knew about what the coach did to her friend but promised she wouldn't say anything.

"I couldn't keep it quiet any longer," Martin said. "After Phillip's death, I knew he [Reynolds] would come after us, so I arranged to talk to Detective Logan."

Before she could talk to him, Reynolds allegedly hit her on the head with a blunt object, Logan said. She ended up in intensive care.

"Williams was so upset about what happened, she checked herself into a motel in Jasper and tried to overdose on pills," Logan said. "She was rushed to Union Hospital and is doing much better now."

"When the coach found out Susan was in the hospital, he went there to stop her from talking," Preston said. "When he got there, he didn't know we switched rooms and started choking me."

Headmaster Jonas MacPharlan said Coach Reynolds worked at Broad Meadow for ten years. When the rape allegations surfaced, former female students admitted Reynolds had attacked them too.

"It's a shame that something like this happened," MacPharlan said. "Our thoughts and prayers go out to the families of the young women he hurt."

"I hope he gets what he deserves," Martin said.

Preston, who was involved in faking the car accident, tried to hang himself earlier this year. When he is discharged, he will be arrested as an accomplice in faking the car accident. McAlpin and Winchester's trial is set for July. Preston's trial date is pending.

To the right of the article, there was a sidebar story about Andy. A file photo of him with his smug grin was over the fold. The headline read, BOY WONDER IS NO HERO.

By Kim Weston

TOWNSEND-Broad Meadow Tigers Andy Winchester was suspended Tuesday for using steroids. The fact that he was taking performance enhancement drugs throws into question the validity of the basketball team's state championship victory.

It has been learned that his collapse at basketball practice in February was a result of mixing marijuana with steroids, authorities said. Former student Terry Dawson was charged with supplying the steroids to Winchester. Dawson implicated Coach Ian Reynolds in the operation.

"Andy Winchester is no hero," said Tilton Wildcats Coach Bill Timko. "Anytime a player uses steroids, it cheats the team and the fans."

A further investigation is pending. Winchester faces a legal battle for allegedly helping to push Phillip Bishop's body off Snake Turn Road.

Logan handed the paper to Lieutenant Winters. When he was finished reading the articles, he tossed it on Frank's desk and said, "You did it."

"I'm glad it's over with, Harry."

"You don't sound so enthusiastic."

"I'm glad Ian was put away, but it's sad what he did to all those poor young women."

"I know."

"They said they're going to testify against him, but it doesn't erase the torment that he caused."

Harry grunted and said, "It takes a long time to get over something like that. If you can ever get over it."

"I can't imagine keeping something like that secret for all those years. Those women are so brave to speak up about it."

"I wish more victims would. Most of them don't because they're afraid the rapist will probably get off on a technicality or something."

"That's what's wrong with the system. We put them behind bars, and a dirtbag lawyer gets them out.

"It doesn't seem right."

Logan sighed and said, "I know what you mean."

Harry was about to respond when the telephone rang. Logan reached over to pick it up and said, "Townsend Police Department. Detective Logan speaking."

"Congratulations, Frank." It was Penny.

"You saw the write-up?"

"Yes, you did a magnificent job. I'm sorry I got so upset about you working so much. You're going to help a lot of people."

"We should go out and celebrate."

"You deserve it."

They decided to meet at his favorite seafood restaurant in Philadelphia.

When he got back to his apartment, Logan checked his messages. One was from his grandfather, congratulating him for cracking the case. When he returned the call, he got the cheerful response he expected.

"You never cease to amaze me, Frank. You did a great job."

"It took a while, but it finally came to me."

"That man ruined a lot of people's lives."

"They're strong, they'll be okay."

"Did you hear from Penny?"

"Yeah, she called me at work. We're going out to eat tonight."

"See, what did I tell you? Quit working late hours and you'll have more time for fun."

He grinned and said, "Whatever you say, Gramps. You want to go fishing on Saturday?"

"I'll see you then."

After work, Logan checked himself out in the mirror and adjusted his tie. He pushed his hair back into place and headed out to his car.

Willy Brown looked up to see Tanya Lowell standing over him. She leaned down to help him pick up the books that the bullies knocked over when they brushed by him again. It was the first time he actually noticed her. She usually sat in back of class. She could have blended into the background, he wouldn't have noticed. That was because she never said anything.

"Are you all right, Willy?"

He huffed and said, "Yeah. I'm so sick of those guys."

"You're better than they are. Do you want to take a walk?"

He hesitated a moment and said, "I guess."

"Come on, do you want to go to the pond?"

He looked at his books and said, "Well, I do have a pile of homework, but I can do it later."

"You shouldn't study so hard. You'll get eyestrain."

He adjusted his glasses and said, "You're probably right."

"Are you looking forward to summer vacation?"

"I can't wait."

"What kinds of movies do you like?"

Rudy went back to Broad Meadow a week later. His stay was short-lived though. Logan arrested him in connection to moving Phillip Bishop's body. He went through the same legal mess as Andy and Chad, and his parents got him out on bail. The trial date was set for July. He would have no relaxing summer vacation before going away to college. He would probably have to put that on hold.

Andy was suspended when word got out about his steroid use. Jonas MacPharlan blamed Ian Reynolds and Terry Dawson and let him finish up at home. His shot at the athletic scholarship went out the window. But that was a minor detail at the moment. He would not have a very good summer either.

The anger students felt toward Chad subsided, and he was able to finish up at Broad Meadow without too many problems. He regretted involving his friends in his mess. He wished he had handled things differently. If he had, none of it would have happened.

Michelle was now recuperating at Broad Meadow. When her relationship with John Fletcher was exposed, classmates were very supportive. The school board met with faculty members to discuss the matter. They decided no real harm was done and let him stay.

Susan was apprehensive about going back to campus. She didn't like the idea of everybody knowing her business. At first, classmates didn't know what to say. It didn't take her long to realize she couldn't concentrate on her classes and got permission to finish up at home.


Lillian MacPharlan cleared the headmaster's house of all her belongings and followed the U-Haul down the road leading away from campus. Her soon-to-be ex-husband remained in the large empty house, proofreading his resignation.

He handed the letter to the board of trustees president and went back to his office. He felt remorseful about the disgrace he brought on the school and could not believe how quickly the fabrics of his life had unraveled.

He cleaned out his desk and placed mementos from a twenty-three-year tenure in boxes. He loaded them in his car and looked mournfully at the landscape before heading out. He passed students on his way down the road but kept his eyes on the yellow line. He could not bear looking at them. He could not handle his fall from grace. They gave him dirty looks and watched his car move down the road and went about their business.

## LOVE'S A CRIME

\* \* \*

Susan was doing her own share of packing. The next day, Chad looked puzzled when he saw an open suitcase on her bed. Boxes were cluttering the floor.

"Don't say anything, her mind is made-up," Michelle told him.

Susan looked at Chad and said, "I think we need to spend some time away from each other."

He held her hands and looked into her eyes. "But I love you. I always have."

She patted his hands and said, "I know you do, but it isn't right for us to be together now. I don't know if it ever will be. You need to grow up some. You aren't ready yet. Phillip listened and was there for me. You never listened. You were too wrapped up in yourself."

"But I tried. I just didn't know what to say. I'm sorry that I acted like a jerk. I wasn't there when you needed me. I wish I could do things over again and make up for all the things I said. Please give me another chance."

"I can't do that. Not now. Too much has happened. We hurt each other way too much."

She laid a dress in the suitcase and pushed down to close it. Then she picked up the bag and walked out, leaving the door wide-open. Chad and Michelle helped carry boxes outside.

When the car was finally packed, Chad asked, "Where will you go?"

"I'll finish up at home. I can take my final exams there."

"Are you going to graduation?"

"I can't. I just want to put this nightmare behind me."

"I'll come see you."

"I won't be there. I'm going to do some traveling after graduation, and I don't know where I'll be."

"When you do know, will you give me your address?"

"We need time apart. I need a fresh start."

"What can I do to make you change your mind?"

Michelle patted his shoulder and said, "It's no use, Chad."

At that moment, Rudy drove up in his yellow station wagon. "I'm all packed and ready to go home."

Chad gave him a funny look. "You're leaving too?"

"I can't hack being here with people knowing everything I did."

Andy climbed out of the passenger's seat and said, "They suspended me. Terrific!"

"What will you do?" Susan asked him.

"I'm just lucky that they blamed Coach Reynolds for getting me hooked on the steroids. They'll let me finish out the year at home. My folks will be wardens, but I'll come back to graduate."

Michelle wiped away tears and said, "It's going to be awfully lonely without all of you guys."

"It's all my fault," Chad said. "If I hadn't been such a jerk, you guys wouldn't be in trouble."

"We got ourselves into it," Rudy said.

"That's right, it was my own doing," Andy agreed. "I should've known better than to get involved with steroids. All I know is that it's been the worst year of my life. It was only a matter of time before I got caught."

"You're really lucky it didn't kill you, man," Chad said. "Mixing drugs is dangerous."

"I know. It's scary, isn't it?"

"Why didn't you talk to me?"

"I didn't want to get in trouble."

"It explains your sudden mood changes," Michelle said.

"Well, I was also upset with faking the car wreck."

"And to think I've been in the same room with you all this time, and I didn't notice anything different with you," Rudy said.

"Don't blame yourself, pal. I was really good at keeping it hidden."

"I thought I was secretive. You win the prize."

"I guess we all have our secrets," Susan added.

Rudy looked at Chad and said, "You'd probably be smart to finish up at home too."

"Where would I go? Life with my folks is strained right now. So I guess I'm better off staying here till graduation."

"You're my buddy."

"You'll be okay, you've just got to take it slowly."

"I know I'm really messed up, but I'll be okay." He hugged Chad and said, "Are we still friends?"

"Forever."

## LOVE'S A CRIME

Andy kissed the girls and hugged Rudy. "I'm sorry I hurt you."

He choked back a tear and said, "It's okay."

They waved good-bye with tears in their eyes as they watched Rudy drive away.

"Will you be okay?" Susan asked Chad.

"I'll be okay. Are you sure you want to do this?"

"I have to. I can't stay here with everybody knowing my business."

He swallowed hard to hold back tears. "Okay, if you really think it's for the best. Will you e-mail me when you're settled and let me know how you're doing?"

"I will." She hugged Michelle and said, "Love you. Thanks so much for being a friend when I needed one."

No words were necessary. Michelle held her in a tight embrace and said, "Good luck, Susy! I know you'll be okay."

"I know. I'm scared though."

"Take it slow. I'll be here if you need to talk. Just give me a call."

Chad held Susan in his arms and wiped her tears with his hands. He kissed her, and she slowly pulled away.

"I love you," he said.

"I know. I love you too." She got in her car and said, "Take care of him, Michelle."

They watched her pull out of the school's entrance and started walking toward the student center.

She put her arm around him and said, "Will life ever be normal again?"

"Not for a long time. Don't be offended if I act like a jerk today."

"I understand."

"Food and drinks are on me."

She limped as they walked down the path. She put her arm around his shoulder for support and said, "Talk to me."

"It all started when I was two and a half—"

# Bibliography

*Scene of the Crime: A Writer's Guide to Crime-Scene Investigations,* Anne Wingate, PhD, Writer's Digest Books, 1992, pp. 41-42; pp. 69-71

*Cause of Death: A Writer's Guide to Death, Murder, and Forensic Medicine,* Keith D. Wilson, M.D., Writer's Digest Books, 1992, pp. 67-68

*Forensics and Fiction: Clever, Intriguing, and Downright Odd Questions from Crime Writers,* D.P. Lyle, M.D., Thomas Dunne Books, 2007, pp. 193-194,

*The Encyclopedia of Forensic Science,* Suzanne Bell, PhD, Facts on File Science Library, 2004, p. 317.